I0818273

Looking for Hope

Looking for Hope

A Novel

Mbinguni

NEW Reads Publications | Jacksonville

Library of Congress Cataloging-In-Publication Data
available upon request.

ISBN 978-1-7357219-0-3 (hardback)
ISBN 978-1-7357219-1-0 (ebook)

Cover Design by Gisette Gomez
Printed in the United States of America
Published by NEW Reads Publications LLC
Jacksonville, FL
newreadspub.com

First Edition: February 2021

PUBLISHER'S NOTE
This book is a work of fiction. Names, characters, places, and incidents and circumstances are the product of the author's imagination or are used fictitiously. Any resemblance to actual persons, living or dead, business establishments, events, or locales is entirely coincidental.

For my grandparents, without whom I would not know the joys of a well-told story.

Contents

Maplewood

One

Our yard was most beautiful when the first hints of spring appeared. Since school ran Monday through Friday and church lasted all day Sunday, there was only one day of the week I could spend fully enjoying the new life budding around me. I would rush through folding laundry and dusting furniture in the morning so I could get to my favorite part of Saturday—the afternoon. The gentle scent of our lilacs invited butterflies to take leave of their busyness and visit for a while. I would watch them flit from flower to flower, while imagining that their conversations sounded like the ladies at Mrs. Pearl's beauty shop. Listening to the robins as they sang about the babies that would soon hatch, I'd lay still on my blanket until my bones hurt, hoping I wouldn't scare any of the creatures away. The newly mowed grass was even and neatly edged, like a haircut fresh from the barbershop. Our grass was thick but you could still see the red clay of Maplewood, Georgia beneath it. I felt as rooted to that clay as the Georgia pine that sat right in the middle of the yard. Our porch chairs had been repainted as white as clouds on a sunny day. Those old wooden boards waited patiently to be occupied by neighborhood fellas who were as cool as October and mahogany-colored ladies with thighs as warm as homemade apple pie. It was on Saturdays that I believed laughter was easy and there would be nothing but good company and food to satiate both belly and soul.

The joy that springtime Saturdays brought me seeped through every part of my seven-and-a-half-year-old frame. My walk had extra pep. My smile was brighter and wider. Even my skin seemed to sparkle in the sunshine. I'm sure that was helped by Momma oiling me down every night before bed. She hated to see a black child ashy and said the oil would keep my skin as soft as the day I was born. That was not a day I remembered, but I trusted my Momma's word. My eyes were as big as half moons and could get me candy, toys, and attention, when batted properly. My hair was like Momma's, long, thick, and dark brown, but not as bouncy or shiny. She wore soft, loose curls that perfectly framed her face, a hairdo she'd copied from Dorothy Dandridge in *Carmen Jones*. I begged Momma to style my hair like that, but I wasn't allowed to wear curls, except on special occasions.

Momma was watching me from the kitchen window as I struggled to keep my bicycle steady on this one particular Saturday in the spring. I'd had a small accident and had warped one of the tires, making it difficult for me to ride. She'd asked Daddy to fix it, but he hadn't gotten around to it yet. There was another broken-down, slightly rusted bike I could use, but my pink bike with stickers on the frame and multi-colored streamers coming out of the handles was the one I wanted to ride. I was so proud of the way I'd decorated that bike.

Pride was a family trait I'd gotten from Daddy. He was also stubborn. According to his gospel, "Maynards didn't lean on nobody and nothing but themselves." My longer-than-average legs were covered with scars because of his stubbornness. Momma warned Daddy that I would ruin my legs, but he said the scars would heal without leaving any lasting damage. If only that were true of all scars.

I could hear the melody of Momma's giggle through the screen door. Her laugh was light and tinkled like the wind chimes that hung from Nana Margie's front porch. Naturally happy, it didn't take much for Momma's laughter to come. My calling my bike stupid after that last spill made her chuckle that time. I always seemed to amuse Momma, but I enjoyed it. The way her face lit up made my annoyance with my bike a small price to pay. It was always a special treat for Momma to really get tickled. When she laughed out loud, her hair bounced with the shake of her body, and her voice would rise higher and higher until no sound would come out of her mouth. Then, tears of joy would run down her face. She'd gasp for air and hold her tummy. I'd only made Momma laugh like that once or twice.

I searched the window for Momma's eyes. Her eyes betrayed her feelings—I always knew when she was about to smile. She'd have to hide her eyes if she wanted me to believe she was mad at me. Momma never looked at me with reproach or agitation; always with love, even in correction. I loved the way her eyes seemed to drink me in whenever I was near, like there wasn't enough of me to see. She looked at Daddy the same way.

I stood watching Momma. Her head was bowed as she worked on something on the kitchen counter. The part of her body I could see shook with the up and down motion of her arms. I'd seen that move before. She was probably shaking the cake in the pan to loosen it for flipping. Her brow was furrowed and her mouth was turned down. When she was done, she wiped the back of her arm across her forehead and exhaled. I could tell she was tired.

Momma had spent all morning preparing for Daddy's birthday and the guests would be arriving soon. She had gone to great lengths to keep this party a surprise. Putting away unnoticeable amounts of money for months, dropping groceries by the houses of family and friends for safe keeping, and not telling me until Daddy left for work that morning because she knew I couldn't keep a secret —they were all a part of her well-laid plan. His 30th birthday would be celebrated in style.

Momma had already explained that I wouldn't have a party this year because we'd had a big barbecue for my seventh and eight would come in quiet and simple. I didn't mind. We would both do anything for Daddy. I knew she longed to hear that laugh of his again. Hearing his laugh would cause a chuckle to bubble up out of anyone's belly, and we had not had the privilege of hearing it since we buried Nana. Finding out Nana was sick with cancer, followed by her death and a fire at the mill had all piled up on Daddy at the same time. He spent so much time trying to manage the remaining mill workers after the shut down, and there was no space for him to get through his grief. That was four months prior, but we still hadn't regained our rhythm. Momma and I were close to Nana Margie, too, and we felt the emptiness of her absence, but her death seemed to leave Daddy a scattered mess. His mind always seemed to be at work, his eyes were never quite focused on what was right in front of him, and the love I used to feel from his heart must have been in the casket with Nana.

Daddy's return home came later and later every day. The skin on Momma's hands should have been chaffed from the number of times she brushed back the curtains looking to see if he'd pulled into the yard. He would come in reeking of alcohol and places best avoided by married men. Even still, when he arrived, dinner was hot and her spirit kind and concerned. She'd always ask, "How was your day?" to which he would respond with a soft grunt. She would serve his food and we would sit at the table and watch him eat in silence.

Momma and I discovered Nana Margie had been Daddy's secret sauce. The recipe just wasn't right without her. He didn't kiss or hug either of us before leaving or when he'd return. He would remain still and seemingly emotionless if we hugged or kissed him. His conversation was stingy, never saying more than "yeah," and "naw," in response to a question that was asked. Daddy could make anyone laugh with his silly antics, like making faces or telling corny jokes. He made no effort to be a clown anymore. He no longer looked to be amused by me either. My dance moves and silly faces didn't even garner a smile from him. He never invited me onto his lap anymore. I tried everything to get his attention. It didn't work. He ignored me, which was as painful as Nana's death to me. Momma would pat me on the head or hug me and tell me to go play in the den or in my room, having witnessed my attempts. Her usual tricks didn't work and so we both stayed out of his way, but kept near enough to move quickly should he have needed something.

Momma hoped the birthday party would return things back to how they used to be. I could read her desperation to help Daddy as if it were one of those big neon signs above her head. She wanted that party to be our saving grace. I overheard Momma telling Mrs. June, her best friend, that Daddy just needed something to show him he still had love on this side of heaven. I couldn't hear Mrs. June's response, but Momma's nodding head seemed to say she was encouraged.

On the day of the party, Momma sent me outside so I would not be underfoot. The scent of warm cake wafting through the air made me wish I was inside with her. She would have allowed me to help her in the kitchen on a normal day, but most times I didn't do anything but make more work for her. She promised, however, to let me lick the excess icing from the spatula and bowl. Yellow cake with chocolate icing was my Daddy's favorite and Momma was the best around town at making it. Her icing was the creamiest and her cake was more moist and soft than all the others, even Nana Margie's. Daddy had no problem saying so either.

"Hannah, I'm finished icing the cake," Momma said. "Put your bicycle away and c'mon in here and clean it up for me. You can go take your bath afterwards. I laid your dress for the party on the bed."

Momma meant business when she called me by my first name. I knew whatever instructions followed, I ought not make her repeat them.

"Yes, ma'am," I said eagerly.

I didn't know which one made me happier. I loved that dress just about as much as I loved Momma's chocolate icing. That dress was special because Daddy said I looked like a princess the first time I wore it.

I raced past Momma, through the screen door and into the kitchen. Just as I was about to stick my finger into the bowl, Momma called out, "And wash your hands!" It was hard to get away with anything when she was around. I looked over my shoulder to make sure she wasn't near, rolled my eyes, washed my hands, then turned my attention back to the sticky, sweet, remnants of icing in the bowl.

The sugar rush only enhanced my excitement. I ran up the stairs, taking them two-at-a-time. I stripped quickly, not wanting to miss a single moment. After drying myself from a lukewarm bath, I wrapped up in the towel and went into my bedroom. My polyester slip and the shiny, cream-colored satin dress were both laid neatly on the bed. The fabric was covered with tiny pink flowers with small green stems and one green leaf. They were spaced perfectly. There was a pink satin belt, which Momma would have to tie once I was in the dress. I had cream bobby socks and off-white shoes that were polished to a high shine.

"Momma!" I yelled.

"Yes, Mouse," Momma responded calmly.

"I got my dress on. Can you come zip me up and tie my belt, please?"

"I *have on* my dress," Momma corrected. "Here I come."

Momma came in, zipped me up, tied my belt, and brushed my hair up into one big ponytail at the top of my head.

"Now go find somewhere to sit still until your Daddy gets here. I don't want you to wrinkle up your dress."

As soon as I sat down outside, Johnny B came gliding up to the porch. Johnny B was always the first to arrive at anything at the Maynard house. As a matter of fact, he was the first to arrive at any event to which he was invited. He was not one to miss a shindig of any sort. Whether it was a church function (even though he wasn't a member of anyone's church) a birthday party, a repast—whatever the occasion,—Johnny B was expected. I don't know if the B stood for a middle or last name, or if it just stood for "be there."

Daddy said Johnny B always dressed to the nines, which I understood to mean he wore really nice clothes. Take his party clothes, for instance. That night, he had on a white seersucker suit with tan pinstripes. His leather oxford shoes matched those pinstripes perfectly. He was always clean-shaven, which displayed his chiseled face nicely, and he smelled good. Sometimes Daddy's cologne could choke the air right out of your lungs. Momma would fuss for five minutes after he applied it. But Johnny B wore just the right amount of something wonderful. He smelled like the woods on a rainy day.

"Hey, lil' Ray," Johnny B shouted.

I didn't look up, hoping to discourage him from continuing. I hated that nickname. Johnny B, or Mister Johnny B to show respect, was a jokester. If he wasn't calling me that name, he was tugging my hair, or trying to startle me. He got on my nerves most of the time. I was mildly amused by him otherwise. His jokes were usually funny and I did love when he would snatch me up and twirl me around. That twirl would end with him handing me a piece of candy or a penny. If it was the latter, I'd use that penny to go buy candy at the corner store.

Johnny B and Daddy had been best friends since they were kids, but they didn't act much like best friends to me. My best friend and I played together as much as we could, and whenever we did, there was sure to be a lot of laughter. When Daddy and Johnny B got together, it was like two big-horned animals head-butting each other.

I was visiting Nana Margie not long before she died and asked her why those two fussed with each other so much. She was tickled by the question. She pulled back the cover and allowed me to climb into bed with her as I'd done many times before. Wrapped in Nana Margie's warm arms was one of my favorite places to be. She used to be plump and warm. Cancer had made her frail and cold, and I had to be careful getting into the bed. She used to always smell of freshly baked bread. Illness changed that. Instead she smelled of medicine and sickness. None of that mattered to me. She still gave the best snuggles. She cuddled me in her arms and I laid my head on her chest as she told me of Daddy and Johnny B's history.

"Well," she said. "Your momma was Johnny B's girlfriend before she was your daddy's wife."

I raised my head to look Nana in the eyes. She stretched her eyes to match my expression and then she laughed. She nodded her head to let me know I'd understood her right.

"Your granddaddy Luther moved your momma's family to Maplewood in her sophomore year of high school. Johnny B loved that gal the moment he set eyes on her. He was always the better dresser and the one that people liked to hang around, so naturally he caught her attention too. Your daddy was quiet and to-himself in school. He liked your momma, but I believe he didn't think he had a chance against Johnny B. Ray ignored his own feelings and the three of them became fast friends. They went bike riding, fishing, to the picture show; they did everything together. Hope liked being with both of them, but Johnny B told anyone who would listen that she was going to be his wife.

"Johnny B decided he was going into the army so he could take care of Hope once they got married. He tried to get your daddy to go with him, but your daddy was more interested in singing with his little band. Johnny B didn't ask your momma to marry him before he left for army school. I guess he thought your momma knew his intentions. Hope and your daddy began spending a lot of time together after he left. She was taking classes over at the junior college, and when Ray would get off from work, he would head over to that college just to walk her home. He would pick dandelions for her because yellow was her favorite color. He even used to write her silly little songs to make her laugh. I don't suppose they meant to fall in love, but that's sure what happened.

"By the time Johnny B returned, it was too late. Hope didn't know how to tell Johnny B, so for a while both she and your daddy kept quiet about it. I told Ray he should be the one to tell Johnny B since he was his best friend. Your momma finally broke down and told Johnny B the truth. He was heartbroken. He left without saying goodbye to either one of them."

"What happened then?" I asked through a yawn.

"He came back two years later. Your parent's house was the first stop he made; they were married by that point and you were two. Johnny B told them both he was okay with the fact that they had fallen in love and he'd like to be friends again. He missed them both. Your daddy and Johnny B ain't never been as close as they were, but they seemed to manage."

"I hope me and Debby never like the same boy," I said as I drifted off to sleep.

Nana chuckled softly. That was the last time I got to nap with her.

I began noticing Johnny B didn't look Momma or Daddy in the face very often after I had that talk with Nana. I could see his eyes soften and sometimes even tear up a little when he did manage to look at Momma. Daddy saw it, too, but I figured he felt so bad about taking his best friend's girl that the guilt outweighed his pride and most times he kept quiet.

When Daddy's guilt wasn't heavy enough, he would remind Johnny B who Momma chose. Johnny B would innocently call Momma "pretty lady," or "sweetheart," and Daddy would quietly warn, "a'ight now," casually slipped in between chuckles. Momma would soothe Daddy with, "Johnny B is harmless. Besides, I married you, didn't I?" She always said this with a smile and followed it up with a long kiss, one of those kisses where a woman would put both her hands on her man's face and close her eyes. Johnny B would look away, but I wouldn't.

"Hey, Mr. Johnny B," I responded as flatly as possible so as not to encourage his teasing.

Johnny B was handsome, but not as handsome as my Daddy. He had never married and had no children, but sometimes I wondered how different my life would have been if he was my father.

"Where's your momma?" Johnny B asked as he quickly scanned the area looking for her.

"She's in the house."

"Well, I guess I'll sit out here and keep you company. You sure look pretty." He smiled and nodded in approval at my dress.

"Thank you," I stuttered. I was caught off guard. Johnny B usually teased, but never complimented. "I wanted to look pretty for Daddy."

"Well, I know he'll think you're the most beautiful girl here, next to your Momma," he said with a wink.

"Hey, Johnny B! When did you get here?" Momma asked as she stepped onto the porch carrying the ham that would crown the center of the table. It was covered with her special homemade glaze and topped with pineapple slices and cherries.

"Let me get that for you!" Johnny B hopped up and slipped the ham out of my Momma's hands.

"Please be careful." Momma never took her eyes off the ham.

I watched both of them from my perch and thought I saw her breathe a sigh of relief once her prized ham was safely on the table.

Momma had invited just about everyone we knew, including Daddy's friends from work and her church friends. Daddy wasn't too particular about the church folk. All the guests were present and restless at an hour past my Daddy's quitting time. She had made Daddy promise he would come straight home. She made up some excuse about needing him to do something important as soon as he finished work.

At two hours past, some of the guests started eyeing the food and complaining that by the time Daddy got there, the flies and ants would have feasted, leaving them nothing. I passed the time in the front room styling my baby doll's hair, but there were only so many styles I could create with the long, black yarn. Tammy was my favorite doll, despite her limitations. She was made out of brown stockings stuffed with a soft, squishy material. Her eyes had been drawn on with white, brown, and black paint. Dark brown thread had been used to shape her ears and nose and make them extend slightly from her face. The same thread had also been used to show the lines separating the fingers and toes, as well as marking where elbows and knees should be. Tammy wasn't hungry, but my stomach was starting to grumble.

"Go ahead and eat, everyone. I'm sure Ray will be here soon," Momma half-whispered.

She slinked into the kitchen with Johnny B in tow. She was hurt and embarrassed that Daddy had not kept his promise.

"I'll go see if I can find him," Johnny B volunteered.

"Thanks, Johnny B. Don't tell him about the party if you can help it."

Johnny B nodded once and left through the back of the house.

Somehow, I knew Johnny B searching for my Daddy was not going to turn out well. I sat in the front room, almost wishing Daddy would stay wherever he was. Whatever he was sure to bring with him was not going to be good for the party. How my Momma and Johnny B didn't know that baffled me.

It was another forty-five minutes before Johnny B returned with Daddy. Daddy's left arm was wrapped around Johnny B's neck and Johnny B's right arm was holding Daddy by the waist. The two of them wobbled into the yard like awkward dancers with four left feet. Daddy wobbled because he was drunk. Johnny B wobbled from trying to support most of Daddy's weight as well as his own. Both of them were big, strapping men, so it was quite an odd sight to see. It would have been downright funny if the situation had been different.

"Johnny B, what's all this! Why you bring me here? I was celebrating my birthday."

Daddy sounded funny; his words didn't come out quite right. His eyes were shiny like glass and he seemed not to realize there were people besides him and Johnny B present. Daddy also must not have realized that Johnny B was not hard of hearing because he was shouting.

"He came and got you for me, Ray. I was trying to surprise you with a birthday party."

Momma spoke through the screen, her words were weighted with disappointment. The guests stood around the table of food acting like they couldn't see how Daddy was acting. They knew just like I did that saying something to Ray Maynard would make things worse.

Daddy shifted his body away from Johnny B but wasn't steady enough to stand on his own two feet, so he tumbled to the ground. Gasps rose from the small crowd and Momma turned and walked further into the house, away from the disapproving and pitying eyes of neighbors and friends.

Johnny B tried to help him up, but Daddy pushed him away. He struggled to his feet and swayed back and forth like a ship on an angry ocean. Johnny B left him there and followed Momma into the house. I stood frozen like everyone else, not knowing what to do.

"Don't you walk away from me, Hope! I want to thank you for this fine party. Johnny B, you come back here. I don't need you tending to my wife!"

Johnny B came back and stood in the doorway.

"Ray, calm down, man. Hope put together this party for you and you ruining it."

"I don't give a damn! Y'all can all go the hell home. I don't need none of them to celebrate my birth with me. I came in this world by myself and that's how I'm leaving. Screw 'em. Maynards don't depend on nothing or nobody but themselves."

At that, the guests started gathering their things, packing extra plates, and tipping out much faster than they had trickled in.

"Ray, get a hold of yourself. What is wrong with you?" Johnny B asked, his voice still a whisper. "I ain't never seen you act like this."

"They fired me, Johnny B. They fired me. After seven years of breaking my damn back at that mill, they fired me. How they just do that, Johnny B? How they do that?" Daddy choked as he burst into tears.

I had never seen him cry, not even at Nana Margie's funeral. Johnny B went back into the house to get Momma and I followed. I felt like I shouldn't witness Daddy breaking into pieces.

Daddy crying, Momma being upset, and Johnny B trying to keep them both calm was all too much to bear. It was confusing and scary to see my family in such chaos. I wanted to find the nearest rock and hide under it until my life returned to normal.

Momma turned from the sink as soon as Johnny B and I came into the kitchen and said, "Johnny B, I just don't understand why he would do this."

Momma's face contorted as she stifled a cry. Johnny B tried his best to make Momma feel better.

"He's real down right now, Hope. They fired him from the mill. His momma just died. Sometimes it's just too much for a man to bear. He got to lighten the load somehow. He think that drink helps with that, but it don't. If he ain't careful, it's gonna cost him everything."

Johnny B sounded as if he was trying to understand it for himself.

My brain began to race. How hard would it be for Daddy to find another job? Did that mean we would have to move? Would we starve? Nana Margie was gone and we didn't have any other family here that we could live with. I worried what losing his job would mean for our family. Even at age seven, I knew that no work meant we were in trouble.

I looked at Momma's face, hoping she would have a smile or an "everything will be alright." Instead she collapsed into Johnny B's arms, leaving the water running over the dirty dishes. Johnny B embraced Momma like you would a child who had just fallen and hurt themselves. He rubbed her back and allowed her to let out all of her hurt and frustration with Daddy. I watched them, hoping they would let go of one another. Surely Daddy would not like to see them in one another's arms. Momma was still sobbing deeply into Johnny's B chest when Daddy stumbled in.

"What in the hell?" Daddy bellowed as if he had just seen a flying pig. "Johnny B, if you wanna live, you get the hell outta my house right now!"

"Ray, it's not what you…" Momma started talking fast as she lifted her head from Johnny B's chest.

"I will kill you if you don't take your hands offa my wife." Daddy glared at Johnny B.

"I only hugged Hope because she was crying. I didn't mean any harm," Johnny B responded angrily. "I ain't never tried nothing with Hope since y'all been together and I don't appreciate you acting otherwise."

"Hope, take your ass on outta this kitchen. Johnny B, I've had enough of you always being in the shadows waiting for my wife to leave me."

"Ray!" Momma shouted.

"Hope, do what I told you to do," Daddy growled.

When Momma didn't move, Daddy thundered, "Now, woman!"

Johnny B let go of my mother. Momma stormed past Daddy and went to wait at the bottom of the stairs. The kitchen, which was not large to begin with, seemed to have shrunk to the size of a shoe box. It felt as if the three of us—me, Johnny B, and Daddy—were standing right on top of each other.

Johnny B turned and looked at Daddy. I could see the hurt and concern in his eyes from where I stood in the corner. I'd eased there while Johnny B was consoling Momma, my presence completely forgotten. I stood perfectly still so as not to draw attention to myself like a roach when a light is flipped on.

Johnny B was shaking as he spoke to Daddy. "Ray, this ain't no way to be talking in fronta people. I don't wait around for Hope to leave you. She loves you, and she ain't going nowhere. I love y'all both, and I just want this family to be alright. I ain't never seen you like this, Ray, and man, you scaring me."

"Don't worry about my family. You ain't got one of your own, so you always trying to tend to mine. Get your own shit. That's why I know you still pining after Hope. You never married nobody after she left you for me."

Daddy's teeth were bared and every word was intended to cut Johnny B.

Johnny B was often asked, in Daddy's presence, why he never started a family. He always answered that he'd rather be free to do as he pleased. No one believed that, not even me.

"You right, Ray. I always loved her, but she made a choice and I decided I could handle staying friends with you both. I ain't gonna let you mistreat her, Ray."

"Who in the hell are you to let me do anything with *my* wife? Get the fuck outta my house and don't you never bring your sorry ass back 'round here!" Daddy yelled at the top of his lungs.

I was afraid Daddy and Johnny B were about to rearrange the furniture in the house.

Johnny B shook his head, walked past Daddy out of the kitchen, and left. The resolute bang of the screen door was like the closing of a friendship. I followed Johnny B's path to the door and peeked out. There were a few guests left. The nosey ones. The ones who would tell and retell all that had transpired with animation and embellishment.

Daddy walked up behind me and yelled through the screen, "Get outta my yard. I ain't gone tell y'all no more. If I come back down these stairs and I see any eyes staring back at me, my gun is gonna do the talking."

It wasn't Daddy's nature to threaten; he was a mild-mannered person. The men whose wives were present without them wouldn't take kindly to them being treated that way. With scornful faces, they gathered the rest of their belongings and left with a lot of teeth-sucking and poked-out lips.

"Mouse, go to your room right now," Daddy ordered.

I did as I was instructed without hesitation. Daddy was right behind me, stomping up the stairs and pulling Momma behind him.

I sat huddled in the middle of the floor of my room as Momma and Daddy spent the next hour hurling hurt back and forth at each other. I couldn't hear exactly what they were saying. My walls muffled the words but not the anger and fear present in that room. None of that could be disguised. I would have welcomed the giggles and strange moans that, on easier days, had irritated me out of my sleep.

I stared at the white bed frame, nightstand, and dresser that Daddy had repainted when he purchased it from the second-hand store. He was so proud to show me my new furniture when I turned five. Momma made a pink quilt and bought some pink sheets. I'd always felt like a little princess in this room up until that night. Now, the room had lost its magic. It seemed darker, almost scary.

Suddenly a thud shook the wall that separated my room from theirs. My entire body stiffened when I heard my Momma yelp like a wounded dog. I had never seen my Daddy hit my Momma or even touch her in a way that was harmful. I hopped up from the floor, walked over to the wall, and placed my ear against the cool, flowered wallpaper.

"Ray, please. Nothing was going on with me and Johnny B. I was upset about you coming to the party late and drunk."

The words were muffled, but I was able to make them out.

"You disrespected me in my own house," Daddy growled.

I heard a loud clap, and Momma made another strange sound.

"Ray, please stop it! Mouse is in the next room. I promise I wasn't doing nothing with Johnny B."

Momma's voice was ragged like she'd been lifting something heavy.

"Well, if Mouse can hear this, she will know not to disrespect a man in the house he pays for, and not to disrespect a man in front of his friends, and not to disrespect a man with someone who is supposed to be his friend!"

With each "not to," I could hear him strike my Momma, and with every strike, a mixture of confusion and hatred began to churn in the depths of my belly. How could Daddy hit Momma? How could he embarrass her in front of everyone at the party? Who or what was inhabiting my father's body?

"Ray, please at least let me send Mouse out of the house," Momma pleaded.

"You go send her away, but don't you dare step one foot out of this house." The voice that came out of him didn't even sound like his. It had no warmth, which was unusual in a home where words had previously been filled with love and joy.

I heard Momma's footsteps as she left their bedroom. They shuffled to a stop just shy of my door. I was just able to remove my face from the wall as she stepped into the room.

"Come here, Mouse."

She beckoned me to her.

I walked over to her slowly. The light caught her face in the doorway, and I could see that it was already beginning to swell.

"Don't cry, sweetie. Daddy is a little upset, but everything will be alright. I want you to walk across the street and play with little Debra, okay?"

I hadn't even realized I was crying.

"Can you walk me over there, please?" I whined.

"You've walked over there plenty of times by yourself. Go on now," she encouraged.

I could tell Momma was trying to make her voice sound natural, but it was different too. I didn't know these people who were once my parents.

Seeing her face like that was making me feel even more panicked. Daddy had lost his marbles and I didn't know what he was capable of. None of this would be happening if Nana was still alive. I didn't know how to fix this now that she wasn't here. I wanted to help Momma, and forcing her out of the house was the only way to do that.

"Please, Mommy," I whimpered.

I was afraid that if I left her there, Daddy would hit her again. I thought if I could just get her out of the house, everything would be alright.

"How about I just walk you to the door and watch you cross the street?" Momma negotiated.

She grabbed my hand and led me downstairs.

"Hope, don't you step one foot out that door!" Daddy yelled from their bedroom.

"Yes, Ray." She sounded like someone else's mother.

"Momma, please walk me across the street."

I grabbed both of her hands and looked deeply into her eyes, hoping I could release whatever spell she was under.

"If I walk you across the street, your Daddy will be very upset with me and I don't want to upset him anymore than he already is," she explained in an effort to calm me down. "Please, be a big girl and go over and play with Debby. Don't worry about me, Baby, I'll be alright. Now, go on."

She kissed me on the forehead and then shooed me across the street like only a mother could.

"I love you. Be home before the sun goes down," she called behind me.

"Yes ma'am. I love you too," I called back as I crossed the street.

Before I could knock on the door of Debby's house, I turned to see if Momma was still watching. She had already turned to go back up the stairs.

I knocked on the door and then sat down on the steps. Staring at my house from this vantage point, knowing what was going on inside, made it look like one of those houses in the spooky movies I wasn't allowed to watch. It didn't look like my home. It couldn't be the same house. It was so different on the inside than it was just a few short months ago.

I got up from the steps and knocked again, then I remembered that Debby and her parents weren't at the party because they had gone out of town for a wedding. I walked back across the street to my house, making sure to look both ways before crossing. By the time I reached the porch, I could hear the shouting and tumbling sounds coming from inside. I ran inside and up the stairs, not knowing what I would be able to do to stop Daddy, but knowing I had to try something.

I pushed their bedroom door open to see Momma squatting, crouched against the wall in the corner, Daddy's knees pressed into the side of her right thigh. In his right hand he was holding a gun, pointed to her head. His eyes were wild and spit was gathered in the corners of his mouth like a rabid animal. Just as Momma's eyes shifted to mine, he pulled the trigger.

Franklintown

Two

They were both lost to me in that moment. My momma was dead and my daddy might as well have been. I no longer saw the daddy whose arms made me feel safe and warm and loved. I no longer saw the daddy who planted kisses all over Momma's face after she'd just cooked a wonderful meal. I no longer saw the daddy who would grab us both by the hands on a Saturday evening and sing to us and dance with us. Daddy was gone and all I could see was Ray. Ray was the person who'd taken away my Momma, and that's what I would call him from that day forward. One moment and one bullet had effectively made me an orphan.

I stood in the doorway, slack-jawed. Momma's gaze was frozen to mine as the life drained from her body. My pretty dress with the pink sash was ruined with her blood, just like my face. Ray turned and looked to the doorway, unsure of who had just witnessed his crime. He stood, gun still in hand, and walked past me and out of the room with no expression on his face. The sound of the shot was still ringing in my ears. I stood motionless, staring at her lifeless form. I waited as my heart pounded so loudly it overcame the ringing. I wondered if he would shoot me like he'd done my mother.

Ray returned in fresh, clean clothes, carrying two towels. He used a wet, blue towel to wipe the blood from my face and arms and a pink towel to dry me off.

"Go change your clothes, Mouse."

I saw his lips move and heard a muffled sound, but nothing registered. I tried to turn and run, but it seemed like cement cinder blocks were connected to my ankles instead of feet.

"Did you hear me? I told you to go change your clothes."

There was no anger or fear in Ray's voice; no shame nor remorse. Just empty space where love used to be.

It felt like my brain had short-circuited. I stared blankly at my father. Then, for the first time, he struck me across my face. The bite of that back-handed slap felt like 20 wasps attacking my left cheek in a synchronized stinging contest. He grabbed me by my arm, spun me around, and hurried me to my bedroom before I could recover.

Ray pulled my ruined dress up without untying my pink sash, which caused the dress to snag on my head. He shook and pulled at the dress and slip until my head popped free. He snatched the first shirt and the first pair of pants he could find out of the dresser drawers. It did not matter that the clothing did not match. Neither one of us considered that the evening would be cool, and I would need a long-sleeved shirt to keep from catching a cold.

Ray proceeded to dress me the way someone would a baby. He pulled the white short-sleeved shirt over my head, picked one arm up and put it through the arm hole. He repeated this with my other arm and did the same for my pants. I remained frozen like a mannequin in a store window while he darted around the house packing our suitcases.

Ray grabbed my wrist and pulled me out of my room. I resisted as he came close to passing by their bedroom. He looked back at me, then at the open bedroom door. He dropped my hand, stepped forward, pulled the door closed, and picked my hand back up. My feet became unglued from the floor. We walked to the end of the hall, but as we approached the stairs, the room began to spin. I'd never experienced the sensation of passing out, but I thought this might be what it felt like. I was light-headed and thought I could fall over and tumble down the stairs at any moment.

"Mouse, I need you to be strong. It's just us two now," Ray commanded.

I couldn't even bring myself to look at him. How could he ask this of me? How could he think I wanted it to be "just us two now" after what I'd just witnessed?

I took a deep breath to steady myself the way I'd seen women do in the movies. I grabbed the rail, which signaled to Ray I was ready to move.

"Good. Good girl." He nodded approval.

Ray grabbed his fedora as we walked out the back door. He stood on the top step as if he was taking it all in for the last time. The sun had eased down from its high perch and had begun to change the color of the sky. Everyone else would be preparing for supper, but we were preparing to catch the last bus out of Maplewood. The little country hamlet was filled with trees as tall as the sky, winding roads that rarely had more than a car or two on them at once, and quiet, unassuming folks who did the best they could by their families and had no idea what had just happened. I had no one who could share in my grief. Ray seemed unbothered, which only served to make me more panicked.

Ray walked and pulled me the three miles it took to get to the station. I silently said my goodbyes as we passed the town I'd loved for the entirety of my short life. We were leaving my whole world behind; the little white school where I learned to read and write, the old wooden church where I was baptized, and the rickety corner store Momma would send me to while she was cooking to grab items she'd forgotten from her grocery list.

I could hear the familiar soundtrack of my life: the crickets chirping, old man Shephard's radio broadcasting Moms Mabley, and someone's baby crying in the distance. The rhythmic crunching of gravel beneath our feet reminded me of the beat to a song Ray used to sing about the day he'd asked Momma to marry him. He'd tap his foot and pat his leg to create the sound of the drum while he'd sing the words.

"Oh, it was the happiest day of my life, when Hope agreed to be my wife. I'm the luckiest guy in the world 'cause pretty little Hope will always be my girl."

How that song made her blush and giggle like a schoolgirl.

The ticket agent at the window of the bus station asked where we were headed. Ray looked up at the board behind the ticket agent's head and asked, "What can ten dollars get in the way of one-way tickets for us two?"

The ticket agent glanced behind himself at the board. He turned his pale face and steel blue eyes back to us, stamped two tickets and said, "Give me the ten dollars."

Ray pulled two crumpled five-dollar bills from the wad of money he had retrieved from his secret stash before we left the house. I'd learned about the extra money and his hiding place the summer before. I stumbled upon him taking money out of the tin can at the back of the garage when I was looking for him. I stopped in my tracks, ducked down, and watched him quietly as he took a couple of bills out of the can and unfurled them. He never saw me, and I never disturbed his can of money.

He straightened the bills out and slid them toward the gentleman through the cutout in the glass, and in exchange received two tickets. He didn't even look to see our destination.

"You'll be boarding two lanes down on the left," the ticket agent called after us.

We boarded the bus and found two seats near the back. The adrenaline I had been operating on was giving way to exhaustion. I wanted to sleep, but I was terrified of what else Ray might be planning. The bus was freezing and I began shivering as we waited to pull out of the station. He reached to draw me into his arms, but I instantly recoiled with a little squeak. He took off his jacket and tossed it onto my lap. I bundled up, curled into a ball and went to sleep against the cold, metal frame of the bus, as far away from him as possible.

We rode for hours. I awoke several times at his prompting. I had no response when Ray asked me if I was hungry, cold, or tired. It would be sensible to say that I thought of running, but I hadn't thought of anything except how my momma looked at her end. I had no idea where we were going or how long we'd been riding. I was afraid of where he might be taking me and what would happen when we arrived, so I allowed sleep to keep me company and give me comfort. I could remember her scent and how my name rolled off her tongue in my dreams. I dreamt that her murder had been a horrible nightmare and that I would wake up and everything would be as it had been before Nana Margie died.

"Mouse, why are your fingers bleeding?" Ray asked during one of the bus' stops.

I looked down and the tips of my fingers, which were raw and bloody. I shrugged my shoulders in response.

"Give me your hands."

Ray wiped my fingers off with a piece of tissue he had in his pocket. I could see that I had chewed my nails so far down that the meat of my nail bed was exposed and tender. I wasn't aware that I was biting myself like that. It wasn't a habit I'd had in Maplewood. Momma would have popped my hand if she'd found me with my fingers in my mouth.

"Now look at you. You look thrown away, like nobody take care of you," he grumbled.

I pushed down the shame of how I looked with my anger and hatred for him. Momma was the one who ironed my clothes fresh off the drying line. She was the one who picked out what I would wear to school and to church. She brushed my hair, tied it down, oiled me up, and said my prayers with me every night. He wanted to fuss at me when he'd taken away the one person who'd chosen to care about how I looked from day to day. I glared at him, hoping he would spontaneously combust.

Finally, we exited the bus for the last time. We were in some little podunk town whose name was unknown to me or Ray. There were a few small, dusty shops on the strip with the bus station, like Harold's Grocery and Meat Market and a local drug store, but they were all closed. It was midday on a Sunday, so most folks were probably in church.

I wondered if anyone in Maplewood was looking for us or if they were looking for me. I wondered if anyone even cared. People in our part of town minded their own business whenever knowing too much was unsafe. Of course, there would be whispers and quiet inquiries behind Momma's death and our disappearances. The police would appear to be interested in finding us. However, with us both gone, no family ties to trace us to, and no witnesses of the crime or us leaving, they wouldn't have much to go on.

We fell right into the crowd walking down the street. Ray reached for my hand, but I withdrew it. I had already come to know I could no longer depend on him for safety or protection. There was no need for his hand. Together, like the tide, we ebbed and flowed with the foot traffic around us. All the people, with skin darkened by genetics and sun, seemed to be headed in one direction, and so were we.

Ray stopped a passerby. "Uh, 'scuse me, sir. You know where me and my daughter could get a room?"

"Yessuh. Gone on down to Fifth Street and take a right. There's a little boarding house about a block up on the left-hand side. See Janie. She'll look after you and your gal," the man replied as he pointed to the street at the end of the block.

"Thank you, man. I 'preciate it."

Ray tipped his hat to the fellow.

We began walking the route the man pointed out. The sun was shining and the air was thick and smelled of a scent I did not recognize. I was beginning to thaw from the ice cold of the bus, but I would gladly brave that cold again to go back in time and be with my Momma.

We passed houses that looked very different from our simple houses in Maplewood. Most of these houses looked like two houses in one, with two doors, two stories, and two car ports — one on either side of the house. Some of them even looked like they had stairs and doors that went down into the ground. Ray had to yank my hand to bring my attention back to walking.

We took the right and there it was: a big two-story pale blue house with white trim, a place that had seen its fair share of transients. This house was not set up like the houses that looked like two-in-one. Its age was evident from the stairs, warped and cracked from years of back and forth. The paint on the railings for the porch had been completely worn off, and left in its place was bare wood that looked dry and brittle.

A withered man in a straw hat sat on the top step of the porch. He gnawed on a piece of the same hat, which was sticking out of the right side of his upturned mouth. We came to know him as West. Simply, West. No one knew if that was his first name, last name, or if that was even his given name at all. No one knew his beginnings or endings, just as no one here would know mine. That was the story of all Ms. Janie's boarders.

"Uh, me and my daughter here need a place to take up for a while. Someone back there on that street told me to see a lady here named Janie." Ray directed his statement at the man on the stairs.

"I'm Janie." A small woman appeared at the screen door. Her eyes were inquisitive and her mouth was set in a way that left her unreadable. Her clothes were plain, nothing special about them that would come to mind immediately if asked to recall them. Her stature was nothing noteworthy either, but those hands…

They immediately drew my attention as she exited the house and walked from the door to the edge of the porch. They were gnarled, like the winding roots of a tree. What those hands had been through was unimaginable to me. She caught my gaze and quickly put her hands in the large pockets on either side of her dress.

"What you need?" Ms. Janie asked.

Ray removed his hat and bowed slightly. "Me and my daughter need a place to stay for awhile and I need work."

"Well, I got folks that pay to live here and folks that work to live here. There's always plenty to do. We need someone to help farm the land back behind the house and we need someone to do repairs to this old thing; your choice. Your work can pay for your room and board and that child can do chores to make her own way. If that deal work wid you, welcome to Franklintown, Virginia. You'll find an empty room on the far-right side of the second floor. Got a little cot we can put in there for the child."

Ms. Janie looked over at me, lowering her head and raising her eyebrows. "You stay from underfoot, ya hear? And mind what I tells you."

I looked down at my feet, wishing there was some way I could disappear. Ray nudged me. I continued to peer down.

"I apologize. She can be quiet as a church mouse. That's what we call her 'cause she so shy." Ray laughed nervously.

I wanted to answer her, but my voice had dug deep down inside me and nestled itself quite nicely underneath my pain.

"That's alright. Seem like she a good child, just quiet. Y'all go on and settle in. Dinner is served around se'm. You can be ready to work fo' day in the morning."

Ms. Janie went back into the house with no question as to who we were, why we ended up here, and how long we'd be staying.

Ray glanced over at me and said, "Mouse, you gone have to talk to folks. People gone think you ain't right in the head if you don't answer 'em."

He circled his finger around his right ear in demonstration of his meaning. Usually, that would have made me laugh.

I watched an ant crawl over my hand-me-down Mary Janes.

"You ain't said nothing since we left Maplewood. Might be better that way," Ray mumbled to himself. "Fine if you don't talk, but you better not cause me ne'er bit of trouble, you hear?"

Ray nudged my shoulder and we entered the house, clambering up the stairs with our suitcases.

The room was simple: a bed, dresser, closet, and a small table with a lamp, none of which were made with any particular care or flourish. I ached thinking about my pretty room back home. I figured I'd better take what this new place had to offer with no complaints. As I ran my fingers over the blanket folded down at the end of the bed, I missed my own bed, my own blanket, my Momma. I choked back the tears and told myself to be a big girl.

Someone knocked at the door. Both Ray and I looked to see who was standing just outside of it. The door was ajar and a young man peered through the open space at us.

"Ms. Janie told me to bring this cot up to this room, sir," the young man finally said.

Ray motioned toward the empty wall.

"Yeah, that's for my daughter. Just put it right over there by the window please."

The fellow looked old enough to be my big brother or maybe even an uncle.

"Yessuh. By the way, my name is Mook. Well, that's what they call me anyway."

Mook's grin was as wide as the door frame in which he stood.

"Alright, Mook. Thank you for bringing this here cot up for me."

My father didn't even glance in his direction.

"No problem, sir. I didn't get your name," Mook said as he continued to grin.

"I didn't give it."

The stern look Ray gave Mook must have spooked him as much as it did me.

"See y'all at dinner," Mook said quickly.

In two seconds flat, he was gone.

As Ray unpacked, he set about the task of telling me who we had become on the trip from Maplewood to Franklintown.

"Mouse, our new last name is Johnson. Same first names so you ain't got so much to remember. Your momma died when you was three. We from Rondale instead of Maplewood and we don't have no other family. Anybody ask you anything else, you tell 'em mind they bidness."

I wondered how much of the trip he'd spent creating our fake past. Rondale was easy enough to remember, it was a larger city right next to Maplewood. I'd only been there twice with Nana Margie; once to find an Easter dress and the other time to visit her ailing cousin. I'd been a Maynard for so long, I worried I might forget the name Johnson. Ray looked over at me for agreement. I bowed my head and pretended to be unpacking what little he'd thrown in my small suitcase.

I looked up again just as he was taking the gun out of his suitcase and tucking it into the back of his dresser drawer. My mouth began to water, which was a sure sign I was about to throw up. I closed my eyes, swallowed the extra spit, and choked down the threat of that nasty, bitter green stuff that would come up if I vomited. When there was no food on my stomach, that was what I got after all that heaving and sweating.

Neither of us spoke the remainder of the night. We both skipped dinner. I was too tired from the trauma of murder and loss combined with the weariness of travel to worry about food. I couldn't tell why Ray stayed in the room. I wondered if he was thinking of Momma and if he felt guilty. He just sat on the edge of the bed with his back to me, staring at the wall.

I washed up in the bathroom at the other end of the hall without having to be told. Then I settled into a restless sleep on a lumpy, unfamiliar cot. It wasn't home, but it was better than the corner of a bus seat.

The sound of the gunshot jarred me out of my sleep during the night. I opened my eyes, unsure of where I was. The bed felt warm and wet beneath me and I smelled the stink of pee. I looked over at Ray's bed. He was still sitting in the same spot, but I could see a small bottle in his right hand. His broad shoulders were slumped and gently bouncing. He wept quietly. He heard me stir and he turned to look at me. I couldn't make out much of his face in the little bit of light from the street lamp outside.

"Mouse? You ok?"

The sadness in his voice created an ache in my chest.

I didn't know how to tell him I'd dreamt of what he'd done. I was afraid to tell him what I'd done.

"I used the bathroom."

I silently prayed he would not snatch me out of the bed and hang me out the window to dry. He dropped his head for a moment, then turned back to me.

"Gone get cleaned up. I'm gone take them sheets off the bed."

I had one more nightgown in the suitcase. I grabbed that and a pair of panties and headed to the bathroom. When I returned, the fitted sheet laid balled up in the corner. He'd covered the wet spot on the cot with a towel. The top sheet and the quilt weren't wet and remained on the bed, pulled back so I could climb back in.

"Put 'em over there, on toppa them sheets. I'll wash 'em in the morning."

I balled up my soiled nightgown and panties and laid them on top of the fitted sheet. Ray laid down on his bed, still dressed in his clothes, minus his shoes.

The sun was beaming into the room when I awoke. Ray was gone and so was the laundry. I could hear Ms. Janie downstairs in the kitchen. I sat up in the bed and rubbed the sleep out of my eyes before hopping up and removing the towel. I hadn't peed the bed much in Maplewood. The few times I did, I remembered Momma scrubbing the mattress and then putting some kind of powder on it to get rid of the smell. I went to the bathroom, and after I cleaned myself up, I soaked my wash rag with water. I took the bar of soap and lathered up the rag as much as I could. I took it back to the room and scrubbed the stained mattress as best as my little hands would allow. I was back and forth to the bathroom sink all morning until I was satisfied that I'd rinsed most of the pee and soap out. I didn't have any of that powder so I decided to let the mattress air dry.

"Ms. Janie made some breakfast if you hungry," Ray said as he returned to the room.

I left him in the room and headed down to the table. Ms. Janie had made grits, eggs, and bacon. She motioned for me to take a seat at the table. She served my food and then placed a fork and napkin on the table before me.

"You sleep ok?"

I nodded my head.

"I saw your sheet and your nightgown out there on the line. I just wanted to make sure you was alright."

I stopped eating. Ms. Janie placed her twisted hand on my back, then took a seat in the chair next to mine.

"Don't worry, child. I'm not upset. I jes' wanna know you alright."

I thought about what might happen if I told her I wasn't alright. I didn't trust Ray not to harm her or anyone else here who might try to help me. I couldn't even find the will to speak about what had happened. I decided not to even try.

Ms. Janie stared at me until I met her gaze. Once I looked her in the eyes and she seemed sure that I'd understood she was concerned, she nodded and stood up from the table. She went on with cleaning the kitchen and allowed me to finish my breakfast quietly.

Ms. Janie pulled a small step stool up to the kitchen sink so I could wash my dishes and silverware. She patted me on the head and told me to go play when I was done. The only problem was I had no toys and no playmates. I went to the room and laid down on the dry parts of the bed instead.

Tuesday morning, Ray announced that I wouldn't be going back to school.

"It's late in the school year. We'll wait 'til August. Guess you get to start your summer early."

I wasn't thrilled about the idea of staying out of school. I enjoyed learning and I was very good at it. My grades were good and my best scores came from spelling, reading, and reading comprehension. Momma said I was smart beyond my years because I liked to read. Nana Margie was always getting books for me to read from the white family whose laundry she did. I wandered around the house with my lip poked out, knowing Momma would have made sure my schooling was a top priority. She'd stayed on me about my schoolwork, sitting with me in the evening to go over spelling words and help me with my math. I supposed I would have to find other ways to stay busy.

Ray had chosen to be the handyman. Ms. Janie's first assignment for him was to paint the house. I'd seen the large buckets with pale yellow dots of dried paint on the label lined up against the back of the house. Yellow was my favorite color and I was excited to see what the house would look like, especially considering I had not seen Ray paint a house before. He seemed like he knew what he was doing from the way he gathered his tools together and began setting up for the task.

Mook had experience with painting and volunteered to help him. I watched as the two of them talked out their plan, set up the ladder, and began applying the new color to the house. It didn't take more than five minutes for Mook to get on

Ray's nerves. Ray's body language showed he was annoyed, though he didn't say it. Mook tried to keep out his way by working on his own section of the house.

Mook was very tall and his skin was a shade of brown you couldn't quite pin down; there were red undertones like the clay dirt in Maplewood. He kept his hair cut low, and his face was bare, but smooth, like he didn't shave to keep it that way. He had a big, bright smile with a dimple in his left cheek. I was fascinated that it was possible to have just one dimple. His legs were bowed, which made his walk stand out. He swayed from side to side more than other men.

Mook often entertained me on his breaks, which he took a little too often for Ray's liking. Ray also didn't care for the fact that Mook had taken a liking to me—not in any fashion other than a teenage boy should like a little sister or cousin. Mook teased me with magic tricks when he'd made a little money from his odd evening jobs. My favorite was when he would pull a penny or a nickel from behind my ear. He'd give me the coin so I could go buy myself some candy.

It took the rest of the week to finish painting, but when they did, they both seemed pleased. Ms. Janie walked out and stood beside Mook and smiled up at the house. She turned and thanked both Ray and Mook for a job well done. Ray nodded and began cleaning up the paint supplies while Mook stood back and looked up at the house, grinning with self-satisfaction.

Mook didn't stay much longer after we arrived; a few months at best. I was sad when I woke up to find he wasn't at breakfast one morning. I'd hoped to see him later in the day. When I didn't, I knew he had chosen to move on. My feelings were hurt that he didn't say goodbye, but no one else even seemed to notice. No mention was ever made of Mook again. I learned that that was life on the road. People would come and people would go; best I not get too attached. It was a bitter reminder that I was no longer in Maplewood and that no place would ever really be a home for me again.

Ms. Janie gave me odd jobs around the house. These were jobs she didn't have time to fool with but still needed to be done nonetheless. My biggest job was to set the table before dinner, a task she taught me how to do.

"You ever learnt how to set a table, child?" Ms. Janie asked one afternoon.

I shook my head.

"Come here. I'll show you once, and after that, you can set the table for all the meals."

I nodded.

I listened intently as she explained what each piece of silverware was used for and where it should be placed. There were five utensils at each setting—a salad fork and dinner fork on the left side, and a knife, teaspoon, and soup spoon on the right. She explained why she set the table for dinner every evening as she was placing the items on the table.

"You know, I always want dinner here to be special. This might be the only meal a person might have on any given day, or maybe they ain't never had nice plates and silverware to eat from. If I never see 'em again after a meal, I want 'em to remember Ms. Janie was kind and gave 'em a belly full."

She chuckled lightly to herself.

Ms. Janie used those gnarled hands so gracefully. I wondered how she could still use them, as badly twisted as they were. Each section of bone between her joints seemed twisted in a different direction. Her hands never seemed to pain her. If they did, she never let on that that was the case. I wanted to ask her about her hands, but even after several months, I still could not use my voice. I couldn't use it even when I was alone.

"Okay, now I finished one. Your turn. Let Ms. Janie see if you was listening."

She cooed like an expectant mother.

I followed her instructions to the letter and she was pleased.

"Now that's just perfect. You alright with me, gal. You alright with me, even if you is mute. I know people think you slow, but I know better. I done watched you since you been here. You swift as they come, and one day, you'll let me hear that voice of yo'r'n. Gone and finish setting the table, and when you done, you can help me put the food out."

She stood for a moment and beamed at my work.

Ms. Janie was so kind to me, and even though I never spoke, she didn't take my silence for rudeness or disobedience. We formed a friendship in spite of my lack of conversation.

Mr. Earl was the next to arrive after me and Ray. He was tall; probably the tallest man I'd ever seen. He was also thin as a rail. It was a wonder his clothes could stay on him because there wasn't much of him for them to hang on. He appeared to be younger than Ray, but older than Mook. Maybe he looked so young because he didn't have a mustache or a beard. His face was clean as a whistle with no blemishes or bumps.

Mr. Earl didn't work in the house or on the land, like Ray or Mook did. Whatever he did to earn money to pay his room and board, he did away from the house. You could usually find him tucked away in his room or in the corner of the parlor reading a book when he was home. He didn't bother much with the men folk of the house, nor did they bother with him. Mr. Earl and Ms. Janie, however, became the best of friends.

When Ms. Janie would have a few minutes to sit still, she'd find Mr. Earl and sit with him. I'd find my way into the same area so I could listen to the two of them talk. Mr. Earl would say something silly, Ms. Janie would howl with laughter, and I'd crack a smile every once-in-a-while. I hadn't really ventured out to try to make friends my age. I felt like no one would like me. I was wearing clothes that were beginning to be too small, I couldn't talk, and I didn't have any nice toys. I was fine with Ms. Janie and Mr. Earl; they had become my friends. They were old enough not to care about any of that other stuff. Having me around to smile at their playfulness was good enough for them.

One afternoon, Ms. Janie taught me how to shine the silverware for the dining table. She left me to do the work. I went and tugged on her apron when I was finished. That was always my signal that the task she had assigned was done.

Ms. Janie walked around the table and looked at each piece of silverware. I held my breath waiting for her reaction to my work.

"Mouse, you follow what I tell you so good most times that when you don't get it just right, I think you doing it on purpose to test me. This ain't quite got the shine I like," Ms. Janie chided gently.

"She ain't got enough elbow grease for that just yet," Mr. Earl piped up from his corner reading spot. "I know how to make it shine. Let that child go play."

Mr. Earl's voice was light and tender. It didn't have the gruffness of most men's voices.

"Alright. You heard Mr. Earl. Off witchu, now. Go play." Ms. Janie gave me a soft smile.

I was kind of relieved. Some neighborhood kids were playing hopscotch outside and I had been listening to their sing-songy rhymes through the open window all afternoon, wishing I could be out there with them.

The kids in the neighborhood were slow to play with me when I did begin going out to play. They thought it weird that I didn't talk and I wasn't in school. A boy my age said as much one day.

I stood on the edge of the large group of kids and watched, trying to seem like I didn't want to be included in their game. A girl who looked a little older than me approached. She had on a dress that was the ugliest shade of green I'd ever seen. Another girl with long, pretty braids on either side of her head was to her left.

"My name is Susie," the green dress wearer stated. "This is Pamela. You wanna come and play hopscotch with us?"

I nodded in return and the circle widened to let me pass. That was the beginning of the Franklintown trio: Susie, Pamela, and me.

The house was quiet, save for Ms. Janie and Mr. Earl talking in the front parlor, when I returned from playing. Ray was nowhere to be found, so I entertained myself in our room. I only had one toy, a small makeshift doll made out of wood that Ms. Janie had given to me. I named her Ruth Anne.

I was bored after having served myself and Ruth Anne several rounds of imaginary tea and biscuits in imaginary cups and saucers. I stood at the top of the stairs thinking about what to do next. I heard Ms. Janie and Mr. Earl in the kitchen. They'd find some work for me to do if I went down now. I turned and wandered down the hall. To this day, I don't know why I went into Mr. Earl's room.

I opened the door and stood in the doorway for a moment to make sure the coast was clear. I slid farther into Mr. Earl's room when I was comfortable enough that no one was coming. His bed was made neatly. Ray never made the bed that neat. The most he did was throw the comforter up to the top of the bed to cover the strewn-about sheets.

There was an old sewing machine on a small table in the corner by the window. It looked like something I could easily break, so I steered clear of it. I decided to investigate his dresser. I had no intention of disturbing anything; I was just being a nosey child.

I opened the highest drawer I could still see into and was confused by what I found. There were women's undergarments, folded nice and neat, in the drawer.

Ms. Janie did not allow unmarried men and women to stay together in her house. She'd mentioned that to Ray one evening when he'd brought a woman over.

"She need to be gone 'fore the sun go down, Ray. Ain't no shacking up in here," Ms. Janie had warned.

I'd never even seen Mr. Earl bring a woman to visit, so why were there women's panties and bras in the drawer?

I opened another drawer and found women's clothing. In the last drawer I could open, I found makeup. I was still trying to figure out what in the world was going on when I felt someone else's presence.

I turned and looked right into Mr. Earl's face. He looked angrier than an alley cat in the rain. He walked over, grabbed me by the shoulders, and shook me.

"What you doing in here, girl? You don't know better than to go putting your nose in other folks' business?"

My soundless crying caused him to release me from his grip.

Mr. Earl started pacing the floor of the room. "Don't look like you came in here to steal from me, so what were you doing?"

Mr. Earl stopped pacing and looked at me with his arms crossed.

I stood looking at Mr. Earl. I had no logical response other than I was curious. I shrugged my shoulders.

"I'm going to have to leave now, you know," he mumbled, more to himself than to me.

I shook my head. I didn't know and didn't understand any of what was happening.

Mr. Earl left the room and walked to the stairway, where he called out, "Janie."

"Yes, Mr. Earl," Ms. Janie responded.

"I need you to come up to my room, please," he said softly.

Ms. Janie came into the room and looked a bit shocked to see me.

"What's going on?" she asked, looking from me to Mr. Earl.

"I came in here and found this child going through my dresser!" He waved his arms around in the air. I knew I was in trouble, but I thought Mr. Earl was being a bit dramatic.

Ms. Janie gasped. She turned to me and said, "Mouse, go to your room right now."

I thought about trying to eavesdrop, but I figured I had done enough for one day.

Ms. Janie came into the room I shared with Ray after a few minutes of talking with Mr. Earl. She sat on my cot and patted the mattress next to her, beckoning me to come sit. I slid over afraid of what was going to happen.

"Now you know what you done was wrong, don't you, Mouse?"

I nodded as I watched her lovingly wipe away the saliva and blood from the tips of my fingers. Ms. Janie never fussed at my bad habit. Once she put hot sauce on my fingers to discourage the biting. It was nasty, but I did it anyway.

"Why would you do such a thing?"

I shrugged.

Ms. Janie sighed as she brushed over her skirt. "Mr. Earl is very afraid that you might tell your father or someone else what you saw in his bedroom. I told him you don't even talk, so you won't tell nobody, but he don't believe me. He's packing his stuff right now. Mr. Earl is my friend and I sho' would hate for him to go, 'specially like this. You help me talk him into staying," Ms. Janie said as she nodded.

I nodded along with her. I didn't want Mr. Earl to go either.

Ms. Janie and I padded back down to Mr. Earl's room together.

"Mr. Earl, I just got through talking to Mouse and she agreed to complete silence on what happened here tonight." Ms. Janie looked at me solemnly, and I nodded slow and hard to show my agreement.

"Now, if she ain't gone tell, and Lawd knows I ain't gone tell, you ain't got to leave."

Mr. Earl stopped packing and sat on the edge of the bed. He looked me over slowly.

"You don't even understand what you saw, do you, child?" he asked.

I shook my head.

"Alright, if you both promise to keep my secret, I'll stay," Mr. Earl promised.

Mr. Earl put his left hand out into the air between the three of us. Ms. Janie put her mangled hand atop his and they both looked at me. I put my small, delicate hand on top of both theirs. Mr. Earl smiled at me and touched my face gently.

Ms. Janie walked me toward the door and told me, "Alright, child. Go get washed up and I'll come tuck you in. Yo' daddy probably won't be back here until the wee hours of the morning."

Over the next few days I held my breath every time Ray was around Ms. Janie and Mr. Earl. I didn't know if they would tell about me sneaking into Mr. Earl's room. I wasn't sure that either one of them would keep my secret just because I'd sworn to keep Mr. Earl's. A week came and went and there was no whipping for being nosey and out of place. I breathed easier as each day passed without the truth being told.

It didn't take long for Mr. Earl to return to his usual self with me. The whole ordeal even became a source of laughter for the three of us. We would often grin at one another when we were all in the same room, reveling in the fact that we had a secret no one else knew.

One day Ray asked, "Why y'all always grinning like the cat that ate the canary?"

"Wouldn't you like to know," Mr. Earl replied.

He gave Ray an unfamiliar look, which made Ms. Janie chuckle. Ray quickly left the room.

Mr. Earl easily reduced grown men to uncomfortable, child-like awkwardness. Both he and Ms. Janie laughed until they cried. I didn't understand why it was so funny, but the two of them laughing made me really happy for the first time since I'd left home.

Three

Ms. Janie, Mr. Earl, Susie, and Pamela became my life lines. Ms. Janie told me stories of some of the more interesting characters who'd come to stay at her house. Mr. Earl tutored me in my classes and sewed matching clothes for me and the doll baby Pamela had given me. Susie and Pamela shared their secrets and desires with me. I soaked up all the love and attention I could from each one of them. God knows I didn't get any of that from Ray.

Ray was around, but he didn't seem to want much to do with me. The feeling was mutual. I wasn't any more bonded to him than I was to a rug on the floor. He worked odd jobs around the neighborhood to earn money to support his drinking. He only stayed sober long enough to do the tasks Ms. Janie gave him for the day. You could find him searching for the bottom of a bottle once his work was done.

I remember one day when he'd found what he was looking for.

"Let's go play outside," Susie suggested.

Pamela looked over at me and I nodded. It was perfect weather and I didn't mind soaking up some sun before it would be time for me to come in and set the table for dinner.

The three of us were busy making mud pies for our play dinner when Ray walked up.

"What y'all doing?"

The hair on my arms stood on end. I wasn't close enough to smell him, but I could tell from his tone he'd been drinking his juice. That's what Ms. Janie and Mr. Earl called it anyway.

"Baking pies for our Sunday dinner tomorrow," Susie answered.

"Ain't no man want no mud pie!"

I dropped my head to hide the tears welling up in my eyes.

"Ain't no man welcome to our mud pie. It's for us," Pamela answered defiantly.

"Ain't no man want a gal with so much lip, neither," Ray countered.

"Fine by me. Too much trouble anyway." Susie cocked her head to the side when she responded.

Pamela and I were shocked. We looked at each other in disbelief. Though I was the only one that was completely mute in our little trio, Susie rarely spoke to anyone outside of us and her family.

My tears dried right up and a sly smile was teasing the corners of my mouth, but I knew I'd better hold on to it.

"Mouse, get on in the house and get the table ready for a real dinner. If you ain't gone talk, you need to at least learn some skills that might help you in this world. Can't feed no man with dirt."

The girls both looked over at me. I nodded at them to signal I was ok.

"Wanna come to church with us in the morning?" Susie asked.

"Naw, she can't come." Ray answered for me.

The girls both came and hugged me before leaving.

"We'll come by tomorrow after dinner if that's okay with your daddy," said Pamela.

She looked over at Ray. He nodded.

The girls left. Ray passed me and went into the house. I released the grin that I'd been restraining. I was glad someone had stood up to him, even if it was only about mud pie. I wished I'd had that strength the day he killed Momma.

His scent lingered on the air after he'd passed. He smelled like the contents of one of his bottles. I'd smelled many of them while tidying up our bedroom on a Saturday morning after one of his Friday-night benders.

Ms. Janie must have seen the whole exchange from inside the house. She called me into the kitchen after dinner was done and Ray had gone to our room.

"You okay?"

I nodded.

"Yo' daddy love you, you know. I think he just have a hard time showing it."

I stood motionless as she patted me on the back. I knew Ms. Janie meant well, but she had no idea who Ray really was. I came to the realization that I hadn't either, until it was too late.

The rest of the summer the girls and I kept our play dates in areas we were sure Ray would not show up. He liked to come and go from the back of the house so the nosey neighbors wouldn't know when he was there or not. We'd play in the front of the house or Ms. Janie would give me permission to go down the street to Susie's house or two blocks over to Pamela's.

Pamela was the first to start creating our own little hand language with me. Susie quickly joined in, and we all made up signs as we went along. They were simple signs, like two hands bent at the wrist to represent a dog, and swipe with a curved hand to represent a cat. When we'd get excited, the three of us could really move fast with our signs. When it was the three of us, we'd only use our language to communicate with one another. I thought they felt special having a secret way of talking that no one else really understood. I felt special that they would do that that for me. Both of them were easy to be with and made me feel like I belonged. They had become sisters to me by the time school started.

The first days of school were easy. Both Susie and Pamela protected me at school just like they'd done in the neighborhood. The other kids left me alone for the most part, since it was evident that Susie and Pamela would not have me being picked on. Every now and then someone would get up the nerve to bother me about why I didn't talk. Either Susie or Pamela would answer, saying it was my business as to why. They'd both taken home a bruise or two for sticking up for me, which didn't bother them one bit.

One day, Winnie decided to lay into me about being mute. Winnie was the biggest, meanest girl in the whole school. She was taller than all the other third graders, and she was built like a football player.

"Must be dumb if she can't talk," Winnie teased.

"She's smart enough to be in her right grade. Didn't you get left back?" Pamela asked.

The crowd that had followed Winnie over to our group on the playground covered their mouths to hide their giggles and smirks.

Winnie's hands balled into fists at her side. Everyone knew that was a sore spot for her, including me.

"You shut up, like your dumb little friend over there."

"Make me."

Winnie charged Pamela at the invitation.

Pamela sidestepped the attack and stuck her foot out to make Winnie fall. The crowd howled with laughter to see Winnie face down in a plume of dust. She stayed on the ground until everyone left the area. Her pride wouldn't allow her to even acknowledge what had happened. No one told on

Pamela when the teacher asked why Winnie's clothes had gotten so dirty during recess. There were no more attempts to tease or embarrass me after that.

My relationship with Ms. Janie and Mr. Earl was just as uncomplicated. They did all the talking, I did all the listening, and it worked out just fine. The routine stayed the same as the years passed. I'd come home from school, and Ms. Janie would give me a snack. Mr. Earl would help me with my homework. If I finished my homework at a decent time, the girls and I could play in the yard. I'd come in, clean myself up, and set the table when it was dinner time. I might see Ray before bedtime, but he usually left Ms. Janie and Mr. Earl to worry about caring for me. On the weekends, I'd hang out with Susie and Pamela from sunup to sundown.

In the two years I'd been there, I still had not spoken a word. We should have kept things that simple.

One evening, I was in the dining room setting the table, and Ms. Janie and Mr. Earl were in the kitchen. I wandered into the room with them after I was done. Usually, Ms. Janie's conversation would depend on her mood. I guess she felt inquisitive on this day.

"Mouse, how come you don't talk to nobody?" Ms. Janie asked. "When you got here, yo' daddy expected you to answer me, and when you didn't, he just said you was quiet. That mean you can talk, you just choosin' not to. You too old now to not be talking."

I shrugged and continued to watch her stir the pot sitting on top of the stove. Mr. Earl sat quietly at the table working on a cross-stitch pillow for the den.

Mr. Earl chimed in, "I bet you got a nice voice. You even look like you could sing real pretty if you wanted. What happened to make you never wanna talk ever again?"

I didn't respond. Most times, their questions were rhetorical, and even if they weren't, I don't think they really expected me to answer. I thought about why I had not heard the sound of my own voice in two years.

Ms. Janie tried encouraging me. "Why don't you try, child? I know you can. I know you got it in you. What happened so bad that you just don't wanna speak?"

She sounded near tears. I was thankful for her concern, but I was fearful of trying to force my voice to return. It seemed to have a mind of its own. I'd tried to influence it once or twice. It was clear to me that it would resurface when it was good and ready.

Ms. Janie stopped what she was doing and sat down directly across from me. She reached those twisted, mangled hands across the table toward mine and looked deeply into my eyes. I wondered if she could see or sense my hesitation. I felt like if I opened my mouth, everything would come spilling out, and then what would happen to my new family?

"I tell you what. I'm gonna tell you a story about how my hands come to look like this, but only if you agree to answer me and Mr. Earl when we talking to you. I don't care if you talk to no one else, but if you gone hang around us, I need to be able to talk and have you talk back. It's been nice having you around, 'cause you just syrupy sweet and cute as a button. I don't have no chil'ren of my own, and you done become like mine. I'd like to hear my own gal's voice. What you think?" she asked.

I wasn't sure why my speaking was so important to her, but I nodded in agreement.

"Alright, we got ourselves a deal. I was about your age when it happened. My momma died when I was two and my momma's twelve underage children were split between the two oldest girls and my grandma. The two oldest girls were married off, and my oldest brother went to find work further north. I was one of the ones sent to Memaw, our grandmother. There was no place for chil'ren who couldn't fend for themselves or earn their keep with our older sisters; couldn't add any stress to they new marriages.

"Memaw was a mean old woman. Bitter and cold as they come, but she was all us three little ones had; me, my older brother James, and my younger sister Tippa. I tried my best to do my chores and stay outta Memaw's way. This one day, I was going to take the clothes off the line, and I told Tippa, who I was also supposed to be watching, to stay put. Tippa was the most mischievous of us all, and James and I took a whollup or two because of something she had done, but she was the baby, and I guess that was our way of protecting her.

"Well, when I came back, I found Tippa in the same spot alright, but she was covered with flour like she was about to be dipped in a hot vat of grease and fried up for dinner. I followed her little flour footprints back to the cupboard and found that she had knocked over the bag of flour in a' attempt to get to the peppermint candies that Memaw only let us have in church. The bag and everything in it were in a heap on the cupboard floor. I tried to clean up the mess, make the bag look like it had never been disturbed, and clean Tippa up before Memaw got back from town.

"I swear that woman must have known how much flour was in that sack down to the smallest grain! As soon as she walked in that cupboard, she turned and looked at the three of us and she asked who had been in her flour. James had no idea what had happened, so he told her he had been out in the barn all day. I just sat there like a bump on a log while Tippa laughed and giggled, all the while looking at her toe peeking up from up under the blanket that was covering her. She had no clue how much danger she put us in.

"Memaw yanked me up by the collar of my shirt so fast and drug me in the cupboard. She told me to get on my knees in the cupboard and put my hands flat on the floor. I was so scared. I didn't know what she was going to do to me, but I knew it wouldn't be good. She told me she was going to teach me not to touch her things without her telling me. She took this heavy brown- and cream-speckled jug down from one of the higher shelves that none of us children could reach. I still to this day don't know what she kept in that jug because I stayed far away from that cupboard unless I was told to go in there. She lifted that heavy jug above her head and smashed it down hard on my hands. I hollered so loud that Tippa cried out, but I heard her cry cut-off real short-like. I think James had put his hand over her mouth so neither one of them got a beating too. She smashed my hands again, but I don't remember feeling anything after that first time. I think I passed out after three times. She never took me to see a doctor, and this is how my hands healed—mangled and ugly."

I stared at Ms. Janie in disbelief. My only references for grandmas had been Nana Margie and the grandmothers of my friends. None of them would ever have done such a terrible thing.

"So child, bad happen to all of us. You can't let that keep you from being you and letting your little light shine. You got a beautiful light in you. You understand Ms. Janie?"

She looked at me with expectation.

"Yes, ma'am," I said, barely above a whisper.

I gasped, taken aback that I'd actually spoken.

That was enough to excite Ms. Janie and Mr. Earl.

"Well, I'll be . . . she does have a voice!" Ms. Janie squealed. Her eyes lit up and she slapped her knee. She seemed so happy for two little words. She hopped up, and so did Mr. Earl. They held hands and danced a little jig around the kitchen, humming a song I'd never heard before.

Every evening at dinner, Ms. Janie's boarders shared their stories. Some would be sad; others would make the whole group burst into laughter. That night, Ms. Janie told one of her stories, and she turned to me for agreement. She said, "Ain't that right, Mouse?" or "Tell 'em, Mouse!" To which I responded quietly, "Yes, ma'am."

Ray hadn't been at ease since we left Maplewood, but this seemed to make him downright nervous. I think he had taken a liking to me not speaking. That, at least, meant his secret was safe. The truth of what he had done was in danger of being revealed now that I seemed to have found my voice. I knew from the look on his face at the table that speaking had been a mistake.

"Mouse, get up."

I awoke to Ray shaking my shoulders, his face hovering above mine. He already had our bags packed and my clothes laid out.

It had to be unreasonably early because there was not the tiniest hint of sun shining through the window. In that moment, I understood what my speaking had meant to him. It meant it was time to move on; time to find another place where we could be anonymous. As long as I started out speaking there, it wouldn't matter; but we couldn't stay in a place where I had once been the little girl who wouldn't talk.

I blinked my eyes to try to dry up the tears that were threatening to form. I would not give Ray the satisfaction of seeing me cry. I searched his face for the thing that Momma must have fallen in love with. I couldn't find any remnant of it. As we walked to the door of the house, my chest tightened with pain.

"You knew this would happen," I whispered to myself.

I had to calm myself. Making a scene wouldn't help anyone, especially not me.

"What?" Ray asked, annoyed.

"Nothing."

We slipped out of the house into the cool, dark night without another word.

Edenville

Four

Ray and I had been riding all day and through the night. I slept in between bathroom breaks and eating the few snacks Ray was able to buy. He'd spent most of his side-job money on our tickets and said he needed the rest just in case he had to pay for a place to stay. Sleep was the only way to avoid both him and my hunger.

At least I was dressed properly for the trip this time. I had on a warm jacket, a long-sleeved shirt, an undershirt, pants, and socks. Franklintown's weather had entered that phase where Mother Nature seemed confused. Early morning coolness, afternoon heat, and unpredictable evenings kept me guessing at what to wear. It was the time of year I hated most in Maplewood. Fall signaled the end of fun. The first cold snap meant no more activities like being sprayed with the water hose, sitting outside eating watermelon, or church cookouts.

Franklintown had made fall bearable with bright, beautiful colors I'd never before seen in trees. Ms. Janie had Ray rake those leaves into piles. Mr. Earl, the girls, and I made Ray mad because we kept using those piles as soft landing pads for our leaps into the air. Mr. Earl even taught me how to press leaves so I could keep the prettiest ones.

I wasn't sure what to expect when we arrived at our mystery destination, but the dropping temperature every time we made a stop told me I should not be expecting warmth. The farther we rode, the colder it became. My legs were stiff and aching by the time Ray nudged me and told me to get up. The sky was dim and the air had an uninviting bite on this new morning in this new town. Though it's magical for a nine-year-old child to witness what happens when hot breath hits cold air, I was too frightened and frozen to enjoy it.

Ray made it clear that my tongue best be bridled in this town.

"I don't care if you talk. In fact, it might be best you don't," Ray half-hissed, half-whispered. "But I swear if you do or say one damned thing 'bout your Momma, I'll choke the life right outta you! Hear me?"

His hand rested on my chest with his fingers and thumb on either side of my throat, almost as if, with a single thought, he could crush my windpipe. I looked at the creases in his face and wondered when he'd become this person. Could losing your momma and your job make you evil? I'd lost my Momma, but I didn't turn into a big old ball of ugly. Why did he change?

I nodded my understanding. He didn't have to threaten me. Loss had already wrapped itself around me and strangled any hope of a regular life right out of my mind.

We went in search of a place that would offer room and board in exchange for work, just as we'd done in Franklintown. In Edenville, it was Sookie's, the local whorehouse. Edenville, Michigan was small, and all the folks of working age were already settled into jobs. Those who were looking were folks who didn't have roots in this town. I had no desire to grow any there.

Sookie's was a two-story house that stood at the corner of Williams and Stark. The house had a simple exterior. Tan in color with white trim and shutters. The roof was covered with shingles that were the same color as the house. The front porch had a small table with two wooden chairs on both sides of the door and a long swing hanging from the top of the far right end. The chairs and the swing had matching gold cushions.

Ray marched right up the stairs and knocked on the front door despite the bystanders that looked at the house and us with their mouths turned up as if they smelled something stink.

The door opened to a statue of a woman looking shocked at our arrival.

"Well, ain't nobody knocked on this front door in ages. Y'all ain't from 'round here," she said with squinted eyes.

The woman looked Ray up and down. Then, she turned her attention to me and studied me for an uncomfortable moment.

"What can I do for you?" She turned her attention back to Ray.

"Me and my daughter here need a place to stay. I can work for you to cover both our room and board."

"Now ain't this something. What's y'alls names and where you from?"

"Franklintown, North Carolina. I'm Ray and this here is Hannah."

The woman inhaled and exhaled slowly. "And how y'all know to come here?"

"I didn't, ma'am. It just looked like a place where I might be able to find what I'm looking for."

"Hmph. You can call me Ms. Sookie." She paused as if she was thinking something over. "Well, I sure do need the help of a big strong man around here. And I need a young lady who can do some things around the house that I just don't have time to do no more. Y'all come on in."

Ms. Sookie shifted her weight back and pulled the door open further while eyeing us both.

"The folks around here let you run this place with no trouble?" Ray asked after looking around at the girls who'd gathered in the study, which we passed as we followed Ms. Sookie.

I thought it was strange that there were only young women living in this house.

"The black folk turn down they noses at us, but they leave us alone. The white folk pretend as if we ain't here. This house sits between both sides of town and it's mine free and clear. We all mind our own business and it works out just fine. This house gonna be a problem for you?"

"No, ma'am… I mean, Ms. Sookie."

Ms. Sookie was larger than life. She dressed in clothes that I had never seen before: smooth, satiny material, brilliant yellows and reds, blues and greens. Every curve of her body was hugged by fabric like a family member you'd loved and hadn't seen in ages. Her shoes had a heel higher than any shoes Momma had worn. The sound of her heels beating the floor created a rhythm that made you want to dance. She almost looked as if she was dancing when she walked.

She had on a lot of makeup, much more than I'd ever seen anyone wear. Through too-blue eyeshadow and too-red lips, I could still see how pretty she really was. I was sure she was far older than she looked, but upon asking how old she was, I was told "never to ask a woman her age."

"You can tend to the grounds and maintain the house, and Hannah can tend to my room. I haven't had a customer in years. I make enough money to pay the bills and live comfortably without having to entertain personally," she explained to Ray.

I wondered what her talent was. Could she juggle? Maybe she could sing. I didn't think she was quite tall or slender enough to be like the dancers in the picture shows. She wasn't exactly fat, but she wasn't thin, either.

"Ray, before the week is out, take Hannah on down to that school. In the evening, she needs to be cleaning my room or in y'all room. I can't have no kids running around here while my girls are trying to work. No man wants to screw a whore with a child around. It reminds them of they obligations at home. They come here to forget about all that… for a while, anyway," Ms. Sookie said wistfully.

What was a whore and what did they have to do with screws? Ray used screws around me just fine when he built stuff. I shrugged off my confusion.

"Well, uh… I don't think Mouse need to go to no school," Ray responded doubtfully.

Ms. Sookie's eyebrows drew together at the use of "Mouse," then relaxed in recognition that he was talking about me.

Ms. Sookie responded matter-of-factly, "Whether you think she *need* to go or not, she don't *need* to be around here looking at grown folk being grown. It ain't good for a girl child. She'll learn when she's old enough what goes on between a man and a woman, but for now, she's too young. If you wanna work here, you gonna have to do as I ask on that one."

"Uh, alright. I'll take her tomorrow."

Ray and I both understood that was the final say on the matter.

"And one last thing, Ray. As the only rooster living in the hen house," Ms. Sookie said as she looked at him long and hard, "stay away from my girls."

To that, Ray simply nodded.

"Now that that's settled, Mouse, let me show you my room and what I need you to do," Ms. Sookie said as she ushered me along the hallway of the first floor.

Ms. Sookie's room was just as lively as she was. The walls were covered in a deep, rich red satin-like fabric. The furniture was white, and all the accessories—the bedspread, lamps, and pillows—were either the same color as the walls or this happy shade of orange that perfectly matched the red. She had art on the walls that didn't look like anything I'd ever seen before.

Ms. Sookie's hair… that was a whole 'nother thing. Her wigs were neatly placed on fake heads on top of their own shelf. They were all big and bright, and there was one for each day of the week. She introduced me to each of them.

"This is Charity. I wear her on Sundays so I can look like a good, God-fearing woman. Faith is for Mondays. Joy for Tuesday. Grace and Mercy, I wear on Wednesday and Thursday," she said of two wigs that were the same style, but different colors. "I wear Patience on Friday and Kindness on Saturday, to remind me not to let these folk get on my nerves."

Ms. Sookie nodded after going through all their names as if she were proud of remembering them.

Her vanity table was covered with makeup, makeup brushes, hair brushes, and combs. These were all items that I had only read about or seen in catalogues. My mother had not worn much makeup and our house was pretty plain in comparison. I was fascinated. I secretly hoped I would be spending a lot of time alone in this room.

Ms. Sookie suggested we take the rest of the day to settle in once she finished showing us around the house.

"It shouldn't be too rowdy around here tonight. Y'all get some rest, and I'll see y'all for lunch."

Ms. Sookie dropped us off at our room.

Ray began moving quietly around the room. I followed suit, and we unpacked our belongings in silence. He took the top three drawers of the tall, brown dresser, and I took the bottom two. There was no discussion about our new lives. He had introduced us with the same names, which was fine with me. It would have been more work to remember a new lie.

Ray grabbed one of the towels and washcloths that Ms. Sookie had given us. He walked out of the room, leaving me to guess he was going to take a bath. I was annoyed that he didn't give me the chance to go first. We both "smelled like yesterday," as Nana Margie would sometimes say. I surveyed the two brass-framed, twin-sized beds in the room. I chose the bed farthest away from the door, searched for a fingernail to bite off, and waited my turn.

When Ray returned, I grabbed the other washcloth and towel and went into the hallway. The house felt quiet and still. I realized that the girls who'd been hanging around when we first arrived seemed to vaporize. I closed and locked the door, then ran some tepid water for my bath.

I returned to the room to find Ray propped up against the headboard of his bed.

"Ms. Sookie seem nice," Ray said softly.

"Yessir."

"Think you gone like it here?"

I was caught off guard. I couldn't remember the last time Ray cared how I felt about anything. I wasn't sure what he wanted from me.

"Yessir."

I watched his reaction. He nodded his head slowly.

"Franklintown was too easy to find us in. It was time to go."

I guessed this was his attempt at apologizing for taking me from Ms. Janie, Mr. Earl, Susie, and Pamela. It didn't matter. There was no apology that could clear him of taking my Momma from me.

"Yessir."

That was the only answer I could muster that wouldn't manage to get me slapped, or worse.

Ms. Sookie called us down to a late lunch. The table was set for two. There was a large bowl of spaghetti in the center of the table. There were plates with sliced garlic bread, chicken wings, and string beans.

"Get y'all a belly full. I don't know when's the last time you had a hot meal," Ms. Sookie told us.

We both inhaled the food. I didn't know if it tasted good or not. I was in too much of a rush to ease the angriness in my stomach.

Ray had excused himself as soon as he was done eating. I continued eating alone. Ms. Sookie came to check on us and sat with me until I finished.

"Where is everyone?" I asked Ms. Sookie as she was clearing the table of our dirty dishes.

"Work at night, sleep all day. They'll smell the spaghetti and come get them some after while."

"What do they do?"

Ms. Sookie stopped moving and looked at me with her head slightly tilted.

"My ladies are entertainers," she answered slowly.

It felt like she was looking for the right words to use.

"What can they do?"

Ms. Sookie sighed with exasperation.

"Chile, all you need to know is this ain't work you want to do when you get grown. Don't matter how you entertain a man, it ain't never enough."

Ms. Sookie took the dishes into the kitchen, leaving me with a million questions. How old did you have to be to become an entertainer? I could sing a little bit. Maybe I could earn enough money to get away from Ray and go back to Maplewood. Maybe I could find a new place to travel since there wasn't anything left in Maplewood for me anyway.

I walked into our room only to find Ray napping in his bed. The food had had the same effect on me and I was ready to lie down as well. I crawled under the sheets and found the bed was cozy and soft. Sleep took me. Neither Ray or I heard any of the goings-on at Ms. Sookie's that night.

Ray escorted me to the school bright and early the next morning. He stood off to the side of my new classroom while I stood in front with what felt like a thousand eyes on me. There were really only forty eyes, but none of them seemed friendly or welcoming. He finished his conversation with the teacher and nodded at me on his way out the door. He seemed to suck the air out of the room with him when he left. There I was, left in a vacuum of unknowing. I willed myself not to look at my feet or bite my fingernails. I knew other children could be cruel. I was determined not to be an easy target.

"Class, this is Hannah Johnson. Everyone say hello to Hannah," the teacher said as she introduced me.

"Hi, Hannah!" the class said in unison.

My real name didn't even sound right. While the last school was given my name, everyone still called me Mouse.

"Hannah, you can call me Mrs. Higgins." There seemed to be a slight air of something in the way she spoke to me, but I couldn't quite put my finger on what it was. It seemed as if she knew she wasn't going to like me even though she had only known me for minutes.

Mrs. Higgins was plain. Her hair was combed back into a tight bun. She wore glasses that dangled from her neck with a chain more often than they were on her face. Her earth-colored dress was slightly too big, though she was a small-framed woman. Her shoes were what I would call boring.

Nothing about her was fiery or eye-catching like Ms. Sookie.

The small school was like Mrs. Higgins—just plain. There were only two classrooms. Everyone in my class looked no older than twelve. The older kids were taught in the other room. I had no concerns that I wouldn't be able to keep up with the lessons because Mr. Earl had been a great tutor. So much so, I had been ahead at the last school when I left.

Mrs. Higgins kept a watchful eye on me at the beginning of class. She eased off once she was certain that I was able to do the work. She picked up a little silver bell from the front corner of her desk and rang it after we'd worked on our English and Math for a few hours. The other children put their books away and I followed suit. Everyone, including Mrs. Higgins, grabbed their brown sacks or lunch pails and headed outside. I didn't have anything but a leftover biscuit and a piece of meat, but I was thankful to have that.

I sat on the outskirts of a group of girls about my age. They all eyed me occasionally, but no one invited me closer. Mrs. Higgins was eating lunch with the other teacher on a bench. I ate my dry biscuit and juicy slice of ham in silence.

Recess followed lunch. I hoped to be invited when some of my classmates began to play a game I knew well. Again, I proved to be semi-invisible. As "red rover, red rover, send Annie right over" was sung by the left side, I walked up to the right line and tried to join hands with the girl on the end. She pulled her hand away like I had been diagnosed with a disease. Embarrassed, I sat down under a tree with my back toward all the fun. I patiently waited alone for the bell to ring. I thought about how Susie and Pamela had taken me right in, and I missed them terribly. I dusted off my fingers and began to chew on my nails while I worried about how long it was going to take for me to make some friends. I wondered if I'd be able to make any at all, considering that folks didn't like where I lived.

I was relieved when the bell rang for us to return to class. As I was walking back to the building, I was approached. Finally, someone wanted to talk to me! I smiled at the girl in the pretty blue dress who was a good foot-and-a-half taller than me.

"Hey, new girl," the girl said in a sing-song way that was syrupy sweet and lime sour all at the same time. I didn't know names yet, but I knew from the way she said "new girl" that she wasn't here to make friends. My smile faded.

"My name is Mou… I mean, Hannah," I corrected her. I had forgotten Mrs. Higgins hadn't mentioned my nickname. She called everyone in the class by their birth-given names. You wouldn't hear any "Toot Toot" or "Pudding" in her classroom.

The girl questioned me, "Don't yo' daddy work at Sookie's?"

I was afraid to answer. I didn't know much about what happened there, but Ms. Sookie made it clear that women who didn't work there didn't like it.

"Yeah," I said flatly as I nudged the rocks on the ground with my feet.

"You know what goes on at Sookie's?" she asked mockingly as she squinted her eyes.

This girl shouldn't know what went on at Ms. Sookie's either.

"All I know is a lot of men come there at night," I answered shyly. Maybe she didn't know. Maybe if I told her, she would like me.

She smirked at me and asked, "Any of them come to see you?" The girls and boys who'd gathered around like a hive to their queen giggled and covered their mouths.

"No," I said as I shook my head quickly.

The girl looked me over and mused, "Hmph. Well, guess it won't be long before you have a caller like Lizzy."

"Who's Lizzy?" I wondered out loud.

"Ask around at Sookie's. You'll find out," the girl retorted. She stared at me intently after that last response. Neither of us said another word, but before anyone could, Mrs. Higgins herded us back inside.

As the crowd headed in, I lagged behind.

"Don't mind Lilly Anne. She's a bag of hot air," a young boy's voice floated in from behind me. I looked up to see the most beautiful dark brown boy walking beside me. Either he walked like a panther or I was so wrapped up in trying to figure out what Lilly Anne meant that I didn't hear him approach.

"She always so nice?"

He chuckled.

"Oh, she's just a charm," he said, clasping his hands and blinking rapidly. "Lilly Anne's daddy owns the only black store in town, so her family has a little more than most. She thinks that means she can treat folks any kinda way. Everybody lets her get away with it 'cause her daddy ain't the one to make mad. I once saw him charge a man twice what he should for some corn meal just because he thought the man looked at his wife," the dark brown boy rattled on.

"What's your name?" I asked.

"Rudolph, but you can call me Rudy. It don't matter that your daddy works at Sookie's. My daddy is in there all the time," he responded, flashing the prettiest smile I'd ever seen besides my momma's. "Momma gets so mad at him coming there, she could spit. But they stopped fighting about it a long time ago when Daddy started back working. He don't go as much, but he still go. I don't know what the big deal is anyway. They just play cards and drink tea. Daddy said when I get his age, I'll understand."

I wanted to know more about Rudy.

"How old are you?" I asked.

"Nine, almost ten. How old is you?"

I paused before responding, "Nine." I'd almost forgotten how many birthdays had passed since leaving Maplewood. There hadn't been any celebrations. No family gathering around. No cake. No candles. Birthday parties were a thing of the past.

"Well, me and my little sister come to town with my momma every evening. My momma works nights in the restaurant across from Sookie's to make extra money, so I guess I'll see you around,"

Rudy said as he picked up his pace. He ran ahead into the classroom. I couldn't help but smile. It seemed like Rudy was offering to be my friend.

It didn't take long for me and Ray to find a new routine. In the mornings, he would scrape together leftover meat and bread for me to take for lunch. I don't know what he did while I was at school, but he was always done and giggling with the ladies by the time I got home. I would go right into Ms. Sookie's room, never without knocking first, and straighten up her room. My first task was to sweep, if the room needed it. The bare, wooden floor would often have strands of wig hair all over it. I'd dust the dresser after sweeping, straighten the items on the vanity table, adjust the "girls" on the wig heads, and straighten out her bed.

The best part of the day came after my chores and homework were done. I would play across the street with Rudy and Beenie, his little sister. Rudy had become my best friend, and I had grown to love Beenie as if she were my own baby sister. The three of us, sometimes joined by Rudy and Beenie's cousin Frank, played all evening until the street lights came on. We played games everybody knew, like hide and seek, and we played games we made up, like mommy and daddy. Rudy and I were usually the parents, and I insisted on a wedding ceremony each time we played. Beenie and Frank were our children. Frank usually got irritated because Rudy wouldn't let him be the daddy even though he was a year older.

What Lilly Anne had said to me kept playing over and over in my head, even though I'd been there for two weeks. I paid real close attention in the halls, in the kitchen, and anywhere I could cross the path of one of Ms. Sookie's working girls, but there wasn't one working for her named Lizzy.

One afternoon, I was milling around in the kitchen. Sometimes Ms. Sookie's cook, Mrs. Jameson, would slip me an afternoon snack. She was a sweet widow, but no matter her disposition or circumstance, no one was immune to the hatred poured on anyone in Ms. Sookie's employ, even if your job didn't include what happened in bedrooms late at night. I was sitting at the table trying my best to look hungry without looking as if I were begging. If Ray caught me doing that, he would have skinned me alive. I knew his rule about Maynards. Even though we had assumed the last name Johnson, the same rule still applied.

A young girl walked in whom I had not seen before. Her walk was slow and moved from side to side like a swing on a lazy summer day.

"Hey, Suga," Mrs. Jameson greeted after she looked up to see who was coming into the kitchen. Mrs. Jameson offered a warm smile for her just as she did anyone else who came into her sacred space.

"Hey, Mrs. Jameson," the girl responded with a smile. The young girl's face was plastered with makeup.

"I saw your Momma the other day, Suga," Mrs. Jameson said happily.

"Did she ask about me?" Suga sounded hopeful.

"No," Mrs. Jameson replied. "But I'm sure she wanted to, honey."

"No she didn't, Mrs. Jameson. She don't care nothing about me now."

I silently watched both women. They looked like they were from totally different worlds.

"Suga, I bet if you went home, she would welcome you with open arms. I know'd you since you was just a little girl. You ain't got no business working here. You barely old enough to be doing the things you doing," Mrs. Jameson said while shaking her head.

"You work here," Suga snapped.

"Not like you do, Suga." Mrs. Jameson exhaled like she was exasperated.

She stopped peeling the potatoes she was preparing for dinner and turned back to Suga.

"I ain't got nothing bad to say about Ms. Sookie, 'cause God only knows where I'd be without this job, but don't let this work keep you here forever. You hear me, Lizzy?"

My head snapped to attention when Mrs. Jameson said that name. Suga glanced over at me.

"Mrs. Jameson, no disrespect, but I asked you not to call me that, and I don't wanna talk about it. I got a customer coming in just a bit. I just came in here to get a glass of water," Suga said, suddenly disinterested in the conversation.

"I hate to see you like this. Don't stay in this place too long. Even if you don't go back home, get out of here and find something else to do with your life," Mrs. Jameson warned.

I was trying to pretend like I wasn't listening. Lizzy, or Suga, looked at me and rolled her eyes. She swayed her narrow hips to the sink with her glass in hand, ran some water in it from the tap, then walked right out of the kitchen without another word.

It was time for me to go tend to Ms. Sookie, so I left the kitchen and made my way to her room. Wherever Lizzy's room was in the house, she must have mastered the art of keeping to herself.

I swept and dusted while Ms. Sookie tended to checking the first wave of guests in for the night. She would have 30 minutes before round two, during which she would come to her room to freshen up. I was brushing Mercy when she came in.

"Hey, darling," Ms. Sookie sang.

"Hey, Ms. Sookie."

Ms. Sookie floated past me and headed to her shelf of wigs. "How you doing today?"

"I'm good. Ms. Sookie, can I ask you a question?"

She paused to give me her full attention. "Sure, baby. What you wanna know?"

"How did Lizzy come to work here?" I questioned in my best nonchalant tone.

"Lizzy? Who is Lizzy?" Ms. Sookie looked up in the air with her hands on her hips.

I was puzzled. How did Ms. Sookie not know her girls' names?

"Mrs. Jameson kept calling her Suga," I hinted.

"Oh, Suga! Ms. Sookie gives all her gals names when they come here. I don't wanna know who they was before they came, and it's best they forget. If they ever knew in the first place, hmph." Ms. Sookie usually referred to herself in the third person, which I always found a little funny. “Why you ask?”

“Someone at school asked me if I knew her,” I answered. “I never saw her until today.”

“Mouse, people in this town don’t sweep around they own front door.”

Ms. Sookie turned around to look for something in the back of her closet. When she turned back around, I must have been looking confused.

“Everybody have they own crosses to bear. You should worry about your own. Don’t think I don’t know there’s some odd reason you and your daddy showed up on my doorstep. I got too many girls here to worry about it, and I needed the help. You want to know what happened to Suga, you be big enough to ask her.”

I took her words as an admonishment. I hadn’t meant to be out of place. I just wanted to understand how she ended up here. Ms. Sookie softened at the tears welling up in my eyes. She grabbed me by the chin and looked at me. It almost felt like she was looking through me.

“You listen here, Mouse. I know those mean kids at that school probably pick on you ‘cause your daddy work here. Don’t you pay them no mind. That don’t have nothing to do with you. They hear what they mommas and some of they daddies say about this place, and they think they hate it without even really knowing what it’s all about. You ignore them and get your book learning, you hear?”

Ms. Sookie’s voice was more tense than I had ever heard it.

I looked her in the eyes and said, "Yes ma'am."

"It ain't but two ways out for a little black girl, your brains or your backside. If you don't get your books, you'll end up working for me or someone like me. You too bright for that. A lot of these girls are, but they never had no one tell 'em. No one ever told me. I like you, so I'm telling you. Mouse, you make the right choice early, or the choice will make you," Ms. Sookie said with the shake of a finger.

If regret had a face, Ms. Sookie was wearing it.

"I hate that I let Suga come work here, young as she was. She was legal age, and I didn't see no other way to help her out of her situation. She didn't have no family to turn to and I couldn't just let her come stay here for free. I knew what happened to her, and it wasn't right and it wasn't her fault. That was the best way I could see to help her get on her own two feet."

I didn't feel like Ms. Sookie was necessarily talking to me, especially after she'd told me to ask Suga what I wanted to know. Before I could say anything, there was a banging at the door.

Ms. Sookie yelled as she tore out of the room, "Who the hell is knocking on the door of my bidness like they the police?"

Ms. Sookie had just told me days before that she was never raided because she made sure to pay the local police officers to stay away from her place unless she called. For their sake, I hoped that loud banging wasn't them.

She snatched the front door open, and there stood Mrs. Pratt with her daughter, Lilly Anne, in tow. When Lilly Anne saw me, she hung her head in embarrassment.

Mrs. Pratt barged past Ms. Sookie.

"Where the hell is my husband?" she demanded.

"You tell me. You should know, shouldn't ya?"

Ms. Sookie looked at Mrs. Pratt with her eyes bucked, her shoulders hunched, and her hands in the air, palms raised.

Mrs. Pratt squinted her eyes at Ms. Sookie. She turned and marched to the bottom of the staircase, dragging Lilly Anne behind her.

"William Lee Pratt, I know your black ass is in here! I brought your daughter so you can explain to her what you in here doing with the girl that used to be her friend! Bring your ass down these stairs!" Mrs. Pratt screamed at the top of her lungs.

Her whole body reverberated as she yelled, and Lilly Anne was being shaken like the drinks Ms. Sookie mixed for her customers.

Mr. Pratt appeared at the top of the stairs. His clothes were disheveled, and he was trying to straighten himself up as he stumbled to the bottom. Suga stayed in the shadows at the top of the stairs.

Mr. Pratt yelled frantically, "Mary, what the hell you doing in here? This ain't no place for you to bring my daughter!"

"Then maybe you can explain why you here, screwing around with someone only a little older than her, no less," Mrs. Pratt responded daringly.

Other guests, including Rudy's daddy, began spilling into the hallway and onto the stairs, wondering what all the commotion was about.

"Let's go," Mr. Pratt said forcefully. He grabbed his wife by the elbow and pulled her toward the door.

Mrs. Pratt turned around and looked directly into the shadows at the top of the stairs. "I know you up there. You ought to be shame. Lilly Anne was yo' best friend. You been lusting after my husband since you was a little girl. I shoulda known then what you would turn out to be."

Suga stepped into clear view and responded, "You shoulda known what yo' husband was and kept him 'way from me. He turned me into what I am, so you got him to thank." She looked Mrs. Pratt right in the eyes and dared her to say something else.

Mrs. Pratt had no rebuttal. She allowed herself to be pulled toward the door.

"At least he gotta pay for it now!" Suga yelled behind them.

Mr. and Mrs. Pratt both stopped dead in their tracks, but they did not dare turn around. Lilly Anne glanced back over her shoulder and I was right in her line of sight. Though I didn't really care for Lilly Anne, this had to be the worst day of her life, and I was sorry to have seen it. I looked down at my shoes so as not to rub in her humiliation.

"Don't you ever come back here, Mrs. Pratt. I ain't turning away no paying customers. If your husband comes here and you don't like it, take it up with him at home," Ms. Sookie warned. With that, she slammed the door behind them.

The next day, I avoided Lilly Anne's glances in the school yard as best I could. Every time she headed in my direction, I'd find another classmate to talk to, and she would turn away. She was itching to get me alone. I had no intention of telling the rest of the class what had happened the night before, but she wouldn't give me the benefit of the doubt.

Lilly Anne finally got her chance when Rudy went inside to use the restroom. I sat alone with the last bit of my lunch. I was a sitting duck, and Lilly Anne had been waiting, stalking her prey.

"If you breathe one word to the rest of the class about last night, I will knock your teeth down your throat," Lilly Anne threatened through tight lips and gritted teeth.

"I hadn't planned on it anyway, so you can keep your threats," I responded casually.

Enraged, Lilly Anne stuck her face close to mine and continued, "Good. And they ain't threats. Ask Rudy."

"Ask me what?" Rudy reappeared, looking confused.

Lilly Anne gave Rudy a nasty glance and left to return to her crew. Obviously curious as to what business she would have with me, her followers swarmed her as soon as she returned. She waved them off and told them it was none of their business.

Rudy scratched his head and asked, "What the devil was that all about, and what are you supposed to ask me?"

"Ah, it's nothing," I said as I turned to head to the swings.

Rudy gave me a long look, then shrugged his shoulders, probably chalking the whole thing up to girls being silly.

Mr. Pratt eventually returned, but I never saw Mrs. Pratt at Ms. Sookie's again.

Five

We were at Ms. Sookie's for almost two years when the new girl showed up on the doorstep like the morning's milk delivery. Ms. Sookie opened the front door only to find this midnight-colored child standing there, legs crossed at the ankle, looking at her sheepishly. Ms. Sookie invited her into the house.

It was strange the way Ms. Sookie handled the girl. She had allowed the girl in, no questions asked. She walked the girl through the house and was speaking to her as if she already knew her. I remembered when Ray and I first arrived. She'd looked at us suspiciously and questioned us before we could even enter the front door.

I stared at this young woman from the hallway. I'd never seen someone so pretty and so dark. I thought the other girls might like to see her too. I ran to tell Lilah—short for Delilah—that someone new was here while Ms. Sookie escorted the girl into the parlor.

Saturdays were usually when the ladies worked their hardest to look pretty. The weekday regulars knew what they were getting, but new clients could be impressed on this last day of the week. At age eleven, I was old enough to help the ladies get ready, and it was a ritual to behold. There was lots of plucking and pulling, cinching and clinching, spraying and spritzing on Saturdays. The stuff they did to themselves made me think twice about becoming an entertainer.

As soon as Lilah put the broadcast out, each of Ms. Sookie's ladies took a break from primping to casually find herself in the parlor. Even Ray was being nosey. He pretended the bar area needed to be straightened.

We hadn't had this much excitement since the dust-up with Mrs. Pratt. I looked over each of Ms. Sookie's working girls' faces. They all tried to act unaffected, but the air in the room felt electrified. Whatever was causing the current, it wasn't the same enthusiasm that I felt. I thought it would be nice for someone new to be around the house. Lilah and Ms. Sookie were the only ones who really entertained all my questions and conversations. The rest of the girls rarely wanted to be bothered. Maybe the new girl and I could form a friendship.

I decided to ignore the obvious irritation of the others and watched Ms. Sookie as she handled the girl like a darkly-colored China doll.

"Come here and let me get a good look at you," Ms. Sookie said as she placed both hands on either side of the girl's waist. "Tiny waist and a young firm ass. Good. Smile, let me see your teeth. Not the best, but not the worst I seen."

Ms. Sookie paused as if in deep thought. She paced a circle around the room. The others pretended to be consumed with pulling at imaginary strings on fabric or wiping the dust off of something or other, though none of them had dusted anything since I'd been in the house.

"Well, you a pretty little thing," Ms. Sookie half-spoke, half-sang. "You got a smile like sunshine. I'll have to be careful wit'chu. You ever done this kind of work before?" Ms. Sookie asked as she gathered the girl's face in both her hands and pulled it closer to her own.

"No, ma'am," the young girl responded bashfully.

Ms. Sookie released her face. The girl clasped her hands behind her back while she looked at her feet and twisted from side to side.

Ms. Sookie eyed the girl sideways. "How old is you?" she asked with a squint and upturned ruby-red lips.

"Eighteen," the girl replied matter-of-factly.

"You sure? You only look like you about sixteen and you got to be seventeen to work with the men." Ms. Sookie placed her hands firmly on her own hips.

Ms. Sookie didn't have any children as far as I knew, but she had what my daddy often referred to as "baby-birthing hips." They were wide like my momma's. I pushed down memories of my momma and thought of how Ms. Sookie's hips looked like a great big pair of parentheses to me, after having learned about them in school recently.

"I'm eighteen. I came here because…"

Ms. Sookie cut her off.

"I don't need to know why you came. I just need to know you old enough, and you know what you doing. I ain't giving nobody no money back, so if I get complaints, you'll have to take the loss. Not me. Got it?"

"Yes, ma'am," the newcomer said with a bowed head.

Ms. Sookie ambled over to her favorite chair, which was embroidered with emerald green silk. That's where she sat when she was entertaining guests as they waited for their appointments.

"You ain't no virgin, is you?" Ms. Sookie asked. Before waiting for a response, she launched into, "I ain't got time to be training you on what to do. You replacing one of my best gals. Hmph. Dimples call herself running off to find love with a man who don't know what she was doing for a living. She'll be hiding from that for the rest of her life. What kinda love is that? Anyway, you know how to deal with a man?"

"Yes, ma'am," the girl responded excitedly.

I hoped all of these questions meant that Ms. Sookie was hiring her.

Ms. Sookie sat back in her chair and exhaled, giving the young girl a long look.

I looked around at the others, trying to figure out what was going to happen next. I found an edge of one of my fingernails that had just enough left to grab with my teeth. I slowly pulled until a thin sliver of nail came off. My fingertip was a little sore and red, irritated by the pulling. I chewed on the piece of nail to try to calm my nerves.

"What's taking so long?" I leaned over and whispered to Suga.

"Ms. Sookie take her time in naming her new girls. A name is serious. Giving a girl the right name can make or break her in this business," Suga answered evenly.

I smiled at Suga, but she returned her attention to the center of the room without a second look at me. I pursed my lips and returned my attention to chewing my piece of nail.

"I think I'll call you 'Sunny,'" Ms. Sookie said as she gave herself a satisfied pat on the thigh. "That smile can light up a room and certainly a man's heart. The only problem is I can't have customers getting too sweet on you. You keep your conversations short, you hear? They'll take one look at that shy nature and see some little delicate flower they gotta protect. I can't have no man getting possessive about my girls."

Ms. Sookie shook her head.

"Yes, ma'am," Sunny responded with a smile, seeming pleased with her new name.

"Mouse, you clean Dimples' old room?" Ms. Sookie asked.

I thought that all of us had been invisible during this naming ritual, but I was reminded that Ms. Sookie had eyes in the back of her head.

"Yes, ma'am." I nodded emphatically.

I had become pretty good at being ahead of Ms. Sookie's requests. I figured that even if things didn't work out with Dimples' new man, she wouldn't be coming back here. Ms. Sookie was so angry when Dimples surprised her with the news she was leaving that she called Dimples ungrateful and told her a man could never truly love a ho. Dimples burst into tears, grabbed up all of her personal belongings, and left without another word. I cleaned her room the very next day, and it stayed just the way I left it.

"Go on and show Sunny here her room and help her get settled," Ms. Sookie said as she popped my hand. "And I told you to stop biting your nails like that. Don't make no sense, you biting yourself until you bleed. Even though you a child, you still represent this house. All them pretty dresses I sew for you, and you 'round here with chewed up nails, looking like a boy."

"Yes, Ms. Sookie," I said as I put my hands behind my back. I usually remembered to keep my bad habit under control during the day. However, I had forgotten to hide my hands before Ms Sookie could notice when I got up from the couch. She took dresses that were too worn for entertaining and tailored them into clothes I could wear. Even though the dresses were made for a girl my age, the loud colors and soft materials made me feel grown, and I didn't want Ms. Sookie to stop sewing for me.

I grabbed Sunny's hand and led her to the winding stairway off the side of the parlor. She looked nervous, and I thought maybe a little conversation would make her feel better.

"Where are you from?" I asked Sunny as I helped her carry her meager belongings to the second floor to the room opposite Suga's. Sunny ran her fingers across the faded and chipped pale blue paint on the banister with reverence before responding.

"Parlortown. It's a few towns north of here."

"Why'd you come here?"

I wanted to know what could make a girl so pretty want to work in this place. Why wasn't she trying to get married like most girls her age?

Sunny's face grew solemn.

"To escape," she said softly.

I wondered what she was escaping, but considering what I was running from, I didn't have the courage to ask. If this was her way out, I could only imagine what she'd left in Parlortown.

Could I be one of Ms. Sookie's girls to get away from Ray?

"What's your real name?" I asked tentatively. Seeing as how she and I were going to be friends, I was curious as to who she really was.

"Genevieve, but I like Sunny better," she told me as she plopped down on the bed.

Sunny rubbed her fingers across the silken lilac bedspread as if it was the finest she'd ever seen. She sat, swinging her legs back and forth while I helped unpack her suitcase, which held four pairs of underwear, two dresses, and a shiny, sculpted figurine of an elephant. I wanted to ask her how she got the elephant, but Sunny looked like she was lost in her own thoughts. I left her alone in the room and went to draw her a bath. No free board. She would have to prove her worth that evening.

I wandered back downstairs.

Ray was drying glasses and putting them in the cabinet behind the bar. I climbed up onto one of the bar stools and watched him quietly. He and I didn't talk much. Honestly, I avoided him most of the time.

"What's the new gal like?" Ray asked.

I immediately regretted that my feet had brought me to the parlor.

"Sunny. Ms. Sookie named her Sunny. I don't know. She seems nice," I answered cooly.

There was awkward silence.

"Where Rudy and Beenie?"

He continued drying the glasses and putting them away absent-mindedly.

"They went to visit his sick grandma."

"Oh, that's why you been hanging around looking pitiful all day."

He chuckled and popped the dish towel at me, threatening to get me with the sting of damp cloth.

I shrugged my shoulders, surprised that he'd noticed.

I hopped off of the barstool and went to see if anyone needed last-minute help getting dressed.

While Ms. Sookie set up appointments during the week, Saturday nights were first-come, first-served. I wanted to see Sunny on her first night, so I decided to hide in the small closet under the stairs. I'd found the crack between the second and third stairs by accident one day. Ms. Sookie sent me in the closet to grab some fresh linen for her bed. There was just enough space for me to see into the parlor. I had been patiently waiting for the right time to use the private space I'd found.

All the girls waited in the parlor, perched perfectly on the chairs and colorfully painted like confections on display in a candy store. None of the girls sat near Sunny, which only made her stand out more. It just so happened the one decent dress she had was buttercup yellow. It cinched at the waist and then flowed out and stopped right at her knees. She looked more like she was going to a church social than entertaining in this house. All of the other girls' dresses were tight and didn't leave much to the imagination. Though the dress was plain, the color radiated off of her smooth, dark skin. She almost looked like she was sitting under a spotlight. I was excited for it to be opening time.

Six o'clock finally came. Ms. Sookie opened the door directly off the side of the parlor and allowed in the seven men who were waiting. While the police allowed Ms. Sookie to operate in peace, she would not be so bold as to allow customers in and out the front door.

Most of the men formed a line. They walked up to Ms. Sookie's stand and gave her a name. She called that particular lady up to the stand and the man and lady went up the stairs to the lady's room. I was trying to work out what kind of entertainment was done with just two people when I noticed that a couple of the men had gone straight to the bar.

Ray sold those men cigars and filled their glasses with liquid, either clear or brown. I heard one say "brandy neat," and the other asked for "whiskey on the rocks." They tipped him when he finished pouring. I was confused by "on the rocks" until I noticed the man who had ordered them was the one with ice.

I turned my attention back to Ms. Sookie at the sound of her voice.

"Mr. Pratt, we don't usually see you here on a Saturday."

Ms. Sookie didn't like Mr. Pratt. I would have known even if she hadn't said as much. I didn't like him either. I'd only crossed his path twice since Mrs. Pratt's visit. The way he looked at me made my skin crawl. Ms. Sookie quickly shooed me out of the room on both occasions.

"Yeah, well… is the rate the same on Saturday?" Mr. Pratt asked.

"Yes, it is," Ms. Sookie replied. "You can go ahead and take Suga up to her room as usual," Ms. Sookie added without looking up from her paper.

She kept very neat records on who visited whom. When I asked her why, she told me to touch my nose. When I did so, she reminded me that my nose belonged on my face and not in her business.

"Actually, who is the new girl over there?" Mr. Pratt inquired quietly. He had a slick smile and his eyes danced like he was looking at a brand new car he wanted to test drive. I'd seen the same look on Ray's face before we bought the used Lincoln we had in Maplewood.

He hadn't asked quietly enough because both Ms. Sookie and Suga looked up at Mr. Pratt in surprise. Mr. Pratt had never visited with anyone other than Suga since I'd lived there.

Ms. Sookie recovered quickly. I moved closer to the crack so I could get a better view of Sunny and Suga. I forgot about the marbles in my pocket, and shifting my body caused a few to drop out and fall onto the wooden floor. The impact seemed deafening in the tiny space. My breath caught in my throat as I dropped my hand on top of them to prevent them from making any more noise. Ms. Sookie's head briefly turned toward the stairs, with her ears perked. No one else seemed to notice, but Ms. Sookie had hearing like a hound. I was terrified she knew I was spying.

After a moment, Ms. Sookie answered Mr. Pratt. "Well, now… that's Sunny, my new gal. You want her to sprinkle a little sunshine in your life?"

I felt like I was in the clear. I settled my nervousness by rubbing my thumbs across my fingers in search of which nails to bite.

"I believe I do. Time for something new," Mr. Pratt commented. He turned his head slightly over his shoulder in Suga's direction, but never looked her in the eyes.

Suga's eyes squinted, and when I followed her gaze, it wasn't directed at Mr. Pratt. It landed squarely on Sunny. There was so much heat coming off of Suga, I thought it would blister the girls sitting next to her. I knew immediately that life here would be difficult for Sunny. Suga would make it that way.

I got bored and uncomfortable after a while. I'd have to remember to bring a pillow to sit on next time I wanted to spy from my secret spot. I gathered up all of the pieces of fingernail that I'd chewed off my fingers and eased the door to the closet open. Ms. Sookie was standing right in front of the door with her hands on her parentheses.

I gasped.

"Mmm hmm. Ms. Sookie sees all. You know that by now. I oughta tan your hide," she said as she grabbed me by the ear.

I dared not make a sound because I didn't want Ray to know what I'd done.

"Your tail should be in your room," Ms. Sookie whispered through clenched teeth and furled lips. "If I catch you spying in that closet again, I'm gonna tell your daddy and let him deal with you."

Ms. Sookie escorted me to my room and closed the door behind her as she left. I felt bad for making her angry, but I didn't understand why she was so mad. It was just a bunch of grown-ups talking.

Hours later, I awoke to a blood-curdling scream. I sat up in bed and looked around the room. My father was sound asleep in his bed. I got up and tiptoed to the door, which I cracked just enough to see Suga in her white cotton nightgown, moving quickly and quietly back to her room.

By the time Ms. Sookie made it up the stairs, Suga, Peaches, and Candy had all stepped out of their rooms. Lilah was nowhere to be found. They all appeared to be half-asleep and confused. I was the only one who knew it was an act on Suga's part.

"What the hell is going on? Where did that scream come from?" Ms. Sookie asked, looking disheveled and annoyed as she got to the top of the stairs.

No one responded. Ms. Sookie opened Sunny's door to the sound of sobbing.

"Sunny… what's wrong with you?" Ms. Sookie cooed.

I inched further along the hallway until I could see into Sunny's room.

"Nothing, Ms. Sookie. It was just a bad dream," Sunny said through snorting and sniffling.

Ms. Sookie sighed. "Alright, child. Get some rest. First night in a new place… I guess that could be a little hard for anyone, but we like our sleep around here. No more of this screaming at night."

"Yes, ma'am," Sunny whimpered.

Ms. Sookie gathered up her pink satin nightgown and walked back into the hallway. As I turned to walk away, Ms. Sookie grabbed my elbow and spun me around.

"Mouse, you see anything?" she asked as she searched my face for answers.

I looked down the hall right into Suga's eyes. Her squinted eyes were a quiet warning.

"No, ma'am."

"Alright. Get back to bed. All of you, back to bed," Ms. Sookie commanded.

Suga and I looked at each other for a long while. She turned first and went back into her room. As I walked back into mine, Ray sat up in his bed.

"What you doing out the room this time of morning?" he asked angrily.

I responded quickly. "I went to get some water."

I hadn't expected him to be awake since he had not heard the scream.

"Don't let me catch you outta bed like that again," he fussed.

"Yessir," I responded, hoping that would end it.

Thankfully, he didn't say anything else, and we both fell off to sleep.

Sundays tended to be lazy. Ms. Sookie wouldn't allow visitors, so that was everyone's day to do as they pleased. Mrs. Jameson had Sundays off, so meals were usually fend-for-yourself. Every now and again Ms. Sookie would get up and cook a breakfast spread so beautiful it would bring tears to our eyes. Sliced ham, biscuits with apple butter, scrambled eggs, hoecakes with pecans and syrup, sausage, potatoes, grits (with red-eye gravy, if she was really feeling good), and sometimes even fried fish. I don't know about any other meal, but Ms. Sookie sure could cook breakfast. There would be so much food the ladies could graze on it throughout the day.

The next morning after Sunny's arrival was one such Sunday. I wandered downstairs, stirred by the mixture of scents wafting into our room as Ray slept.

"Morning, sweetie pie," Ms. Sookie greeted me.

"Morning, Ms. Sookie. Mmmmmm-mmmmm, I can't wait to dig in! You made my favorite," I sang as I rubbed my hands together. I loved Ms. Sookie's hoecakes.

"I sure did, but I need you to do one thing for me before you sit your little self down at the table. Go round up everybody, including your daddy."

I was a little confused. Still, I answered, "Yes, ma'am."

None of the ladies wanted to wake up, not even for that glorious breakfast. I was met with shoes being thrown at doors, cuss words shouted at me, and downright rude insults. They all knew if Ms. Sookie wanted them, they better see their way down to the table. So they came, drowsy eyes, unkempt hair and all.

"I'm so glad y'all came down to share in this bountiful meal with me. I thought it would be nice to welcome Sunny with a family breakfast. Sunny, how you feeling this morning?" asked Ms. Sookie.

"I'm alright, Ms. Sookie. You didn't have to go through all this trouble," Sunny said as she grinned.

"Wasn't no trouble, Sunny. I did this for each of these girls sitting at this table. Ain't that right, ladies?"

All the ladies nodded in unison.

"You see, I want you to feel welcomed and like a part of a family. I'm like your momma, and you all should be like sisters. Right, ladies?" Ms. Sookie asked pointedly.

Again, heads bobbed up and down, though some were slower to bob than others.

"And mommas see everything, even when they don't see," Ms. Sookie said forcefully.

With that, she looked right at Suga. Suga bowed her eyes as if to look at something interesting in her lap.

"And Momma won't have her girls fighting over no man, especially not one who ain't worth a hill of beans," Ms. Sookie said with a bang of her hand on the table.

Everyone jumped at the loud sound of her heavy hand on the oak table. Suga got mad when Ms. Sookie said that. She hopped up from the table and stormed off. Lilah moved to go after her, but Ms. Sookie shot her a glance that easily said that her behind better remain glued to that seat.

"Your friend will be fine up there by herself. She can come back down and get something to eat when she comes to her senses," Ms. Sookie said to Lilah.

Ms. Sookie said grace and then the rest of us reached for what we wanted in earnest, but soon enough, we were all laughing and joking. Ms. Sookie's cooking seemed to have a way of encouraging that behavior.

After I'd nearly eaten myself sick on hoecakes, syrup, and sausage, Ms. Sookie called me to her side. She passed me a foil-wrapped plate and told me to take it up to Suga. I did as she asked, though anywhere near Suga was the last place I wanted to be.

That walk up the stairs and down the hall seemed like it took forever. I knocked on Suga's door, but there was no response. I opened the door but did not immediately enter the room. Suga had good aim, and I wasn't always fast enough to dodge whatever she could get her hands on to throw.

"Ms. Sookie told me to bring this plate up to you," I said as I offered her the plate.

"What for? She don't care nothing about me. She got a new favorite. Sunny."

Suga said "Sunny" like it tasted of dirt.

"Ms. Sookie loves us all," I responded as I walked further into the room.

"What do you know?" Suga spat back at me.

"I know you went into Sunny's room last night," I said with a roll of my neck.

"Shut up or I'll give you just what I gave her," Suga threatened.

I dropped the plate on her nightstand and left her wrapped up in all the hatred that could fit in that room. I'd seen what that kind of bitterness could do to a person. I didn't want it to snake itself around me too.

Six

I woke up to use the bathroom in the middle of the night and saw Ray crawling back into bed. When he heard me stir, he quickly laid down and closed his eyes as if he'd never left that spot. He added a snore for good measure. I didn't know where he was sneaking in from, but I knew it couldn't have been good.

The next night I pretended I was sleeping so I could follow him out of the room. The only problem was I actually fell asleep. I jerked awake hours later remembering my mission. I looked over, and his bed was empty. I sat up and eased myself down to the floor. In my stocking feet, I tiptoed down the hall and put my ear to Sunny's door. I heard nothing. I went to Lilah's door and heard what sounded like a chainsaw. When I got to Suga's door, I heard Ray's deep voice and her giggling like a schoolgirl. If Ms. Sookie knew that Suga was still entertaining after hours, especially with him, she would kill them both. I shook my head and tiptoed to the toilet. As I sat on the cold seat, I dreaded where this road would lead. Ms. Sookie had been very clear that he was supposed to stay away from the girls.

I could barely look Ray or Suga in the face the next day.

"Mouse, you been acting a little strange all day. What's wrong?" Ms. Sookie asked.

If I told, we might be made to leave, or it would anger Ray. I wasn't a fan of either outcome.

"Nothing," I responded.

Ms. Sookie looked at me for a long time before she went back to stitching a new skirt for me on her sewing machine. This skirt was made from a purple satin dress that had become too ragged of use and repair for Lilah to keep wearing.

I wondered if Ms. Sookie suspected what was going on in her house.

As if my thoughts had beckoned her, Suga appeared and knocked on Ms. Sookie's door.

"Yes," Ms. Sookie answered.

"Ms. Sookie, I need to talk to you for a moment," Suga said quietly.

"Ok. What about, dear?"

"Alone," Suga said, looking over at me.

"Mouse, give me and Suga a minute, baby. I'll let you know when I need you to try on this skirt again," Ms. Sookie said, dismissing me from the conversation.

I couldn't resist listening in, so I closed the door behind me and walked away loudly. Then I turned back and crept close enough to put my ear on the edge of the door without my feet showing underneath it.

What did Suga have to talk to Ms. Sookie alone about? If she told Ms. Sookie about Ray, our lives in Edenville would be over. I'd have to start all over again someplace new.

"Ms. Sookie, I think I wanna stop this line of work."

"Well, I ain't never been one to force a girl to do this kind of work. But what other kind of work you gone do, Suga? You got something else lined up?"

Ms. Sookie sounded concerned.

"No. I haven't really thought that far," Suga responded.

"I see. Is this because of a man?" Ms. Sookie asked sharply.

"Well…" Suga said hesitantly.

"I figured as much," Ms. Sookie said with a long sigh. "I knew you been acting different. Now Mouse acting funny…" Ms. Sookie's voice trailed off momentarily. "Suga, when are you going to figure out that most men only use you until they use you up, then they onto something new? Who is it, Suga?" Ms. Sookie demanded.

Suga was quiet.

"Oh, nothing to say now? You came to me because you want to get out of the business, but you gotta keep your love for this man hid?" she asked angrily. "Do what you want. I don't care. I beg y'all not to give your heart to no man. I give you a way to take care of yourself, and this is how you repay me."

"Ms. Sookie, I thank you for what you done. You took me in when no one else wanted me, but you can't expect me to do this forever," Suga pleaded.

"I don't, Suga. In fact, I want better for you. I just don't want you going off with some man if he ain't gone treat you right. I love all y'all girls. You young and I should have half-expected this. I thought maybe you'd been hurt enough to learn that love is a fool's game." Ms. Sookie sounded defeated, like someone who was just tired of trying.

"I ain't made my decision yet, Ms. Sookie. I was just telling you what was on my mind. You been good to me. I didn't want it to be no surprise to you if I do decide to go," Suga said solemnly.

"I understand. You still ain't gonna tell me who he is though?"

Again, there was no response.

"Hmph. I hope it's not Mr. Pratt. If you think he's gonna leave his family and run off with you, you gonna get disappointed," Ms. Sookie preached.

"No, ma'am. It ain't Mr. Pratt," Suga assured her.

"Alright. Well, you just let me know what you decide. Either way, I'll be here for you. I appreciate you coming to me like a woman."

I eased away from the door and sat down on the bottom stair. I hurriedly took the little doll out of my pocket and began playing with it to make it seem as if I'd been sitting there the entire time. Suga strolled past me and right up the stairs without a word.

"Mouse!" Ms. Sookie called.

I ran into the room.

"How many times I told you to stop chewing up your fingernails like that?"

I looked down at my fingers and saw they were irritated and bleeding.

"Lawd, why do you keep doing this? That's a sign of bad nerves, but what your nerves bad about?" Ms. Sookie asked.

The questions came so rapidly, I just stood there and blinked at her. I had plenty for my nerves to be bad about.

"Never mind," she said absently as she pulled the skirt off the sewing machine. "Here, try this on."

I began taking off my play pants when Ms. Sookie asked me, "Mouse, you know who Suga been hanging around with?"

I looked at the floor. Ms. Sookie could read me like a book, so I would have to play this cool. I hated lying to her, but I couldn't afford to tell her the truth.

"No, ma'am," I lied sweetly.

Ms. Sookie looked at me for a moment as I pulled the skirt up and fastened the hook at the top.

"Well," she said matter-of-factly, "that looks quite nice on you. Change back into your play pants and get on out of here. Go find Rudy to play with or something. I got some things to think about while I finish up this here skirt."

"Yes, ma'am."

I headed to my room to grab my dolls so Rudy and I could use them as children if Beenie was going to be uncooperative, as she sometimes was. Before I could leave the room, Suga cornered me by standing in the doorway.

"What you told Ms. Sookie?" Suga asked calmly.

"Nothing," I responded, trying to push past her. She was unmovable.

"She said you been acting funny. Why's that?"

Suga tilted her head like a dog does when it hears an unfamiliar sound.

"Maybe because I know you and Ray are sneaking around like some rats," I said, standing my ground.

I was close enough to Suga to smell that she'd had toast with grape jelly for breakfast. I would not give an inch. I would not allow her to think she could scare me anymore.

"What do you even want with him anyway?" I growled.

"I ain't want nothing. It's what he wanted. Besides, he nice to me. He sings me little songs and brings me flowers."

Those were things he did for Momma. It was like he was spitting on her dead body. I balled my fists up at my side to keep from socking Suga.

"I'm gone tell Ray you been talking our business to Ms. Sookie," Suga threatened.

She knew the weakest spot on which to apply pressure.

"If I had told Ms. Sookie, you think either of us would be standing here now?" I asked.

"Naw… I guess you right. But if I think for one minute you gonna tell Ms. Sookie, I'ma tell Ray. I got yo' daddy wrapped 'round this little finger right here," Suga sneered, holding up her pinky finger. "I'd rather not make things hard between us, seeing as how I might just be your new momma," she said slyly.

"You will never be my momma," I said bitterly.

Heat rose from the tips of my toes to the top of my throat. If I could have opened my mouth and blown fire on Suga, I would have.

"That's right. Your poor momma died. She was sickly, right?" she asked mockingly.

"If that's what he told you," I said with a smirk.

I thought about the fact that my father was capable of murder. If my sweet momma could push him to it, certainly so could this heffa.

Suga paused, looked me over, then turned and walked toward her room. She looked back over her shoulder. "Just remember, this can go easy or it can go hard. All depends on you."

Sunny was coming out of her room just as Suga was passing. Suga gave her a once-over and kept walking. Sunny looked down the hall at me with her face screwed up as if to ask what that was all about. I shrugged my shoulders and walked over to her door. She grabbed my hand and pulled me into her room. We sat on her floor and played jacks until it was time for her to get ready for the evening.

I laid awake in bed that night, fearing a middle-of-the-morning wake-up by Ray. I dozed off at some point. I assumed Suga had kept our little conversation to herself when I opened my eyes in the same bed the next morning.

The sneaking around between Ray and Suga continued through winter and into spring. Ms. Sookie's suspicions only became more and more heightened. She watched Suga closely and took note that even when Suga wasn't working, she rarely left the house. Most of the girls would at least get out and go to the store or the diner when they wanted something different than Mrs. Jameson's cooking.

Ms. Sookie called me into her room on a pretty Saturday morning. I was moving around the house doing small chores to get the place ready for the evening.

"Mouse, you dumped the garbage in Suga's room yet?"

"No, ma'am."

"Good. When you collect it, bring it to me instead of taking it to the big can out back. Understand?"

"Yes, ma'am."

"And don't tell nobody what I asked you to do," she warned.

It seemed like a strange request, but I did what had been asked. When I brought her the paper bag filled with trash, I hung around to see what she would do with it.

Ms. Sookie rummaged around in that bag. She angrily threw the bag down with a grunt.

"That heffa. She done missed her monthly," Ms. Sookie said to the ceiling.

"Monthly?" I chirped.

"Lawd, ain't nobody explained your monthly to you?"

Ms. Sookie had brought her right hand up and placed it over her heart. Her mouth was open in awe.

I shook my head. Ms. Sookie patted the mattress beside her.

"Baby girl, how old are you now?"

"Almost twelve."

"Twelve. I was about your age when it happened to me. Listen, you are soon going to have your first monthly cycle. It's when your body changes and you will be able to have a baby," she began.

I already regretted that I had asked.

"Your body releases an egg every month. If that egg don't get what it need from a man to make a baby, then your body gets rid of the egg by bleeding. You bleed from your flower for five to seven days," she said, pointing at the area between my legs.

Ms. Sookie sat looking at me expectantly when she finished.

I felt like I wanted to faint. I would bleed from between my legs for five to seven days?

"Don't be afraid, Mouse. It's natural and it means you a woman," Ms. Sookie said, trying to sound encouraging.

"I don't want to be a woman, then," I grumbled.

Ms. Sookie howled with laughter. When she finished laughing, she dried her eyes and threw her arm around me. She pulled me into a sideways hug.

"Well, baby, you don't have much choice in that. Mother Nature determines when you become a woman," she said with a pat on my thigh. "I been looking at you and I think your time is soon coming."

"So how does the egg get what it needs from the man?"

Ms. Sookie blew out a long sigh.

"I think I done told you enough for today. That's a conversation for another time."

She chuckled.

I was so consumed with the bleeding from my flower and becoming a woman, I wasn't concerned with what Ms. Sookie had figured out from Suga's garbage. All I had time to worry about was praying away womanhood.

I asked Lilah about monthly cycles, and she told me all the gory details. I learned the tricks they used to keep from becoming pregnant before I understood how a woman became pregnant in the first place. Lilah showed me the pads that women wore. They looked horrible and uncomfortable. I finally understood why the girls had one week off during the month. I always thought Ms. Sookie was just being nice. She knew no one wanted to entertain when they were bleeding into a big pillow between their legs.

I endured the rest of the season with lots of worry, but without any bloodshed. Even the promise of summer wasn't enough to ease my concerns. Instead of it being a time of fun and freedom, it was a time of confusion and fear. I was confused as to what was happening to my body and fearful of what becoming a woman meant for me. My breasts were starting to protrude. I was having a harder time managing the smell under my armpits, and hair was starting to show up in places it hadn't been before. I'd never been fat, but my bottom and hips were starting to change shape.

My body was betraying me, and other people were noticing.

"Mouse, here go you a bra."

Ms. Sookie dropped the folded-up bra on my bed.

"I have to wear this, Ms. Sookie?"

I was repulsed.

"Yes. I told yo' daddy you needed one, and he gave me some of his tip money to go buy it from the department store."

My cheeks felt hot. I suddenly understood why he'd given me a strange look after I'd taken a bath and changed into my nightgown a few nights before. I held the bra up and looked at it in disgust. I'd helped the ladies with theirs enough times to know how to put one on, but with all their crying about how uncomfortable they were, I wasn't interested in ever wearing one.

I did as I was asked and wore the bra to school the next day. Rudy gave me a couple of strange looks, too, but didn't dare say anything. I was beyond aggravated between him acting weird and the newness of wearing something snug around my chest in the heat.

The folks who were from Edenville didn't react to the heat of summer any better than I did. I was annoyed, but I knew this was mild compared to Maplewood summers. That had been a different kind of heat. Those summers were so hot, sometimes you felt like you couldn't breathe. Ray would bring both Momma and me a cool treat on those days. Edenville summers felt like you were surrounded by heat, but a cool breeze from a fan would blow by you ever so often.

I was tickled at how everyone was bothered by what I considered to be mild weather. I thought at the end of the school year everyone would be happy. Instead, the teachers were irritable, no one wanted to play during recess, and even the students didn't have much to say to each other. A few said it was too hot to talk. When we had to be outside, they all tried to find somewhere to enjoy some shade. Mrs. Higgins regularly complained of a headache after recess because of all the little musty boys and girls cooped up in the tiny school room. Ms. Sookie, on the other hand, didn't mind the heat at all. She would often say, "The heat brings me more money. Wives are too hot and tired to be bothered and we have just what they men need—a cool drink and a hot bed."

The first day of the last week of school proved to be worse than bras and heat. My stomach started cramping like nothing I'd ever felt before. It was so bad, I felt like I would throw up. I asked Mrs. Higgins if I could be excused to the bathroom. I pulled down my panties and almost passed out. There it was; what I'd spent all of spring and the beginning of summer dreading. My lily-white panties were crimson in the crotch. If it hadn't been for Ms. Sookie, I wouldn't have known what was happening at all.

I had no idea what to do and didn't have any sanitary napkins with me. I wadded up some toilet paper and stuffed it in my panties. I wiped myself clean as best I could, and I prayed Mrs. Higgins would let me go so I could get home before any more damage could be done.

I walked back into the classroom as calmly as I could. Thankfully, Mrs. Higgins was not lecturing, and I could walk up to her desk without the whole class staring and being nosey.

"Mrs. Higgins," I whispered. "I need to go home."

"Home?"

She looked at me confused. Thankfully, she'd been just as discreet in her tone as I had been in mine.

"Yes, ma'am. I just got my monthly for the first time. I need to wash out my underwear, and I don't have any sanitary napkins," I explained quietly.

"Oh, child. Okay. You go on home. I'll have Rudy bring your books and assignments. You drink some hot tea and lie down," she said sweetly.

Though Mrs. Higgins had never really been mean to me, she hadn't ever been particularly kind either. This was the first time she had ever shown me any sweetness.

I turned and walked out of the classroom. I glanced back at Rudy, who had a puzzled look on his face. I nodded, and he nodded in return. He knew he would find out what was going on later.

I walked home as quickly as I could. When I got there, Ray was outside, pulling Dollarweeds. He was preparing the flower beds for new plants that would flourish in the summer heat. My favorites were the Plumeria with their bright pinks and yellows. He looked up at me walking past.

"Mouse, what you doing outta school?"

He was ready to yell at me.

"I threw up and Mrs. Higgins sent me home," I lied.

He shook his head and went back to digging.

I made a beeline for Ms. Sookie's room and knocked on the door. She was playing with her hair and make-up in the mirror of her beautiful pearl-white vanity table with the gold embellishments.

"Hey, baby. What you doing here? You didn't get in trouble down at that school, did you?"

Ms. Sookie's face was drawn up in concern.

"No, ma'am. I got my monthly," I responded with tears in my eyes.

The shock of seeing blood in my panties for the first time had worn off, and now the weight of being a woman was resting on my chest.

Ms. Sookie gasped and then pulled me into her bosom with the tightest, but best hug ever.

"You just wait right there," she told me.

Ms. Sookie got up from her vanity, went into the bathroom, and came back with some sanitary napkins.

"You been cramping?"

"Yes, ma'am. My stomach hurts real bad."

"Okay, let's go upstairs and get you all cleaned up. Ms. Sookie is gonna show you how to take care of yourself. I'm gone fix you right on up. How does that sound?"

I nodded.

"Go grab some clean underwear and meet me in the bathroom," she instructed as she walked me to the bottom of the stairs.

A few moments later, Ms. Sookie met me in the bathroom. She started running hot water in the tub then poured some white stuff that looked like sugar into the water.

"Okay, while that's running I want you to take off your panties. We need to rinse the blood out in cold water while it's still fresh," she told me.

I took off my panties and threw the soiled toilet paper into the toilet and flushed. I was so ashamed of the mess I'd made, I wadded up the panties before passing them to Ms. Sookie.

"Mouse, you ain't gotta be embarrassed about your monthly, especially not around women folk. It's natural. You a woman now. I know this got to be hard without yo' momma, so I'll do my best to teach you what she would want you to know," she said lovingly.

Ms. Sookie rinsed my panties out in the sink with cold water. She sprinkled some soap shavings onto them and scrubbed the two sides together until they were almost as white as when my father bought them.

"Since your daddy use this bathroom, I'll take these down to my bathroom to dry," she said with a nod while putting some strange-looking leaves into the warm bath water and turning off the spigot.

"I put some epsom salt in that water, and these here are peppermint leaves. This is an old trick my momma taught me that will soothe that stomach pain you got," she shared.

I watched her stir the water as if she was a witch hovering over her cauldron of brew.

"Okay, Mouse. Get in and soak in that water until I come back for you."

I sat in the tub of hot water, feeling like stewed chicken. Eventually the water began to cool and I could feel that the cramping had eased. I was almost asleep when Ms. Sookie tapped on the door and told me I could get out.

Ms. Sookie showed me how to place the sanitary napkin into my clean underwear. She gave me a nice, soft nightgown to put on and walked me to the bedroom. The nightgown swallowed me up, but it was so soft I didn't care.

"I told yo' Daddy that you sick and not to worry. Me and the girls are gonna take care of you.

If you don't feel well enough to go to school tomorrow, you can stay home," Ms. Sookie informed me.

She tucked me in and told me that Mrs. Jameson would be in in a bit. I was beginning to think that becoming a woman wasn't going to be so bad after all.

There was a tap at the door a few moments later, and in came Sunny.

"You got your monthly!" she exclaimed.

"Ms. Sookie told you?" I yelled.

"Only 'cause she excited. She thinks it's a special thing."

"What do you think?" I asked in earnest.

"I think it's a curse. Just stay away from men folk."

Sunny kissed me on my forehead before leaving.

Mrs. Jameson came with some lavender tea and butter cookies soon after Sunny left. Butter cookies were my favorite. They were shaped like flowers and had holes in their centers. I liked to put it on my finger and eat my way around the cookie until it was gone.

Mrs. Jameson set the tea and cookies on a side table.

"How you feeling, sweet girl?" Mrs. Jameson asked.

"I'm okay," I croaked out as dramatically as I could. I hoped that would earn me some more butter cookies.

Mrs. Jameson rubbed my belly and looked at me with a sweet, understanding smile.

“Okay, I’ll be back to check on you in a bit, and I’ll bring your dinner up when it’s ready. You drink your tea and then try to take a nap. When you wake up, you should feel a whole heck of a lot better.”

After a hot bath, warm tea, and butter cookies, I did fall asleep easily. I woke up to Mrs. Jameson bringing me a bowl of soup and crackers. It wasn’t the dinner I had hoped for, but it did just fine.

“That Rudy came by and dropped off your books. I put them over there in the corner. He was showl concerned about you. I told him you’ll be alright,” Mrs. Jameson said.

Ms. Sookie came back one last time before the evening got started. She wanted to make sure I was feeling better.

“What about cleaning the girls’ rooms?” I asked.

“Don’t you worry that pretty little head of yours, Mouse. We’ll manage. Get some rest now,” Ms. Sookie assured me.

I slept so well, I did not hear Ray come in or out of the room. I remembered opening my eyes and seeing him standing over me, pulling the covers up to my chin. I thought I must have been dreaming because that was something he would have done back in Maplewood, before Nana Margie died.

I woke up at six, my usual time for a school day. Ray was already gone from his bed. I assumed Ms. Sookie had already talked to him about me staying home if I wasn’t feeling any better. I grabbed one of the pads Ms. Sookie had given me and headed to the bathroom. The house was already beginning to get warm, and the cool tile felt good on my feet. I sat on the toilet and changed my pad, rolling the used one up in toilet paper and burying it at the bottom of the wastebasket.

I stood and began washing my hands in the sink. As I looked up at my reflection in the mirror, my breath caught in my throat. I was looking at Hope Maynard. I was so overwhelmed with my monthly coming, I hadn't plaited and tied up my hair. With my hair loose, I was her spitting image. I put my hands up to my cheeks. I turned my head from side to side. I examined my face from every angle.

The tears came hot, fast, and unexpectedly. The pain of not having my mother bubbled to the surface before I had time to push it back down into the place where I wasn't so aware of it. I only cried harder when I thought about having my first monthly cycle without her. I loved Ms. Sookie, but I wanted my momma. Thanks to Ray, I'd have all those big moments without her. My first boyfriend, graduating high school, my wedding, and motherhood would all happen without her.

I grabbed my washcloth and put it over my mouth in an effort to stifle the sound of my sobs. I didn't want Ms. Sookie or any of the girls to hear me. There was nothing they could do to help me when I couldn't share the truth. I forced myself to take long, deep breaths until I was calm enough to turn on the faucet and wet my washcloth. I wiped my face and decided to sit on the side of the tub for a few moments. I chewed on my nails while I thought about how to get through this day. I decided I would go to school.

I also decided I would not put my hair up in my usual large afro ponytails. My first act as a woman would be to wear my hair wild and free. I picked my hair out so that it was as big as possible, grabbed my books, and headed out to school.

I passed Ray as I rounded the side of the house. He was still fiddling in the flower bed. He looked up at me and his face went pale, as if he'd seen a ghost. I knew he'd seen what I'd seen in the mirror that morning. It gave me just a little satisfaction to have scared the hell out of him for just a moment, but then some other emotion washed over his face. He looked sad for what felt like a split second. His body shuddered, then he lowered his head and went back to tending to the garden.

I spent most of my walk to school thinking about that split second. I had to shake it off so I could focus in class.

I walked into the classroom feeling confident, wearing womanhood like a badge of honor. All the girls seemed to know I had come into my own. Even Mrs. Higgins gave a smile and nod when I took my seat. All the boys just stared in awe of my big hair and the spunk in my stride.

As soon as Rudy had a free moment, he asked me about what had happened. I made up an excuse about tummy troubles and gross stuff coming out of both ends. I gave enough details for him to be satisfied with my explanation.

"Whatever happened yesterday, you sure look like you feel better," Rudy commented.

I laughed and nudged him.

The rest of the day, all I worried about was changing my pad in enough time that I wouldn't make a mess of my underwear. Ms. Sookie had given me a purse and put several pads in it. I'd give Mrs. Higgins a look and she'd simply nod her head. I'd quietly head to the restroom with my purse and do what I needed to do.

Ms. Sookie was even more protective of me after my monthly started. She did allow me more time around the grown folks, under her watchful eyes, of course. While I wasn't allowed in the parlor, no one fussed about me going to bed super early anymore. I had to go to my room by nine on school nights, and on weekends, I could stay up until eleven. On Fridays and Saturdays, I would sit quietly and watch couple after couple walk up and down the stairs. On the way up, the couples smelled of flowers and musk. On the way down, they smelled of sweat and another scent I didn't recognize.

One particularly hot Friday night, I was sitting on the stairwell just off the parlor. A new fella walked into Ms. Sookie's like he owned the place. He wore a brown cowboy hat, a dingy white button-down shirt, a pair of suspenders, khaki pants, and some black work boots. The short, stocky man was not only unimpressive in stature; he wasn't easy on the eyes either. He needed a haircut and a good shave. There was a scar across his left cheek, and his left eye was a bit hazy.

He sized up the crew in the parlor. All of the girls had already had at least one customer so far. Traffic had slowed, and everyone seemed grateful for the break, considering it was hotter than fish grease in the parlor. There were no windows in the room, and the open windows in the other rooms were only helping to circulate the heat. Their sideways glances indicated that none of them were in any rush to be the object of his attention. After observation, each girl returned to finding the best way to keep cool. Iced drinks were only for the paying customers.

"Hello, sir. How can I help you?" Ms. Sookie asked kindly.

Her face looked like she knew the night was about to go sour.

"Seems like you should already know what I want," the man said dryly.

"Well now, sir. All women like flowers, but each woman has a preference of what flower she likes best. Ms. Sookie aims for everyone to have the flower they like best."

"Hmph," he replied. He looked around the room and his eyes rested on Sunny.

I saw a bit of panic in Ms. Sookie's eyes. It was a flash of the look my momma had before…

"Oh, Sunny. She has a regular who should be here any moment. What about Lilah over there?" Ms. Sookie asked, interrupting my thoughts.

Sunny remained seated, looking confused. Lilah shot Ms. Sookie a look, then smiled and nodded at the gentleman.

"If that Sunny got an appointment, I'll pay twice what that fella was gonna pay," the man countered.

Ms. Sookie looked at Sunny, then back at the gentleman.

"I'm sorry. He's a long-standing customer, and I can't ignore his scheduled time," Ms. Sookie said with an apologetic nod.

"Fine. How about that one over there?" he said, pointing at Suga.

All of a sudden, Ray slammed a glass down on the bar top. Everyone's head jerked toward the bar to see what had happened.

Ms. Sookie's eyes grew dark.

"Is there a problem, Ray?" she asked.

"Suga booked too," Ray replied.

"Booked wit' who?" Ms. Sookie said with a tilt of her head.

"Me," he responded.

Suga didn't say a word or move. However, a smirk turned up the right corner of her mouth. The corner only I could see.

"I can't see that since you ain't allowed to take up with none of my girls," Ms. Sookie sneered.

"Ms. Sookie, I know we had an agreement, but he can't have Suga," Ray said matter-of-factly.

"Why, you ungrateful..." Ms. Sookie whispered, then looked up at me perched on the stairwell.

Whatever she was going to say stalled on the tip of her tongue when she remembered I was there. If she'd only known what I thought of him, she wouldn't have bridled her tongue.

"Your bartender can tell you who can have what girl?" the fellow asked.

"Hell nawl," Ms. Sookie responded. "Sir, you go ahead and take Suga up to her room. She'll show you the way."

"If he touches her, the police gonna come here tonight. You don't want that, Ms. Sookie, and neither do he," Ray warned.

"Naw, I don't believe *you* gonna want that," the stranger replied.

Ray took the blue-and-white dish towel from his left shoulder, wiped his hands on it, then he tossed it on the bar.

"Ray, stay your ass behind that bar. You don't run none of these girls. If you and Suga got something going on, *despite* my rules, you gone have to take that up with her after work hours," Ms. Sookie ordered.

Ray strode around the bar and stood next to Suga.

"Sir, kindly pick another girl," he said politely.

"I done picked the one I want," the man replied.

It was obvious his heels were dug in, and there would be a battle over Suga.

"We ain't got time for this! Suga, get your ass on up them stairs, or I swear when you hit the ground, the dust won't settle on your backside before I have a new girl in your place. Play wit' me iffin' you want," Ms. Sookie bellowed as her nostrils flared.

I hadn't ever seen Ms. Sookie that angry. Suga started to rise, but Ray placed his hand sternly on her shoulder. She looked up at him, pleading in her eyes. He did not move his hand.

The man turned to the group in the parlor as if he were performing in a play, "I would say let's settle this outside like gentlemen, but you'd have to be one. How you get mad when a man wants a whore? That's what she is, ain't she? Lent to any man with a few coins."

"Say one more word," Ray growled.

"Mouse, go to your room," Ms. Sookie snapped.

I didn't move.

"Now!" she yelled.

I jumped up and ran to the top of the stairs, but there was no way I was going to miss what was going to happen. I was too frightened that the man would kill him. As much as I disliked Ray and tried to avoid him, I couldn't stand the thought of losing my only living parent. He may not have been a good father, but he was all the blood family I had left in the world.

I didn't see it, but I heard the sound of a switchblade. Ray did not carry a knife, so I assumed it was the other man.

Ms. Sookie's voice floated to the top of the stairs. It was calm, almost silky, "Now, listen. You already got one scar on your face and a bad eye. I'm real good with this here switchblade, and if you make me use it, you're gonna have matching sides. I don't want no trouble in my establishment. I'll deal with my employee, but I'm gonna have to ask you to leave for the night."

I eased to the other side of the stairwell so I could see the man. I watched as he eyed Ray and then Ms. Sookie.

"Ain't no tail worth all this trouble. Shame a man can't even come pay for a sweet taste because a rat done soured the well," the man said slickly. "Hmph. Glad I won't see another sunset in this raggedy place."

The man turned and walked out the door, closing it quietly behind him. Everyone must have been holding their breath, because we all exhaled at the same time.

"Everybody except Ray and Suga, go on outta my sight! Sookie's is closed for the rest of the evening. I don't wanna see none of y'all until tomorrow."

All of the girls got up and headed upstairs. None of them looked at me as they passed on the way to their rooms. Sunny stopped and stood beside me.

"Mouse, c'mon in my room with me," she offered.

"I want to hear what Ms. Sookie is gonna say," I told her.

She shrugged and left me there. I sat, legs crossed and feet tucked beneath me so no one would know I was listening.

"What the hell going on here?" Ms. Sookie asked. I couldn't tell who she was talking to, but Ray was the one to speak next.

"Ms. Sookie, we ain't mean for it to happen." He whined like a child who'd been caught with his hand in the cookie jar.

I spit out thin slivers of nail. I had no idea where the pieces had landed and didn't take time to look for them.

"Please don't tell me you two fools think y'all in love!" Ms. Sookie hollered.

"But we is," Suga replied.

"You ain't got the sense God gave an alley cat. Love? This man done watched you sleep with man after man and you think he love you? He know about the baby?"

"The what?" Ray shouted.

Ms. Sookie chuckled.

"Guess not. You ain't stopped working and ain't even told this man you expecting? I didn't want to believe either of y'all would go against my wishes. This summer heat got y'all half crazy." Ms. Sookie sucked her teeth. "Ray, I hate to do it, but you gotta leave tomorrow. Suga, you think you so in love, you can go with him. Just think about how Ray gone provide for all four of y'all in a boardinghouse."

"Ms. Sookie, don't make me leave. I promise I won't cause you no more trouble. Suga can find another job, and I can stay on here. Mouse loves you and the girls. I don't want to have to move her again," he begged.

His plea couldn't have really had anything to do with what I needed. I was motherless because of him.

"I love Mouse, too, but you blatantly disrespected me, Ray. I can't let you stay here.

Honest to God, I don't want Mouse to leave, but maybe it's for the best anyway. My heart skipped a beat when I thought that man was gone ask for her. She getting to an age where she don't need to be around this anyway. It's final, Ray. Y'all best be gone from here early in the morning. Suga, you staying or you going?"

There was a pause before her answer. I wished I could see their faces.

"I'm going. I love Ray," Suga said quietly.

"Fine." Ms. Sookie turned and started up the stairs. I stayed low and scrambled into Sunny's room.

"What happened?" Sunny asked with wide eyes.

I bursted into tears.

"Suga is pregnant for Ray and Ms. Sookie making us all leave!" I sobbed loudly.

"Oh no!" Sunny cried.

She grabbed me and squeezed me like I imagined a big sister would. I sobbed until my eyes could no longer produce tears. She went to the bathroom and brought back a cool, wet rag to wipe my face.

Sunny made me sit up on her bed before pulling her old tattered suitcase from underneath it. She laid it carefully on the bed, opened it, and pulled out the sculpted elephant I'd seen on the day she moved into the house. She handed the elephant to me.

"I want you to have this elephant. It's the only thing I have to remember my momma before she died, but it's the only thing I can give you to remember me," she said sadly.

"I can't take your elephant, Sunny," I whimpered.

"Yes, you can. You hold on to it until we meet again. You and Ms. Sookie was the only ones kind to me when I got here. You lost your Momma just like me. You hold on to it for both of us, okay?"

"Okay. I promise to keep it until we meet again."

I fell asleep in Sunny's room, and we were both awakened early in the morning by a light tap on the door. I thought it was Ray looking for me, but when the door cracked open, it was Ms. Sookie.

"Sunny, it's some breakfast waiting on you downstairs. I want to talk to Mouse for a minute," she said softly.

"Yes, ma'am."

Sunny squeezed my hand as she got up to leave.

Ms. Sookie looked tired and sad, like she hadn't slept much that night. She sat on the edge of the bed and held her arms out to me. I scooted to the bottom of the bed and right into her arms.

"You are becoming a young lady, Mouse. Young ladies don't belong here. I was already thinking it may be time for you to leave me, so what your daddy and Suga did just made the decision for me. You know I don't *want* you to leave, right?" she asked.

I looked up into her eyes and saw the pain there. I nodded my head.

"If you ever need to come back here, don't you hesitate, and I don't mean to work neither. You always have a place to lay your head and a woman who loves you," she said, nearly weeping.

Ms. Sookie pulled me into her bosom and hugged me tighter than I'd ever been hugged before, even by my own momma.

"You go on and wash up and then come downstairs to get you some breakfast. Your daddy and Suga already up and waiting for you. I asked Ray to let me come get you up."

I went to my room to find my clothes already laid out on the bed for me. I brushed my teeth, washed my face, and combed my hair. While I dressed, I thought of how I'd seen the way Ray looked at Suga when he thought no one was paying attention. I couldn't stand it. It was the way he'd looked at Momma. He would walk by and brush her hand with a sweetness I hadn't seen in years. I disliked Suga even more.

Suga was only seven years older than me. I couldn't stomach the idea of having the nineteen-year-old in a relationship with Ray telling me what to do. I thought about running off and hiding in the hope that Ray and Suga would just leave without me, but I knew he wouldn't. He would be too scared of what I would tell without him around. I would just be delaying the reality of us leaving Ms. Sookie's.

I went downstairs and everyone was at the kitchen table. We all ate in silence. Mrs. Jameson quietly packed some food for the three of us and gave the wrapped food to Suga with a hug. She then walked over to me and bent down to give me a quick peck on the cheek. I could see tears had welled up in her eyes and were threatening to run down her face. She wiped at them quickly.

Ms. Sookie couldn't take another minute. She got up from the table, handed Suga an envelope with the last of her pay, and left the kitchen. The rest of the girls each hugged us one by one and solemnly walked us outside. I looked toward Ms. Sookie's room and could see that she was watching.

The three of us set off toward the bus station with no destination and no plan for the future.

Hemings

Seven

Ray had some money saved from his tips, but not enough to buy three bus tickets with money to spare for a place to stay when we arrived. Suga dug in her bag and happily gave him the money for our fare, but told him to choose where we were going. He picked a place named Hemings, which was only two towns west of Edenville. It seemed that Michigan would keep us for a little longer.

On the ride, Suga and Ray talked about places they could look for employment once we arrived. I watched him smile at her and touch her stomach, and I saw a flash of the man he used to be. I wondered if that's how he'd been when Momma was pregnant with me. The longer I watched the two of them, the more my temperature rose.

I was so angry at those two for getting us thrown out of Ms. Sookie's that I kept my mouth closed. Anything I said would have gotten me into trouble. It was all I could do to keep myself from crying. The first chance I could find, I planned to run back to Ms. Sookie's. Thanks to Suga's loud mouth, I knew all I ever had to do to get back there was to save up three dollars and fifty cents.

"Mouse, you ain't said nothing the entire trip. What's the matter wit'chu?" Ray asked.

I glared at both him and Suga and responded, "I'm fine."

"Stop biting your nails like that. What's wrong with you?" Suga chided.

I continued chewing while looking her right in the eye. She wasn't *that* much older than me, and she would not be the boss of me just because Ray had taken a liking to her. Suga looked at him for reinforcement. I looked at him, willing him to take up for me. He turned his head to look out the window, avoiding eye contact with both of us.

"Ray, you ain't gone say nothing?"

He looked at Suga, then me.

"Mouse, you know Suga pregnant. You can't be upsetting her. The baby..."

I tuned him out with thoughts of ramming my fists down both their throats. I took my fingers out of my mouth instead.

It was only an hour-and-a-half ride to Hemings. We stepped off the bus into the devil's den. The summer of 1961 was in full swing. The sun wasn't even at its highest point, and I could see the wavy lines of heat coming off the road. I was miserable thinking of the three of us having to walk around in this inferno looking for work and a place to live with our suitcases in tow.

Hemings was buzzing with activity. The bus depot was right at the edge of downtown and Saturday was a shopping day. There were women dressed in their pedal pushers and plaid tops with their hair in freshly-pressed pin curls. They were all carrying brown paper bags with groceries and supplies for the week. The few men that were around were all working in the shops on the main strip.

Suga sidled up to an older woman sitting on a bench outside of the butcher's shop.

"Ma'am, we new to this town. Could you tell me where me and my husband can find work, please?" she asked with a sweetness I'd never seen before.

"Well," the woman said and paused. She looked at Suga and then Ray before she continued. "Most of the menfolk work over at the pulpwood mill. That's just down the road a few miles. Most of the ladies work tending laundry and chil'ren for white families 'cross town."

When Ray heard there was a mill, his face lit up. Suga did not look pleased about her options.

"Thank you, kindly," Suga said to the woman with a nod. She turned and looked at Ray.

"I'm gone head over to that mill and see if they hiring. You and Mouse go see what you can find out about you a family to work for and getting Mouse in school," he instructed.

Suga and I looked at each other. Neither one of us was thrilled about being stuck with the other, but we didn't have much choice in the matter.

Ray took off walking. Suga looked around and then decided to go back to the lady on the bench.

"I'm sorry to bother you again, ma'am," she said softly.

"Call me Mrs. Althea, honey. What you need now?"

"Do you know where I might go to get one of those jobs and to see about getting my..." Suga struggled to figure out the appropriate way to refer to me. "My stepdaughter into school," she finished.

"What's your name, darling?" Mrs. Althea asked.

"I'm Suga, and this here's Mouse."

"Come with me. I can help you get yourself set up. I suppose y'all looking for a place to stay too," she said, looking over the rim of her cat-eye glasses.

"Yes, ma'am," Suga said, nodding urgently.

"Mmm hmm," Mrs. Althea hummed with a certain knowing.

Mrs. Althea was short and round. She had to scoot herself up the edge of the bench in order for her feet to touch the ground. She rocked her way into a standing position with some grunting and heavy breathing. Once standing, she wasn't much taller than me, and she was almost as round as me, Suga, and Ms. Sookie put together. Her graying hair was pulled into a bun at the nape of her neck. Her glasses had a pearl chain that could hold them around her neck when they weren't on her face, which I suspected was for the sole purpose of preventing her from losing them. It had taken a lot of material to make her plaid dress, and I wasn't sure that plaid was a great choice for a woman of her stature.

Mrs. Althea had us follow her home, which had been a twenty-minute walk to the north side of town. When we arrived, her husband, Mr. Kenneth, was sitting in a rocking chair on the porch.

"There's my sweet Althea," he sang with a raspy voice.

Mrs. Althea's skin was too dark brown to show any signs of blushing, but she laughed and swatted at Mr. Kenneth as he reached for her hand.

"Y'all put those suitcases down right over there. This is my husband, Kenneth Alexander. He is retired from that old mill and 'round here on my nerves more hours of the day than you can count."

They both laughed at her little joke.

"Bernadette!" Mrs. Althea yelled.

A beautiful young woman came trotting to the screen door.

"Yes, Momma?" she asked with raised eyebrows and her hands on her hips.

After seeing that her mother had brought company, she opened the screen door and stepped out onto the porch with the rest of us.

Bernadette looked to be in her mid-twenties, around the same age as most of the girls at Ms. Sookie's. She certainly dressed differently than them. Her calf-length tan pencil skirt and her white collared blouse were very neatly-pressed. Her black shoes were closed-toe and had a strap across the top, with a modest heel. Her dark brown hair was in soft, tight curls that were pinned back on one side and framing her face on the other. She had a smile that sparkled and eyes that twinkled. I liked her immediately.

"Didn't you tell me the Richardsons were looking for a worker?" Mrs. Althea asked.

"Yes, ma'am. I think they still are. Ruby had to quit since she's about to have another baby, and she doesn't plan on returning," Bernadette explained.

"Call Ruby and see if you can get Mrs. Richardson's number. This young lady is new here and needs a job. This is Mouse and she needs to get into school. She looks about the right age to be in your class," Mrs. Althea told Bernadette.

"Hi, Mouse! How old are you?" she asked me.

"I'm twelve," I responded proudly.

"Well, my Momma is right. I'll be your teacher! You can call me Ms. Bernadette," she said with a huge smile.

She stretched out her hands to me. I reached out, and she grabbed my small hand in both of hers.

Suga cleared her throat.

"Ah, yes," Ms. Bernadette said. "Let me call Ruby and get the number."

"Bring some lemonade back with you, would you? I'm sure these young ladies are parched after that walk from downtown," Mrs. Althea said.

Ms. Bernadette returned after a couple of minutes with a beautifully-painted pitcher filled with cold lemonade on a tray. There were three glasses and a piece of paper with a number written on it as well. She put the tray down and handed the number to Suga, who took it with a small smile. She then served me, Suga, and Mrs. Althea some lemonade. Mr. Alexander already had a glass of something light brown sitting next to him on a small table. Ms. Bernadette must not have been thirsty.

I could feel Suga's uneasiness, though I wasn't sure why she would feel that way. The Alexanders had been nothing but kind to us. Everyone else must have felt it too. Mrs. Althea offered to walk us back into town, but Ms. Bernadette insisted she would take us. We grabbed our suitcases and followed her lead.

"Suga, I would suggest you call the Richardsons as soon as you find a place and get settled. Do you have another name you use?" she asked as we walked back the way we'd come.

"No," Suga responded.

Her eyebrows were pulled in and her forehead creased.

"I only ask because the Richardsons are very well-to-do. When you call, you don't want to introduce yourself as 'Suga…' not that there's anything wrong with your name," Ms. Bernadette said apologetically.

"I guess 'Suga' ain't fancy enough for them white folk," she added with a little edge.

Ms. Bernadette had only tried to be helpful, and Suga was about to bite her head off. She turned her attention to me instead.

"Mouse, do you like to read?" she asked.

"Yes, ma'am. I love to read!"

"Oh, good. English is my favorite subject to teach. What was the last book you read in your class?" she quizzed.

"*Rabbit Hill.*"

"Oh, I love that one. Talking animals are always fun," she said with a laugh.

I laughed too. Suga stared straight ahead.

We were still about a ten-minute walk away from the center of town when Ms. Bernadette stopped and thought for a moment.

"Mother told me I should bring y'all to Mr. Hamilton's. He takes in boarders and he just had a family of three leave not too long ago," she said. "Here, follow me."

The three of us cut down a side path that led to a small house sitting in a clearing. A tall, hefty, handsome gentleman was sitting outside on the porch.

"Well, hey, Ms. Bernadette! What brings you around here this afternoon?" the man asked.

"I have some new friends who need a place to stay, Mr. Hamilton," Ms. Bernadette responded.

"It's just the two of y'all?" Mr. Hamilton asked with mild concern.

"No," Suga piped up. "My husband is over at the mill looking for a job."

"I see. Well, I do have room, but your husband will need to come and talk to me about the rate and such. I only handle business with the man of the house," Mr. Hamilton said.

"Yessir," Suga responded.

We resumed our walk in awkward silence.

"Suga, what's your husband's name?" Ms. Bernadette asked.

"Ray," Suga answered flatly. "Ray Johnson."

I thought "Maynard" in my mind.

"Did you and Ray discuss where to meet once he was done at the mill?" Ms. Bernadette prodded.

"No, we didn't exactly make a plan for any of this."

It was evident that Suga was agitated.

"Okay. Well, why don't the three of us go wait at Mister's All-You-Can-Eat. You two must be starving. You can get a little snack," Ms. Bernadette said cheerily.

"Ray got all the cash with him. We'll just sit here on this bench and wait. We don't need no charity," Suga said as much to herself as to Ms. Bernadette.

"Suga, I'm sure you don't need charity. However, I am not going to leave you out here in the heat waiting on Mr. Ray. I've got enough cash to get us all a soda and a donut. And besides, Mister's is much cooler than it is out here," Ms. Bernadette said reassuringly.

I was grateful when Suga agreed. My mouth was dry as cotton. We walked the two blocks over to Mister's. When we entered, it seemed the whole room turned its attention to Ms. Bernadette. The older women hugged her. The men waved at her, and the children ran to her and hugged her around a thigh or her waist. Suga and I found a quiet little table near a corner to sit while she said her hellos.

After a few minutes, Ms. Bernadette came over to the table and sat with us. Right behind her came a teenage boy, tall and lanky as a light pole. His jet-black hair had been straightened and was high in the front and sloped down smooth in the back. I'd never seen anything like it. Most men in Maplewood and around the other towns we'd been in either had about an inch or two of nappy hair or were in various stages of bald. I looked over at Suga, whose eyebrows were drawn together again, creating lines on her forehead.

"Hey, Ms. Bernadette! Who are your new friends?" the young man asked.

"Hey, Al! Oh, these two young ladies are new in town. This is Suga, and this is Mouse," she answered.

"Hello, Suga and Mouse. Pleased to meet you. What can I get for you ladies today?" he asked with a smile.

Al's white pants and shirt were pressed so crisply they probably could have stood there without him in them. His red bowtie was perfectly tied and centered between the two points of his collar. His white apron was clean, and the belt was wrapped around his narrow waist twice and neatly tied in the front.

"I think we will each have one of Mister's glazed blueberry cake doughnuts and a soda." Ms. Bernadette ordered for all of us.

"Coming right up!" Al exclaimed.

Al returned with our order after just a few minutes. I bit into that glazed blueberry doughnut and thought I must have just bitten into a piece of heaven. The glaze was sweet and the cake doughnut was soft, moist, and fluffy. Ms. Bernadette smiled when she saw my expression. She winked at me.

"I thought you might like that," she said with a sneaky smile.

Suga gave no reaction to the doughnut. Ms. Bernadette just smiled at her despite seeming a little disappointed at her lack of excitement. We ate our treats and drank our soda without any conversation while the soft buzz of chatter surrounded us.

Al came over every so often to check on us. Ms. Bernadette walked over to the counter to pay for our snacks. She whispered something to Al before returning to us.

"Bernadette!" a voice called out.

All three of us turned our heads toward the door. I looked back at Ms. Bernadette, and the smile she was wearing took up most of her face. Whoever this man was, he was special to her.

The man walked over to the table, wrapped his arms around Ms. Bernadette, lifted her off her feet, and spun her around in a circle.

"Jimmie!" she exclaimed.

"I went down to the house looking for you, and your daddy said you were in town. Let me look at you!" Jimmie said excitedly.

He put Ms. Bernadette down, and she spun around so he could take her in.

"I didn't know you were coming home. When did you get back?" Ms. Bernadette asked.

"Just now, sweetheart. I didn't tell you because I wanted it to be a surprise."

Jimmie was tall as a pine tree, with broad shoulders. He was thin, but not skinny like Al. His skin was rich, dark brown, like a new leather belt. His black hair was cut low, and his mustache and beard were neatly trimmed. I'd thought my father was the most handsome man I'd ever seen until that moment. The uniform he wore only made him look more handsome in my book. I'd once heard Lilah say there was nothing more fine than a man in a uniform, and now I understood what she meant.

Jimmie looked over at me and Suga, then back to Ms. Bernadette.

"Jimmie, this is Suga, and this is Mouse. They are new in town, and I was showing them around. We are waiting on Suga's husband to come back from the mill so they can go get a place to stay with Mr. Hamilton. Ladies, this is my beau, Jimmie."

Jimmie nodded and said, "Pleasure, ladies."

He turned his attention back to Ms. Bernadette.

"I thought I would pick you up and take you for a ride," Jimmie said shyly to Ms. Bernadette.

"Oh, Jimmie. If I had known you were coming home today, I would have fixed myself up. Plus, I don't want to leave the ladies here all alone, seeing as how they are new here. It's getting late and

Suga's husband should be back from the mill soon," she explained.

"Well, why don't we all go look for him, and once we get these two in his care, you and me go for a ride?"

Ms. Bernadette looked at us, and Suga gave a single nod of approval. As we were standing up, Ms. Bernadette gave Al a look. He hurried over with a sack full of those amazing doughnuts and handed them to me. Suga opened her mouth to protest, but Ms. Bernadette laid a hand on her shoulder and smiled. Suga kept her mouth closed, but her face said she didn't appreciate what Ms. Bernadette had done. Ray was likely to be unhappy with it as well.

The four of us walked down the street and were almost back to the bus station when we saw Ray coming up the road. He had an extra spring in his step.

"There y'all are! I hoped I wouldn't have to look too far for ya. I went down to that mill and they hired me right on the spot! Even let me work a few hours today to learn the job. Mouse, what's that you got there?" he asked.

"Some doughnuts from Mister's," I answered softly.

I prayed silently that Ray would not embarrass me in front of these people who had been nothing but kind to us.

"Well, y'all ain't had no money, so how you pay for that?" he asked, looking at Suga.

"Ms. Bernadette paid for it," Suga answered quickly.

"It was nothing. They walked all the way out to my parent's house and all the way back to town. I knew they had to be a little hungry, and I knew as the man of the house, you were probably carrying all the money. Please, don't be upset with them. I insisted," Ms. Bernadette explained.

"Fine. How much that stuff cost?" Ray asked Ms. Bernadette as he dug in his pocket.

"Don't worry about it. Please," Ms. Bernadette pleaded.

"Naw! If you don't let me pay you back, I'm gone take that as an insult. Johnsons don't depend on nothing and nobody but themselves."

"Sir, please. Bernadette was only looking after your ladies as a kindness. If you insist on paying back a kindness, you will hurt her feelings. I don't like for my gal's feelings to get hurt," said Jimmie.

Ray looked Jimmie up and down. The uniform must have persuaded him to accept the gesture without further fuss.

"Thank you. Y'all c'mon," Ray said hurriedly.

"Suga, do you remember the way back to Mr. Hamilton's house?" Ms. Bernadette asked.

Suga nodded.

Ms. Bernadette and Jimmie told me and Suga goodbye and headed back toward Mister's to hop in Jimmie's car.

"Did you find out about work and school?" Ray asked in a huff.

"I got a number I need to call for work, and that Bernadette is gonna be Mouse's teacher," Suga replied.

"Gimme one of them doughnuts. I'm starving, and we gotta see how much rent gone be before we spend any more money," he said, snatching the bag from my hands.

Ray and Mr. Hamilton worked out the details of our living arrangements while Suga and I waited on the bench outside. Once they came to an agreement, Ray waved us into the house.

Our space was a small apartment on the back side of the house. The outside was old and run-down. Its faded paint looked to be the same shade as the one on the house, but the house had received new coats over the years. Inside, there was one bedroom that held a rickety bed frame with a worn mattress with springs sticking out. Across from the bed was an old, damaged brown dresser. There was one bathroom we would all have to share. Then there was a living room with a couch, which would double as my bed, plus a chair and a very small kitchen. The walls, however, were beautiful.

The walls were made of deep, rich, brown wooden panels. The panels had ridges in them and were arranged in the shape of an upside-down letter v. It looked like something that might belong in a church or a courtroom, not an old raggedy house. I wondered why someone had thought enough of this little space to make the walls look like that.

While the walls were magnificent, the rest of the house wasn't as nice as Ms. Janie's or Ms. Sookie's. But we would make do.

Once we were settled in, Suga went to the main house to call the Richardsons. When she came back, she said she was expected to go by the house the next day to interview with Mrs. Richardson. We finished the rest of the doughnuts in the bag and the food we'd brought with us, then we each washed up for bed.

While Ray was in the bathroom, I heard Suga struggling in the room. I went to the door to see what she was doing. She was trying to push the exposed springs back into the mattress so she could make up the bed and make it as comfortable as possible. She was stuffing the holes with raggedy pieces of white cloth she must have found in the bathroom.

"Mouse, come help me with this," she said, grunting.

I walked over to where she was bent over the mattress, and she handed me some cloth. It was that thick terry-cloth material.

"Stuff that into that other hole over there. Try to make sure you cover that spring," she instructed.

I was tempted to make the spring stick out more. I thought better of it and plugged the hole as she'd directed. By the time we'd finished, you could barely tell the mattress had been such a mess.

"Help me make up the bed," she demanded.

"Your *husband* will be out of the bathroom in a minute. Why don't you ask him to help you?" I asked sarcastically.

"'Cause I asked you," she said with squinted eyes.

I sucked my teeth and grabbed the sheets that Mr. Hamilton had provided off the top of the dresser. I wasn't in the mood to have trouble with Ray for irritating a pregnant Suga. Everything was, "You know Suga pregnant," and, "You shouldn't upset a pregnant woman," blah, blah, blah. I was beginning to think he was excited about this baby, which only made me dislike Suga even more.

When we finished dressing the bed, I hurried back to my sanctuary. My couch bed. It was not a sofa bed. There was no mattress, just worn, uneven cushions that were beige with bright pink and yellow flowers. I thought the cushions might have once been white because there were a few small areas where that was the actual color. It smelled faintly of cigar smoke, and there were a few small burn holes on the cushion at the foot of my bed.

I covered the cushions with a thin sheet, then laid down and pulled the other thin sheet on top of me. Ray came out of the bathroom and went into the bedroom with Suga, closing the door behind him. He had not thought to leave the bathroom or kitchen lights lit. I was in new surroundings with nothing but heat and darkness for companionship. In every other house, we'd been in the same room together. Now, things would be different. Suga had changed everything. I stewed over the situation I was in until I fell asleep.

Before the sun rose the next morning, I heard strange noises coming from the bedroom. I sat up on the couch and looked over the back of it toward the room door. Someone must have woken up to use the bathroom in the night, because the door was slightly open. I eased off the couch and lightly planted my feet on the floor. I rose slowly and inched my left foot forward. I hadn't been here long enough to have learned which floorboards would creak and which would remain silent. I moved slowly, testing each board before putting my full weight onto it. I didn't weigh much, but one wrong move could still give me away.

As I moved closer, the sound grew louder. I could hear heavy breathing. I wondered what in the world the two of them could be doing. I slid along the wall until I could lean over and peak into the room. I was horrified by what I saw. Ray was laying on the bed on his back, eyes closed. He was naked, but I couldn't see all of his body. Suga was naked, sitting on top of him. Her breasts were bare and her belly was beginning to poke out like she had eaten a cantaloupe whole. Her legs were on either side of Ray's waist and she was moving up and down, with her head thrown back. Every time she came down, she groaned and he exhaled deeply.

I inhaled sharply, and Suga must have heard me. Her head jerked and she looked directly at me, standing in the doorway, stupefied. An unfamiliar smile washed over her face. Ray's eyes remained closed. I turned and ran to the bathroom. I heard Suga cackling behind me.

The noises grew faster and louder. I cupped my hands over my ears and closed my eyes as tightly as I could. I had no idea what they were doing, but I was afraid of what she might be doing to him. As evil as he'd become, I hoped she wasn't putting some type of spell, or what the old people called "a root," on him.

Is she a witch?

Someone knocked at the bathroom door, and I opened it. Suga stood in the doorway in a thin bathrobe with a look of satisfaction on her face.

"I need to use the toilet," she announced.

"What were you doing to my father?" I asked suspiciously.

"You'll learn one day," she replied.

"I don't want to know how to cast evil spells on nobody," I whispered.

Suga laughed hard and long. She held her belly with one hand and wiped tears from her eyes with the other.

"Is that what you think I was doing?"

I just stood there and looked at her.

"Chile, me and yo' daddy was doing what men and women do. Maybe one day I'll tell you all about it," she said smugly.

When we walked past each other sideways in the small door frame, her poked-out belly rubbed against mine. Then, she closed the bathroom door in my face.

I stood staring at the door, wanting to barge back into that bathroom and tell her she should really be afraid of what Ray could do to her. I decided that whatever he might do, she would have it coming.

I gave my bed its daytime transformation. I folded the sheets up and stuffed them behind the largest pillow on the couch. I changed into my play clothes and sat on the edge of the cushion. I was still worried.

Ray went to Mister's and purchased a small breakfast for the three of us to share. He made sure Suga had as much as she wanted, then he and I split the rest.

"We ain't got much to spare until I get paid. Suga, here go five dollars to get some groceries tomorrow. Get some canned beans, chicken, and stuff that's gone fill us up and last until I get paid on Friday. What time you gotta go talk to them white folk?" he asked.

"I gotta be there by one o'clock. The missus said that should be enough time for them to get back from church and have lunch," Suga informed him.

He nodded his head in satisfaction. I ate the last of my biscuit.

"May I be excused?" I asked.

"Mmm hmm," Suga replied.

After discovering I could be dealing with a bonafide witch, I got up from the table without so much as a look or roll of the eyes. I decided it might be in my best interest to just steer as clear of her as possible.

I went to the den, Suga went to get dressed for her interview, and Ray dressed to go hang out with the fellas from the mill.

"Mouse, I'm going into town. You go with Suga," he said before walking out the door.

I examined my fingers instead of rolling my eyes at him.

When Suga was finished getting dressed and taming her coarse hair, she told me to come on. She had a piece of paper with directions written on it, which she must have gotten from Mrs. Richardson when they spoke. I wiped the blood from my fingertips on the underside of my shorts and followed her out of the door.

Suga led the way as I lagged behind. When we lived at Ms. Sookie's, all I'd ever wanted was for Suga to be my friend. Now, all I wanted was for her to disappear. I watched her sway her pregnant hips from side to side, switching like windshield wiper blades on a rainy day. Her walk had a steady rhythm, like a good bass line in a song. And like a good bass line, Suga had Ray dancing to her beat.

"Keep up, Mouse. I don't wanna be late to these people house. Gotta make a good impression. This a chance to be a respectable woman," she said, more to herself than me.

"You and Ray ain't really married, so how you gone be respectable?" I asked.

Suga spun on her heels. The move stopped me in my tracks.

"You don't know what the hell we is. And even if we ain't, yo' daddy love me, and he love this baby too. You best remember that. You make him choose, you gone getcho' feelings hurt," she growled.

Tears welled up in my eyes. I'd already known that pitting myself against Suga would be a bad move for me. Realizing that she knew it, too, cut me deep. There was nothing left for my momma in Ray's heart. I knew because I was her spitting image. If he could look at me and feel nothing, then she was a long, lost memory to him.

"Why you choose Ray? Why didn't you stay with Mr. Pratt?" I howled.

"'Cause he ain't want me no more and yo' daddy a better man anyways. I ain't got time for this, Mouse!" Suga yelled. "And you best watch yo' mouth 'fore I tell yo' daddy you calling him by his first name."

Jimmie and Ms. Bernadette pulled up beside us in his car.

"Hey, y'all! Where y'all headed?" Jimmie asked.

"I got that interview over at the Richardson's today," Suga replied.

Ms. Bernadette looked at me. I tried to hide that I was upset.

"Suga, since you have to do that interview, why don't you let Mouse come with us? You can come by the house and get her when you're done. Jimmie and I will drive you back to town," Ms. Bernadette asked hopefully.

Suga nodded.

"She was getting on my nerves anyway. Y'all take her and I'll come to the house to collect her when I'm done."

"You remember how to get there?" Ms. Bernadette asked.

"I believe so."

Suga was curt in her response, but I didn't care. I grinned and ran to hop in Jimmie's shiny car.

"Mouse, don't be no trouble," Suga said before turning to continue down the road.

Ms. Bernadette slid over so I could get in next to her. The seats were covered in thick, clear plastic with bubbles all over it that reminded me of little kernels of corn. I spent the next minute pushing the bubbles in on themselves. Ms. Bernadette looked over at me and raised her right eyebrow. I stopped.

Jimmie's car was a gold-colored Electra 225, or what most people called "a deuce and a quarter." I knew that nickname because Ray wanted one and talked about them all the time. We never could afford one, but he sure liked to dream about when he would be able to. The paint on Jimmie's had shiny flecks that sparkled in the sunlight. The seats were cream-colored, and the dash was a dark-brown material that looked like wood. It was a beautiful car. I looked over at Ms. Bernadette snuggled up against Jimmie and wondered if this was how Ray and Momma used to be.

"Mouse, we are going to Momma and Daddy's house for lunch. You hungry?" Ms. Bernadette asked.

I nodded greedily.

"We've got some good news. I'm glad you'll be there to hear it."

She shifted over in the seat and wrapped her arm around me. I smiled up at Ms. Bernadette.

"What's the good news?" I asked.

"You'll have to wait until we get to the house."

Ms. Bernadette giggled, then looked over at Jimmie, who was smiling so hard his cheeks must have hurt. I was fine with waiting to hear the news with everyone else. I was just happy to be with them and not Suga.

"Hey there, Mouse," Mrs. Althea said when I walked through the door.

Her face lit up when she saw me. I felt warm.

"Hey, Mrs. Althea," I responded.

I walked over and hugged her, then Mr. Kenneth.

"I'm so glad you could join us for lunch!" Mrs. Althea said happily.

"Me too!"

Ms. Bernadette, Jimmie, and I all went to wash up at Mrs. Althea's instruction. My eyes grew with excitement as I walked into the dining room and looked over the spread before me. Everyone chuckled as they took their seats. Mrs. Althea motioned for me to come sit on her right side. Mr. Kenneth was to her left, at the head of the table. Ms. Bernadette and Jimmie were on the other side, with Jimmie seated directly across from me.

Mr. Kenneth told us all to join hands. Jimmie reached across the table for mine and I quickly grabbed his. Mr. Kenneth began saying grace. I eased my eyes open to look around the table. Ms. Bernadette and Jimmie were staring at one another with funny looks on their faces, the same look my father and mother once had for each other. I closed my eyes and put my head all the way back down until Mr. Kenneth was finished.

"Amen," he said.

It felt like he had prayed for twenty minutes. The fried chicken was directly in front of me, and all I could think about was how good it smelled.

"Amen," everyone else said in unison, except for me.

Mrs. Althea began passing dishes to Mr. Kenneth. Once Mr. Kenneth took his portion, he passed the dish to Mrs. Althea. The dishes went around the table in this order until everyone had all they wanted on their plate.

"That message was sho' nuff good today, wasn't it, baby?" Mr. Kenneth asked Mrs. Althea.

"Sho' was," she responded. "That Reverend Miller know he can preach!"

I had not been to church since we left Maplewood. Ray didn't take me, and when I was invited to go with others, he made up excuses as to why I couldn't. Either I didn't have anything to wear, or I had been sick the night before, or we were of a different faith of the invitee. He always found a way to keep me from going.

"Momma and Daddy, Jimmie and I have a bit of news," Ms. Bernadette interrupted.

Mrs. Althea looked up from her plate while Mr. Kenneth kept right on shoveling food into his mouth. Mrs. Althea nudged him with her left wrist.

"Oh, um… yes, what's that, you say? Y'all have some news?" he asked.

"Yessir. I've asked Bernadette to marry me, and she's said 'yes,'" Jimmie responded.

Mr. Kenneth's face gave him away. He tried not to smile, and so did Mrs. Althea. Ms. Bernadette looked from one to the other, then to Jimmie.

"You two knew! And you didn't say a word!" Ms. Bernadette yelled.

"Well, it wasn't our business to mind," Mrs. Althea responded.

"What kind of man would I be if I didn't ask your father for your hand first?" Jimmie said to Ms. Bernadette.

She pretended to pout about being left out. Mr. Kenneth rose from his seat and walked over to Jimmie. Jimmie stood, and they shook hands, then embraced. Mr. Kenneth bent over and kissed Ms. Bernadette on the cheek. Ms. Bernadette stood up from her chair and ran over to her mother. First they embraced, crying tears of joy. Then, Mrs. Althea took her hand to examine her ring. Mrs. Althea looked up at Jimmie and winked in approval.

The rest of the meal was a bundle of tears and laughter. Everyone carried on over the ring, where they would hold the ceremony, the babies to come. There was such joy in their house. It was so beautiful it almost made me sad. I longed for the days when my family was like theirs. I'd never have the chance to tell my mother that the love of my life had proposed.

After eating a slice of sweet potato pie, I wandered outside and sat on the steps of the porch. A dusty old cat came and rubbed itself against my legs. I wasn't a fan of cats, but I didn't mind the company. I rubbed its patchwork-colored fur and listened to its intent purr. Ms. Bernadette came out and plopped down beside me after a few minutes.

"Mouse, you okay?" she asked.

I nodded.

"Does this mean you won't be my teacher?" I asked.

"I'll be your teacher, Mouse. Jimmie and I haven't made any plans to leave just yet," she responded.

That didn't give me much reassurance. I knew how quickly someone could up and relocate.

"Ms. Bernadette, have you ever seen a witch in real life?" I whispered. I looked over my shoulder to be sure no one else would hear my question.

"Well, I don't believe so, Mouse. Why do you ask?"

"I think Suga is one."

"Why do you think that?" she asked with a look of concern.

"Because I saw her bouncing up and down on my father and they were naked. They were making weird sounds and they both looked like they were in some sort of trance," I told her.

The look of concern eased from her face and she started laughing. My feelings were hurt that she would laugh at me. I turned my head so that she would not see the tears forming.

Ms. Bernadette grabbed my chin and turned my face toward hers.

"Oh, Mouse! I'm sorry, sweetheart. I was not laughing at you. I just know what you saw and how you could possibly mistake that as Suga putting a spell on your daddy. In a way, I suppose she is," she said with a smile.

I was even more confused.

"What does that mean, Ms. Bernadette?"

"Well, what you saw happens between two married people that care for one another. Suga is not a witch, and what you saw was natural," she explained.

I thought about telling her that Suga and Ray were not married, but that wouldn't do anything but cause trouble for me. Then I thought about her and Jimmie.

"So, you and Jimmie do that too?" I asked in awe.

Ms. Bernadette blushed.

"Jimmie and I are not married," she responded cautiously.

"So, only married people can do that?" I pressed.

Suga wasn't a witch, but she and Ray shouldn't be doing whatever it was they were doing.

"Only married people can do what?" Jimmie asked from behind the screen door.

"Okay, that's enough on that subject," Ms. Bernadette said quickly.

She and Jimmie exchanged a look. He did not question our conversation any further.

We had been joined by the rest of the family by the time Suga came switching up to the house.

"Mouse, come on. We gotta head back to town and get ready for tomorrow. I gotta be at work bright and early," Suga said into the air without looking at anyone in particular.

"Suga, you welcome to come and grab a plate for you and your husband," Mrs. Althea offered.

Suga stepped closer to the porch.

I was starting to get annoyed at the lie of marriage between Suga and Ray.

"I know with that interview today, you ain't had no time to cook. Go on and take some of this food with y'all."

I watched Suga, whom I had decided was no longer a witch, wrestle between hunger and the repercussions she would likely face from Ray for bringing home food. Hunger won.

"Thank ya kindly, Mrs. Althea," Suga responded.

Suga went into the house and came out with a basket holding three plates and a whole sweet potato pie. I knew what I was going to have for breakfast tomorrow.

Jimmie and Ms. Bernadette drove us back home. Ray wasn't there, so Suga told me to go ahead and get my clothes ready for the next day. I took a bath, and once I was finished, Suga and I sat down to share one of the plates we had brought home. There were no tears of joy or laughter at this table. There was only food, Suga, and me.

Suga and I went our separate ways after supper. I converted the couch, and she went into the bedroom. I didn't even realize I had drifted off until I was startled out of sleep by a loud bang as the door to the apartment flung open and hit the wall behind it.

Ray came in stumbling. I stayed perfectly still on the couch.

"Suga!" he bellowed.

Suga appeared in the doorway of the bedroom. She looked uninterested.

Ray said something that sounded like, "Did you get the job?" Suga nodded. He stumbled toward the bedroom. Suga moved aside to allow him through the door. She closed both doors, and I drifted back to sleep until morning.

Eight

I was awakened by the sound of Suga's voice yelling my name.

"Mouse! I know you can hear me. Get your tail up! Now! We gotta get going in a few," she hollered.

Suga was moving quickly back and forth between the bedroom and the bathroom.

I looked around. It was still dark outside. There was a dirty plate and a coffee mug on the table, which meant Ray had already eaten and left for work.

I propped myself up on my elbows and asked, "Well, why I gotta go? I ain't gonna be working."

"I ain't gonna leave you here all by yourself," she said while she kept moving.

I threw myself back against the couch. We were just in the middle of summer and I was already ready to go back to school.

I sat up, gathered myself and my thoughts, and went into the bathroom to brush my teeth, wash my face, and comb my hair. I put on my clothes and then straightened up the couch. I was ready by the time Suga grabbed her purse and lunch sack. We set off to the Richardson's house together.

Suga reached into her lunch bag and passed me a slice of sweet potato pie. I ate greedily. Mrs. Althea's pie was so good, I immediately wished I hadn't scarfed the slice down so quickly once it was gone.

It took about fifteen minutes for us to arrive at the Richardson's house. Day was just breaking as Suga knocked on the back door. A white woman opened the door and stepped aside to allow us into the kitchen.

"Mornin', Mrs. Richardson. This here is Hannah. Remember I told you about her."

"Good morning, Lizzy. Yes, I remember. You remember to keep her quiet and out of the way," Mrs. Richardson reminded Suga.

"Yes, ma'am."

Suga gave me a quick look to make sure I understood. I nodded acknowledgement.

Mrs. Richardson was the palest white I'd ever seen. Her reddish-blonde hair was pulled up in a beehive on top of her head. She had very pretty features and freckles on her face. She was dressed in a cream floral-print dress that complimented her figure and showed off her legs.

"Mr. Richardson will be ready for breakfast in a bit, so you better get started. I've already shown you around the kitchen, so you should be able to find everything you need. He likes his eggs sunny-side-up and his coffee black. Make some toast and grits to go with those eggs," Mrs. Richardson ordered.

As Mrs. Richardson was talking, Suga was already putting on an apron and gathering what she would need to make the morning meal. She pointed to me, telling me to sit on the little bench that was positioned by the back door.

"Since it's summer, Julia won't be up until around 9. She likes pancakes, scrambled eggs, and bacon. I've got a terrible headache, so I'm going to lie down."

Mrs. Richardson gave a tight smile, turned, and left the kitchen.

Suga already had the pot of grits on the stove, and she was pulling out the bread for the toast. I hadn't known Suga could cook, let alone move so quickly in the kitchen. I watched her flow with skill from one item to the next. By the time the coffee was ready, Mr. Richardson strolled into the kitchen.

Mr. Richardson was a stout man. He was wide, but not fat. He was kind of built like an ox. He wasn't particularly good-looking, but he had a pep in his step and a twinkle in his eye.

"Good morning, Lizzy. Who's this young lady?"

"Mornin', Mr. Richardson. This is Hannah," Suga answered.

"Well, good morning, Hannah," Mr. Richardson said to me with a wink.

"Good morning," I replied with a smile.

"How old are you?" Mr. Richardson inquired.

"Twelve, sir."

"You and Julia are the same age. You'll meet her when she decides to get her lazy bones up," he said slyly.

He spoke to me as if the two of us had a secret.

Mr. Richardson ate his breakfast, drank his coffee, and read the morning paper that Mrs. Richardson had left on the table for him.

"Thank you for that fine breakfast, Lizzy," Mr. Richardson said as he stood to put on his suit jacket.

"You welcome, Mr. Richardson."

"Alright, ladies. I'm off to work. Tell the missus I'll see her at dinner tonight."

Suga nodded, and Mr. Richardson left through the back door.

I wasn't allowed to move from the bench unless Suga needed me to fetch something, move something, or wipe something down. She treated me as her personal assistant. I was thoroughly bored until Julia bounced into the kitchen.

Julia was peppy like her father and was shaped up like him too. But she had fiery red hair and freckles like her Momma. Her hair was in two ponytails at the sides of her head with a perfect part right down the center. She had on jean pedal pushers and a yellow button-down shirt that was the color of buttercups.

"Good morning, Lizzy!"

Julia's eyes lit up when they wandered over to me on the bench.

"You must be Hannah! I'm so glad to meet you! After breakfast, we can go play outside in the backyard."

It was obvious that Julia could barely contain herself. It made me excited that she wanted to play with me so badly.

"Morning, Ms. Julia," Suga said tightly.

"Hi," was all I could muster up to say.

Mrs. Richardson floated back into the kitchen.

"My God, Julia. You know I hate when you wear that yellow shirt your grandmother bought you. It looks horrible against your red hair, dear," Mrs. Richardson fussed. "I don't know why my mother-in-law insisted on buying you clothes when she had absolutely no sense of style. That gene will not be passed on to you," she mumbled under her breath.

I didn't think the shirt looked so bad. I thought it made Julia look bright and happy.

"This is my favorite shirt, Momma," Julia argued.

Suga laid a plate with pancakes, scrambled eggs, and bacon in front of her.

"Here you go, Ms. Julia. Enjoy."

Mrs. Richardson patted her daughter on the head and left the kitchen.

I sat and pretended I wasn't envious of Julia's breakfast. The pie had worn off and my stomach was looking forward to lunch time.

Julia finished her food and gave Suga her plate. She walked over to me on the bench and stood with her hands in her pockets.

"Would you like to go outside with me?"

I looked over at Suga, and she nodded.

"Okay," I responded.

Julia grabbed my hand and pulled me up. She opened the back door, and we ran out into the yard. There was a wood stump turned up on one of its cut ends that functioned as a seat for Julia. I sat on the ground.

"I'm so happy I have the rest of the summer to play with you. The kids around here don't really like me. They pick on me because I'm not from here and they tease me about my red hair," she confided.

"I got teased because I wouldn't talk after my father…" I trailed off.

"After your father what?"

"After my father moved us away when my momma died," I finished. I'd almost messed that up.

"Why'd you stop talking?"

Julia's face was scowled up at the thought of me not speaking.

"Sad, I guess," I responded as I shrugged my shoulders.

"Guess that's as good a reason as any to stop talking. Sure wish I'd thought of that when we moved here."

"Somebody died?" I asked.

"My Granny. My daddy's momma. She was the sweetest person ever and made the best chocolate chip cookies I ever had in my whole life. I was real sad after she died. She gave me this shirt, and I wear it as much as I can, even though my momma hates it," Julia explained.

"I think your yellow shirt is pretty," I reassured her.

"Why, thank you, Hannah!" Julia exclaimed. She clasped her hands under her chin and batted her eyelashes quickly.

We both giggled.

"You stay right here. I'm going to go inside and get my tea set. We are going to have tea and crumpets when I return."

I'd never heard of a crumpet, but she seemed so eager, I thought it to be a good thing.

Julia returned with the dainty floral tea set. To my disappointment, the tea was imaginary and our crumpets were made of dirt. Nevertheless, Julia and I played as if we were entertaining the most important guests in all of Hemings.

By lunchtime, we were both dirty and starving. Suga called us in so that she could give us lunch. When she saw us, she pursed her lips in agitation. I was sure Julia was the only reason I hadn't gotten blessed out about how I looked.

"You girls go get washed up," Suga said quietly.

Julia went to grab my hand, but Suga grabbed me by the shoulder.

"Mouse, you need to use the bathroom back here," Suga instructed.

She looked me sternly in my eyes.

"But I want her to come back here with me," Julia said in defiance.

"Ms. Julia, Hannah has to use the bathroom back here," Suga responded calmly.

"But why?" Julia asked.

"She just do."

Suga was trying to keep her voice soft, but she was losing her patience.

"What's the problem in here? I told you all that I have a headache." Mrs. Richardson said as she walked into the kitchen.

"Lizzy won't let Hannah come wash her hands in my bathroom," Julia whined.

"That's absurd, dear. They have a special bathroom back here attached to the kitchen," Mrs. Richardson said.

I was beginning to catch on.

"But Momma..."

"Not another word about it," Mrs. Richardson scolded.

I turned and went into the help's bathroom to wash up. I was too hungry and excited about the sandwiches on the table to care.

When I returned to the kitchen, I went to the counter to grab a plate. Before I could, Suga snatched me back. She pointed to the bench and handed me a piece of room-temperature fried chicken wrapped in a piece of paper towel.

When Julia walked into the room, she looked from me to Suga to the table. I figured she was beginning to catch on too. She made a plate of half a sandwich and potato salad, and she stomped into the dining area where Suga instructed her she would take her lunch.

As soon as she was out of ear shot, Suga started in on me.

"Mouse, you done lost your rabbit mind? You gone get me fired on my first day! You can't be 'round here acting like you belong with these white folk!"

Suga was whispering, but the urgency in her voice was evident.

I sat on the bench, cold chicken unchewable because my mouth was dry with embarrassment. I hadn't thought of myself as any different than Julia, but I could see I was very wrong.

"I'm gonna have to see if Ms. Bernadette will let you come over there with them while I'm at work. You and that Julia ain't gone be nothing but trouble together."

Suga shook her head as she washed the dishes in the sink.

Julia returned to the kitchen after she finished eating. Suga was in the bathroom. Julia wrapped another sandwich half in some paper towels and put it in her pocket. Suga walked in the room and looked us both over.

"Can Hannah and I go back outside?" Julia asked with squinted eyes.

"Yes, but you go on ahead. I'll send Hannah right out," Suga said warily.

Julia walked slowly through the kitchen and to the back door. She looked over at me and then went outside, closing the door behind her.

"Mouse, I'm gone let you go out and play with that girl. But you be careful. She don't understand the rules, but you best understand 'em. Y'all can't do the same things, and if anything happen to her, it's gone automatically be yo' fault. Watch yo' self. If you feel like she might get you into some trouble, you come right back to this kitchen before that happen. You hear me?"

"Yes," I responded.

"I can't afford to lose this job, Mouse. Go on. Get."

Suga shooed me through the door.

I found Julia on the same stump from earlier.

"What did she say?" Julia asked.

"To stay out of trouble," I answered.

Suga had let the wind out of my sails. I was afraid to even play with Julia.

Julia pulled the sandwich out of her pocket and handed it to me.

"Did you even get to eat?" she asked.

"I ate some fried chicken," I responded.

Although the sandwich looked good and I was still hungry, my pride wouldn't let me take it. Julia hadn't offered the sandwich with any pity, but after not being allowed to use her bathroom, I thought better of accepting. I hadn't used the name Maynard in years, but Maynard blood still coursed through my veins.

Julia and I spent the rest of the afternoon in the backyard. Suga called us in when it was nearing dinnertime. We washed up in our separate bathrooms, and I had to help set the dinner table. Suga and I cleaned all of the pots and pans while the family ate. Once they finished, we cleared and cleaned the table, washed the dirty dishes, and bid the family a good evening.

"See you in the morning, Lizzy," said Mrs. Richardson.

"That was a fine dinner, Lizzy," Mr. Richardson chimed in.

"See you tomorrow, Mouse," said Julia.

I waved.

Suga smiled and said, "Thank y'all. See you tomorrow."

I was happy about having made a friend in Julia, but miserable at the thought of having to work alongside Suga for free for the rest of the summer.

"You like Julia?" Suga asked quietly.

"Yes," I responded.

"I'm sure she like you, too, but white folk like Julia can be dangerous."

"Dangerous how?" I asked puzzled.

Suga stopped walking to look at me.

"Because she from a place where she didn't deal with black folk a lot. She don't know the order of things, and that's dangerous. If she pull you into something, one of two things gone happen when the shit hit the fan. The white folk either gone say you done it, or that you tricked her into doing it. Either way, you the one gone pay the price. I know we ain't always seen eye-to-eye, but you is Ray's child. If you get in trouble, I'm gone have to deal with him, so it's in my best interest to keep you straight. I'm gone call Ms. Bernadette when we get home and see if you can go over there at least a couple days a week until school start. The less time you spend with little Miss Julia, the better," Suga explained.

Suga turned and started walking again. I started walking slowly behind.

"Are you gonna tell my father?"

"Ain't nothing to tell," she said dryly.

We made it to the store just in time to spend that five dollars before it closed.

"We still got some leftovers from Mrs. Althea, so we can finish that up for supper. Tonight, I'm going to soak these beans and bake this chicken. Tomorrow morning, I'll stew up these tomatoes with okra and corn. All I gotta do when I get home tomorrow is cook some rice and cornbread. Then, before we go to bed tomorrow, I'll put the beans on with some ham hocks, and that should last us the rest of the week until your daddy gets paid," Suga planned out loud.

I let Suga talk without any interruption from me. I wasn't a fan of lima beans or okra, corn, and tomatoes, but neither she nor Ray cared what I liked.

Suga called Ms. Bernadette before Ray got home from work.

"You going to Ms. Bernadette on Mondays, Wednesdays, and Fridays. Tuesday and Thursday, you will still come with me," Suga announced when she came back into our apartment.

That meant the next day would be another with Suga and the Richardsons. Though I liked

Julia, I wasn't exactly mad about getting to spend more time with Ms. Bernadette.

Ray made it home just before I was set to go to sleep. Suga served him warm food with a cold demeanor.

"Here's your dinner, Ray."

"Damn, that's how you gonna give me my food?"

"What's wrong with the food, Ray?"

"Nothing wrong with the food. I'm tryna find out what's wrong witchu."

"I'm just tired and I feel like I don't do nothing but work. I barely get to see you, and when I do, you tired or you been in the bottle."

Ray sighed. I pretended to be reading a book.

"Suga, I ain't in the mood for this. I work all day so I can keep a roof over all y'all heads, and I'm tryna get us ready for this baby. What else you want me to do?"

Suga began to walk away from the table in a pout. Ray grabbed her hand.

"Look, after the baby get here, I promise things will change for the better. We will be a real family."

I'd had a real family once. I closed my book, rolled over, and pulled the top sheet all the way over my head. I didn't want to hear anything else he had to say. I poked my fingers in my ears and squeezed my eyes shut, hoping to drown him out, along with the future he was planning with a woman other than my momma.

The morning routine at the Richardson house was much the same as it had been the day before. However, when Julia came into the kitchen, she was much less excited. She ate her breakfast quietly and then cooly asked if both of us could go outside to play.

"What's wrong with you?" I asked Julia out of curiosity.

"My momma was some mad with me after y'all left yesterday," she responded.

"Why?"

"Momma said blacks and whites ain't the same, and I need to know my place and yours," she answered quietly.

"Yeah. Suga, I mean Lizzy, said pretty much the same thing to me yesterday," I assured her.

"Daddy came into my room later and told me momma and her people think like that, but he doesn't. He said it was okay if I don't, either, but I would have to be careful around people who do," she explained.

"Do you?" I asked.

"No. I don't see what the big deal is. If you get cut, you're gonna bleed red just like me. We are not different, and anyone who thinks so is just plain old stupid," she said in anger.

I couldn't help but smile.

"Let's make a pact," Julia offered. "When it's just the two of us, we are as close as sisters. When it ain't, we hide how we feel, but we don't act mean or ugly with one another."

With that, she spit in her hand and stuck it out. I spit in my hand and grabbed hers, and we shook on our vow. Spit oaths were just as binding as blood oaths, but I don't think either of us had the courage to cut ourselves.

"Suga is making me go to my teacher's house on Monday, Wednesday, and Friday, so I won't be here tomorrow," I told Julia.

"That's just awful, but I guess two days is better than none," she reasoned.

"Ms. Bernadette is nice though."

"Yeah, but she'll probably have you reading and doing math and all kinds of boring stuff."

I shrugged my shoulders and wondered what Ms. Bernadette would have me doing.

The rest of the day was easy. Julia and I found different games to play in the safety of her backyard. We only went in the house to grab water or use the bathroom until it was time for lunch and for me to go in and help prepare for dinner.

Once Suga and I cleaned up, we headed home.

"Seems like Julia minded her manners today," Suga commented.

"Her momma had a talk with her," I responded.

"I see. And how she feel about that talk?"

"She didn't like it very much, but Mr. Richardson agrees with Julia."

"Mmm hmm. I figured she must'a got that stubbornness of hers from her daddy. Well, you two just be careful it don't get you both into some trouble you can't get out of," Suga warned.

I didn't say any more. I didn't want to talk anymore about it. Adults were so confusing to me.

How could two twelve-year-olds being friends cause any trouble?

When we got home, Suga made the rice and cornbread, and we ate that with baked chicken and stewed okra, tomato, and corn, just like she'd planned. I was bathed and in bed by the time Ray made it home.

The next morning, Ms. Bernadette stood waiting at the fork in the road to pick me up.

"Morning, ladies," she greeted us.

We both responded in kind.

"Mouse, behave," Suga instructed.

Suga nodded at Ms. Bernadette and turned off toward the Richardson's. Ms. Bernadette turned, and we walked toward her parents' house.

"A little birdie told me you made a friend out at the Richardson's," Ms. Bernadette teased.

"Yes, ma'am. Her name is Julia. I like her a lot, but it seems like nobody really wants us to be friends."

"Well, there might be some people who don't want you to be friends, but I think most times that's just fear, is all."

"But fear of what?"

Adults were too complicated.

"Black folks have plenty to be afraid of when it comes to white folks. White folks are afraid of the unknown when it comes to black folks," she explained.

I didn't really understand. I looked at Ms. Bernadette and waited for her to explain more. She looked at me and sighed.

She continued, "Black folks have been on the receiving end of some pretty bad things that white folks have done to us just because they are afraid. They are afraid that one day we might pay them back for the way we've been treated in this country."

"You mean like slavery?" I asked.

"Yes, and other bad things that you are too young to really know about," she answered.

"That was so long ago though. If Julia and I can be friends, all black and white folk can be friends, right?"

"It would seem that way, but there are folks on both sides that are much older and can remember some of those awful things just like they happened yesterday. Both my parents are grandchildren of slaves. They can tell some stories about times that would make you cry, Mouse. There's a lot of hurt on our side and a lot of fear on theirs. That's passed down from generation to generation."

Ms. Bernadette was looking off toward the house like she was remembering something from long ago.

"Nobody passed anything down to me," I said. "I didn't know much at all about white people before Julia and I met, but she's nice to me and I'm nice to her. Why can't it be that simple?"

I really wanted to know.

"It just isn't, Mouse. I can't really explain. I know. I've got a book I think you should read. It might just help you understand what I mean a bit.

It's at the house. You think you'd like to start on it today?"

I wasn't all that excited to have to read a book during my time out of school. But if I wanted to understand what was so bad about Julia and I being friends, I figured I'd better give the book a chance. Plus, reading this book might help me gain good favor with Ms. Bernadette when school started.

"Okay. What's the name of it?" I asked.

"*To Kill a Mockingbird*, by Harper Lee," she answered.

I wanted so badly to ask Ms. Bernadette what in the world killing a bird had to do with black and white folk, but I thought better of it. We didn't say much else for the rest of the walk. Mrs. Althea was busy in the kitchen making breakfast for Mr. Kenneth when we arrived.

"Hey there, Mouse!"

"Good morning, Mrs. Althea. Mr. Kenneth," I nodded in Mr. Kenneth's direction to bid him hello.

"Have some breakfast, sweetie?" Mrs. Althea asked.

"If it's no trouble."

Mr. Kenneth sucked his teeth.

"Ain't no trouble, Mouse. This woman cook like she feeding an army at every meal. If you don't eat some of this food, she and I both gone be big as this house. Bernadette show ain't gone eat none of it 'cause she tryna fit into a wedding dress come next spring," Mr. Kenneth advised.

He and Mrs. Althea shared a laugh. Ms. Bernadette rolled her eyes and tried to act annoyed by the conversation, but she couldn't hide the excitement in her eyes.

"Well, I'll be glad to eat her share, then," I said.

They all laughed loudly at my response.

Mrs. Althea made pancakes that were soft as clouds but had the perfect crisp on the edges. She served them piping hot, and I slathered them with butter and Alaga syrup. The bacon was cooked perfectly, not too hard, not too soft. And the scrambled eggs were fluffy as could be. I noticed her trick was to add a little water to them while she was beating them.

After we all ate breakfast, Ms. Bernadette led me into a fancy room toward the back of the house.

"What's this room?" I asked.

"Some call it a sitting room, but I use it as a library," she answered.

There were only four medium-sized bookcases against the right wall of the room. They weren't very tall. I could reach every book on them. The walls were painted a light green color, similar to a grape. There was one sofa the color of butterscotch. The other chair looked like it was made for you to lay on—the top end was raised and the rest of it was flat. It was the color of split pea soup.

Ms. Bernadette walked over to one of the bookshelves, bent down, and ran her fingers across the books of the top shelf. She stopped when her finger landed on the book she wanted.

"Ah, here it is!"

She pulled the book out and turned it around for me to see.

"*To Kill a Mockingbird*," I read aloud.

"Here, you sit on this chaise and read for a while. I'm going to go help Momma clean up the kitchen."

She pointed to the split pea soup chair.

I took the book from her hands, thanked her, and settled in for some reading. By the time Ms. Bernadette returned, I was already taken by the story. I liked that the main character was a girl, and she was around the same age as me.

"So, what do you think so far?"

I could tell she was hopeful that I would like the book too.

"I like it, but I don't see what this has to do with me and Julia."

"You will. Why don't you take a little break?"

She handed me a pretty bookmark covered in painted ladybugs from the desk in the corner.

I placed the bookmark in between the pages and laid the book down on the chaise.

Ms. Bernadette and I went outside for some fresh air. Mr. Kenneth was sitting in his favorite chair on the porch, and Mrs. Althea was sitting on the other side of the table, across from him.

"Momma, you remember Mrs. Nancy?" Ms. Bernadette asked Mrs. Althea.

"Why, of course. Why would you ask me a question like that? We was the best of friends for many years," Mrs. Althea responded.

"What happened between you two?" Ms. Bernadette pressed.

Mrs. Althea stopped her knitting to look long and hard at Ms. Bernadette. Then, with a sense of knowing, she started knitting both her story and the hat she'd been working on.

"Well, the two of us had come up friends. She was what other uppity whites considered po' white trash. Her people were decent enough, and though they didn't much like the two of us being friends, they didn't put up a fuss about it. My parents couldn't stand it, but my father's thoughts on it was that we was gonna find a way to spend time together. He decided to just let it figure itself out.

"It did just that when we both turned fifteen. Nancy and I walked down to the five and dime. Back then, colored people weren't allowed in the store. We really weren't allowed on that side of town, and we sure betta not be there once the sun went down. I'd given Nancy a penny to buy me a piece of penny candy. My cousin Ralph had given her a penny too. Well, when Nancy came out of the store, she gave me my candy but did not have any for Ralph. Nancy didn't have her own penny and had used Ralph's to buy the candy she had in her mouth. Ralph kicked up a fuss, enough for the store owner to come out and see why this colored boy was making so much noise in front of his store.

"Ralph told the store owner what happened, and Nancy denied it. The store owner didn't even ask if I knew what happened, and I was too afraid to say anything. He was red in the face with anger, assuming that Ralph was calling this little white girl a liar and a thief. It just so happened Ralph's father, my uncle, was making a work run through town. He beat Ralph like a dog and made him apologize to both the store owner and Nancy. Nancy smiled and accepted the fake apology."

Mrs. Althea stopped talking, but she was still knitting frantically. I understood the point of Ms. Bernadette asking the question.

"Why did Nancy lie?" I asked.

"Because she could, and she knew she could," Mrs. Althea responded.

"Why did your uncle beat Ralph? Didn't he know she was lying?" I questioned.

"He knew. He also knew what kind of trouble Ralph would be in if he didn't fix it. He beat Ralph to save his life. Back then, and even now, you just don't go around calling white folks a liar and a thief."

Her hands were shaking.

"Did you ever talk to Nancy again?" I asked quietly.

"No. After that, I didn't want to be friends with her. If she could almost get my cousin killed over a stupid piece of penny candy, what more was she capable of? I would have given her my candy if I'd known she wanted a piece that bad. That's just how close I thought we were," Mrs. Althea said as she closed her eyes.

"I still see her in town every now and again. She tried to apologize once, but I couldn't stand to hear it. Ralph and his daddy was never the same after that day. All over a penny candy," she said quietly.

"Ms. Bernadette, may I go back to the reading room now?"

I was tired of adults trying to make me feel like Julia was evil. She just didn't think like the rest of the white folk.

"Sure, Mouse," Ms. Bernadette responded.

I continued reading *To Kill a Mockingbird* until late afternoon when I heard Jimmie's voice and went out to see what was going on.

"Hey, Mouse!" Jimmie exclaimed.

"Hey, Jimmie."

"Woooooah, that was pretty dry. I thought I was your friend!" he teased.

I smiled half-heartedly.

Jimmie looked over at Ms. Bernadette. She raised her eyebrows and pursed her lips.

"Come on and take a walk with Jimmie." He grabbed me by the shoulders and steered me toward the back door. "We'll be back when the food is ready," he said over his shoulder to Ms. Bernadette.

"Alright, what's wrong with my friend?" he asked once we were outside in the yard.

I shrugged.

"Naw, you gotta do better than that, Mouse."

Jimmie looked at me with one eyebrow raised. He got down on one knee so we could be eye-to-eye.

"I'm just so mad," I said. "Everybody is against me and Julia being friends."

I stomped my foot in outrage.

"And who is Julia?"

"Mr. and Mrs. Richardson's daughter."

"Oh, so she's white," he said with a nod. "Mouse, I don't think people don't want y'all to be friends. We all know how dangerous times are right now. Did you know some states have fought over schools being integrated and that young black children are getting hurt because of it?"

"No…what's inta…"

I struggled to repeat the word.

"Integration," he interrupted. "Integration is where both black and white students go to the same schools, in the same classrooms."

I didn't know anything about that, so I shook my head.

"Some white folks are especially angry because they don't like black folks. Julia may not act like that, but lots of people around her will. There may come a day where she's too afraid to stand up for what's right, or she may even turn on you to keep from being picked on herself. We've all seen it happen, even with adults. I've seen it time and time again in the military. Guys who are nice to me in the field don't say a word to me when we get back to base. Bernadette, Mrs. Althea, Suga, none of us want to see you get hurt. Julia might just surprise us all, but if she don't, we don't want you to be caught off guard by it," he explained gently.

I nodded. Jimmie stuck out his hand for me to give him five. When I tried to slap his hand, he pulled it back so that I would miss. I couldn't help but smile, because I never could hit his hand before he moved it. He stood up and patted my shoulder. We went back into the house and ate lunch. While my food tasted like sawdust, everyone else seemed to enjoy their meal.

I asked to be excused and went back to the sitting room to continue reading. Between Suga, Mrs. Althea, Ms. Bernadette, Jimmie, and the book, I was getting a crash course on race I never asked for.

I was almost glad when it was time for Suga to pick me up.

"Mouse, Suga should be here soon. Let's go sit out on the porch," Ms. Bernadette told me as she stood in the doorway of the room.

"Can I take the book with me?" I asked.

"You mean may I take the book with me. Sure, you just have to promise to bring it back. It's one of my favorites."

"I will."

Suga picked me up, and the rest of the evening routine went as normal. After supper, I curled up with the book to continue reading. I was more than halfway through. While some of the characters were just as everyone had been telling me, there were still white characters who did right by black people. Atticus Finch was defending a black man as hard as he could because he knew he was innocent, even at the expense of his own family's safety. They had to know that not all white people were bad.

Suga had softened her disposition when Ray arrived home. She sat with him while he ate, and they talked. I felt like I was invisible, so I behaved that way. I stayed quiet and continued to read my book until I fell asleep.

I woke up the next morning with the book laying on my chest, opened to the last page I could remember reading. Tom Robinson had just finished testifying, and I couldn't wait to find out how everything would turn out. Before I could dig back into the book, Suga informed me it was time to get up. I was excited to go see Julia so we could talk about the book.

"What's that you reading?" Suga asked as we walked.

"*To Kill a Mockingbird*," I replied.

"Hmph. I never much liked reading. You like it?" Suga asked, looking at me curiously.

"I love it! It's like going to another place without ever leaving your room," I said excitedly.

"I'm not real good at it. Maybe when the baby come, you can read to it," she said shyly.

"Okay," I said quickly.

I was shocked. It was the first time Suga had been kind of nice to me. I hadn't really been all that happy about the baby, but thinking of reading to him or her was nice.

I looked over at Suga and smiled. She smiled back.

We arrived at the Richardson's house, and Suga jumped right into preparing breakfast for Mr. Richardson. I sat on the small bench and went right back into the book.

Mr. Richardson ate breakfast without too much fuss and parted with the normal goodbyes. Mrs. Richardson seemed in a really good mood that morning. She sat and ate breakfast with her husband and was still sitting at the table when he left.

"Are you enjoying that book, Hannah?"

"Yes, ma'am," I responded.

I'd learned to keep conversations with her short and to-the-point.

"The girls in the book club selected that book just to see what all the fuss over it was. That just isn't my kind of reading. It was absolutely horrible how that poor girl was treated," she said.

"What poor girl? Scout?"

I was sure she wasn't talking about Mayella.

"Oh, I don't remember her name. The girl that black boy raped," she said, flustered.

Suga looked at me, eyes wide. I opened my mouth to correct her, but Suga slowly shook her head. Even though Suga didn't know what the book was about, she knew from my face that it wasn't a good interpretation. I closed my mouth and said nothing. I just looked at Mrs. Richardson.

"All manner of women have to be careful around black boys."

She scooted her chair back from the table, brushed her skirt down, and exited the kitchen.

Suga and I looked at each other for a moment. Suga turned to the sink and began washing the pans she'd used to cook breakfast. I was angrier than snake spit, but there was nothing good that anger could do. I pushed it down into my toes along with my growing dislike for my friend's mother and kept reading.

Julia bounced into the kitchen, happy as a lark. I had to tell myself that she was not like her mother before I opened my mouth to speak. She immediately picked up that something was off, but she knew not to address it with Suga in the room. When she finished her food, we went outside to our usual spot.

"Hannah, you okay?"

"Yeah. I was just a little annoyed by something your mom said at breakfast."

Julia shook her head.

"What did my mother say?"

"She said women had to be careful around black boys."

I parroted Mrs. Richardson.

"I'm not surprised. I'm sorry she says crazy things. I don't know why she is the way she is."

Julia sounded resigned to her mother's behavior. I hadn't wanted to make her feel bad.

"It's okay. I know you don't feel like that," I reassured her. "None of my family or friends call me Hannah. You can call me Mouse."

I hoped sharing my nickname with her would change the mood.

"Mouse? Where did that come from?" she asked with a grin.

"I used to be really quiet, even before I stopped talking," I responded. "Look at this book Ms. Bernadette gave me to read. It's pretty good."

I showed off the book.

"I told you she would make you read," Julia moaned.

"You should read it too. Can't you go to the library and get a copy?"

"I guess."

Julia didn't seem convinced she would be interested.

"C'mon, then we can talk about it together. I promise that if you go get the book, I'll wait for you to catch up with me to finish it."

"Alright," she said reluctantly.

Julia and I played the rest of the day. After serving the family dinner, Suga and I headed home. I didn't know what I was going to do with myself for the evening since I'd promised Julia I would stop reading the book until she could catch up. I'd have to wait until the following Tuesday to see how far she'd read.

Friday was a fun day with Ms. Bernadette. Instead of having me read in the study, she decided to take me on an adventure.

"Mouse, we are going to the lake!" Ms. Bernadette exclaimed as Suga dropped me off at our usual meeting spot.

"The lake? I can't swim," I responded.

"Well, we don't have to get in the water. We can sit by the edge and enjoy the day," she said.

I shrugged my shoulders. We walked back to the house where Jimmie was waiting. The car was already packed up, and even Mrs. Althea and Mr. Kenneth were excited.

"C'mon, gals! We gotta get down to the lake early to get a good spot. Beautiful day like this, everybody who ain't got to work is gonna be at the watering hole!" Mr. Kenneth shouted.

Ms. Bernadette, Jimmie, and Mrs. Althea were laughing.

"We're coming, Daddy!" Ms. Bernadette yelled back.

She looked over at me and said, "Last one to the car is a rotten egg!"

With that, she took off running. She'd caught me off guard, so my start was later than hers. I pumped my legs as hard as I could, but they proved to be no match for the stronger, lengthier legs of Ms. Bernadette. She was breathing much harder than me, though.

"Mouse, you let that old woman beat you?" asked Jimmie.

Ms. Bernadette turned her head slightly to the right, raised her eyebrows, and put her hands on her hips.

"Well, she had a head start," I said, trying to save face.

"I did," she said. "Next time, I'll give you more warning."

We all laughed some more as we piled into the car. Mr. Kenneth tilted the seat up at an angle and helped Mrs. Althea climb into the back. He climbed in behind her and pulled the seat back into place. I hopped in the front with Jimmie and Ms. Bernadette. Off we went to the local lake.

Jimmie parked the car in a shaded area where there were plenty of other cars. The men carried the food, the women carried the blankets, and I carried the towels.

I helped Ms. Bernadette and Mrs. Althea spread the blankets out into a nice big square where everyone could have their own little area. After we were all settled in, Mr. Kenneth took off to the water. Jimmie went right behind him.

"I sure would love to get in, but I don't feel like fighting with this hair tonight," Mrs. Althea said.

"Me either, Momma," chimed Ms. Bernadette.

"I don't care about my hair. I can't swim," I said.

Both ladies chuckled.

"Well, next time you can bring a bathing suit, and I'll teach you. Sound like a plan?" Ms. Bernadette asked.

I nodded excitedly.

The only lake in Maplewood was not one in which you should swim. Gators made the water unfriendly, and there were no pools on the black side of town. None of our other stops had anywhere for black folks to swim either. I wondered what it must have been like to grow up right near this lake and to swim here every summer.

"Mouse, I got you something," Ms. Bernadette said with a grin.

She'd interrupted my daydream.

"You got me something?" I asked, making sure I'd heard her correctly.

She pulled a package from behind her back. It was a small cream-colored notebook with pink flowers all over it. There was a silky pink ribbon attached to the notebook, and it had a pink pencil connected to it. It was so beautiful. I'd never received such a gift before.

"It's beautiful. Thank you," I said quietly. "Why did you buy me this?"

"Since you like to read so much, I thought you might like to try your hand at writing. You can write stories, poems, or just your thoughts about things. You can use it like a diary, if you want," she responded.

"I love it!" I squealed.

She handed me the book. I ran my hands over the hard outer cover as well as the soft pages inside. I wanted whatever I wrote in the notebook to be special.

We spent the rest of the day lounging, reading, laughing, and eating. As the day began to cool and people were starting to pack up, Mrs. Althea pulled an uncut pound cake out of the picnic basket. It was covered with a thin lemon glaze. When she cut into the cake, I could tell it was moist. My mouth started watering.

It looked like Momma's pound cake, and her pound cake had always been my favorite. Hers was light and fluffy with the perfect amount of sweetness. It didn't matter much to me if she added a glaze or not because the cake itself was so sweet. Glaze only added another layer of flavor for me to enjoy.

I grabbed a napkin and held it out so I could get my slice. A car parked near our area backfired just as I reached out. I was instantly back in Maplewood, looking at Momma as the gun went off.

When I came back to myself, the slice of pound cake was on the ground, my pants and shoes were wet with pee, and the Alexanders were looking at me with their eyes bucked and mouths open.

Ms. Bernadette snatched up one of the blankets from the ground and wrapped it around me as I began to cry.

"It's okay, Mouse," Ms. Bernadette whispered.

"What's wrong with the girl," I heard Mr. Kenneth whisper to Mrs. Althea.

Mrs. Althea promptly shushed Mr. Kenneth.

Most of our things had already been packed, so while Ms. Bernadette ushered me to the car, the rest of the family packed up our remaining items and followed quickly.

We quietly filed into the deuce and a quarter in the same order from the morning. I was last in, wrapped in the blanket. Ms. Bernadette put her arm around me and allowed me to rest my head on her bosom. I was embarrassed and worried about how I was going to explain to Suga and Ray that my big almost-a-teenager self had peed my clothes.

Ms. Bernadette took me to the bathroom when we arrived at the house.

"Mouse, take those clothes off. Here is a washcloth and towel, and here's a long shirt you can put on when you finish washing up. I'm going to go wash these clothes for you. You can go right across the hall into my room when you finish, okay?"

I nodded. My eyes began stinging with the threat of more tears. I took a breath. I did not want Ms. Bernadette to see me cry again. I'd already embarrassed myself enough for one day.

"I'll be right outside the door. Pass me your clothes once you get them all off," she said.

Ms. Bernadette stepped out of the bathroom, closing the door behind her.

I undressed and cracked the bathroom door only wide enough to pass the clothes through. When I was sure she was gone, I sat down on the side of the tub and plugged the drain. I turned on the warm water and waited for the tub to fill. Once there was enough water, I eased down into the tub. No soap. Just water and a wash rag. I only wanted to be in the water long enough to rinse the pee smell off.

I rinsed off. Unplugged the tub. Dried off and put on the shirt Ms. Bernadette had given me.

A few minutes later, Ms. Bernadette found me sitting on the floor of her room. The shirt was large enough on me that I could have my knees up to my chest and the shirt pulled down over my legs. I sat there looking at my bloody fingertips.

"Mouse, what happened at the lake today?"

I sat silently gazing at the brownish-colored carpet on her floor.

"Sometimes when a car backfires, it sounds like a gun. Is that why it scared you today?" she continued to pry.

I quickly glanced at her, but looked back down at the carpet.

"You know you don't have to be afraid to tell me anything, right? I see you are biting your fingernails so low that your fingers bleed. I've seen you do that before. Is that something you do when you're scared or nervous?"

Again, Ms. Bernadette was met with silence.

She rubbed my back for a bit, looking off into the distance.

"I've got to go check on your clothes," she said as she got up from the floor.

A few minutes later, Mrs. Althea showed up with that slice of the pound cake I'd wanted so badly. I now had no desire to eat it.

"I brought you some cake, Mouse," Mrs. Althea said in a chipper voice. "Bernadette is trying to hurry up and dry your clothes 'cause Suga is waiting on you.

I know my eyes grew to about twice the size when I jerked my head toward Mrs. Althea.

"Don't worry, child. We told her I accidentally spilled a whole pitcher of punch on your clothes, and you were a red, sticky mess. Told her we couldn't send you home like that, and Jimmie and Bernadette will give y'all a ride home so you won't be too late. She's eating some of this pound cake. She fine," she assured me.

I relaxed a bit. At least I wouldn't have to do the work of coming up with a reason as to why I had to bathe in their home and wear their clothes. Ray would skin me alive if he found out about this.

"Mouse, you been through something. I don't know what it is, but we can all see that. Whatever it is, if and when you feel alright enough to tell any of us or all of us, we will be right here to listen. Bad things don't have to own us. They can only do that if we let them," she said quietly.

Mrs. Althea eased her round self up from Ms. Bernadette's bed. She rubbed my head and left me with my thoughts and that piece of pound cake.

There was a light tapping at the door about ten minutes later. I didn't say anything. Ms. Bernadette cracked the door and came in with my clothes, fresh from the dryer. I'd never seen a black house with both a washer and a dryer. I made a mental note to go check them out if I was ever allowed to return.

"Here you are, sweetie. All clean," Ms. Bernadette said with a sweet smile.

"Thank you," I said quietly.

"When you're dressed, Jimmie and I will be waiting to take you and Suga home," she said.

Ms. Bernadette turned to leave, but I stopped her.

"Thank you for everything, including the journal you gave me. I'm sorry I embarrassed myself and your family today," I explained.

"Mouse, you didn't embarrass yourself or us. We love you dearly, and we all know you reacted out of fear from that car backfiring. There's no reason to be ashamed of that," she assured.

She grabbed me and hugged me.

"Now, go on and get dressed, or none of us will have any pound cake left. Suga is eating enough for her and that baby."

I smiled, and she took that as her cue to leave. She closed the door behind herself. I dressed quickly. I was ready to get home and go to bed.

"Well, there's Christmas," Suga said dryly.

When I was dragging to get ready, Suga would call me Christmas. One day I asked her why, and she explained that Christmas took forever to come, and that's exactly how slowly I moved.

Jimmie and Ms. Bernadette took us home with no further pee incidents.

Nine

On the days I was allowed to go to work with Suga, Julia and I continued to play and read the same books so we could discuss them. I'd find new books for us to read on the days I spent with Ms. Bernadette. Those two routines filled out the rest of my summer.

I'd read or write in my journal in the evenings if Suga didn't need my help cooking. Spending all day on her feet as her stomach continued to grow was beginning to take a toll on her. I could see she was struggling, and I didn't mind helping. The more I helped to lessen her load, the nicer she became toward me. Things had gotten so good between us, you could almost say we had become close.

With only four more months before the baby was supposed to arrive, Suga was beginning to collect items for its arrival. Blankets, hats and socks, cloth diapers, and bottles started appearing in our one-room apartment. Even Ray was preparing. He came in one day with a used crib that was in really good shape. He was so proud, and I could tell that Suga was very appreciative. They put the crib in their room. I was appreciative of that. I didn't know much about babies, but when Angie (my friend in Maplewood) got a little sister, she said she couldn't sleep most nights from all the noise. I wasn't interested in losing sleep because of a hollering baby. The only thing I was interested in was whether it would be a boy or a girl. The suspense was killing me.

Summer break would be over in two weeks. Julia and I both knew we wouldn't get to see each other as much once school started. Even though desegregation had started to happen all around us, the children of Hemings would remain separated by race for this school year. Lots of things had changed, but folks weren't ready for their children to start mingling.

I'd asked Suga if I could go to work with her every day for the remaining time. Suga and Ms. Bernadette agreed to it.

"Well, it's only two weeks. Y'all been doing good all summer. I guess can't much happen before y'all go back to school," Suga said with a sigh.

I thought she was just too tired to put up much of a fuss. The baby seemed to be taking all of her energy.

"I've got an idea," Julia said.

It was only the first day of the two weeks, and Julia was already making plans.

"What's that?" I asked.

"Have you been down to the lake?"

Julia's eyes were full of mischief.

"Yeah, Ms. Bernadette and her family took me."

I was reluctant to answer. I hadn't thought about the lake since I'd peed myself.

"We went on the Fourth of July. The fireworks show was beautiful," Julia responded.

Ray was bone tired from work and hadn't really been in the mood to celebrate the Fourth of July. We'd eaten a simple dinner at home even though the Alexanders had invited all of us over.

"We could walk over there and hang out. There's sure to be a lot of kids there since it's this close to break being over," Julia suggested.

I didn't really want to go back to the lake after what had happened. What if it happened again? How embarrassing would it be to have to come back to Julia's house with peed-up clothes in front of Suga and Julia's family?

"I don't think that's such a good idea. Besides, white folks hang out on one side, and black folks hang out on a different side. How would we be able to go together?"

I was hoping by pointing that out, it would save me from this horrible idea.

"Nobody will bother you if I say you're with me!"

"I don't want to get into trouble, and that's exactly what this plan sounds like."

"I thought you were more adventurous, like Meg," Julia pushed.

Julia was referring to the main character in *A Wrinkle in Time*. It was true, Meg had courage, but she was also lily white.

"Meg was a white character in a book," I said flatly.

"I know. But you still remind me of her," Julia teased.

I was flattered. I smiled. But I still knew better than going to the lake.

We agreed to ride her bike downtown instead. She pedaled while I balanced myself on the rods that stuck out from the back tires. I knew if Suga or Julia's mother saw us, that would be the end of me, but Suga was working and Mrs. Richardson was probably taking her usual afternoon nap. She rarely went into town.

We were passing all of the places I was used to seeing.

"Where are we going?" I asked.

"Just a little farther. There's a little shop that sells these delicious butter cookies. Mommy and Daddy have an account there, and I can get us some on their bill."

I began to notice that there were very few people that looked like me down on this end of town. Uneasiness crept up my back and settled on my shoulders.

"I don't know, Julia. Doesn't look like I should be down here."

"It's fine. We're just going to get some cookies. You can stay outside with the bike if you want. It won't take me but a few minutes."

Julia stopped the bike in front of this cute little bakery I'd never seen before. There was a display in the window with all kinds of sweet treats. If I'd had enough money, I would have taken one or two of everything. I saw three trays of the butter cookies Julia had mentioned. Then, I saw Mr. Richardson. He was with a woman that was not Mrs. Richardson. I looked over at Julia. She had noticed him too.

Mr. Richardson took the white box, tied shut with a beautiful purple ribbon, from the store clerk and handed it to the woman. She giggled, leaning over to give Mr. Richardson a thank-you kiss on the cheek. Julia and I could not hear a sound since we were still on the outside of the store. Everything seemed to play out like a silent movie in slow motion.

The woman had silky blonde hair with just a bit of bounce and curl. Unlike Mrs. Richardson, she was small and dainty. Her freckled face was pretty, and her smile was straight out of a magazine ad for toothpaste. Her dress was perfectly fitted for her tiny waist. She looked at Mr. Richardson with stars in her eyes.

I glanced back over at Julia. Her arms were stiff at her sides, and her hands were balled up into tight fists. I thought I saw a faint cloud of smoke just above her head. She was wearing the same face she usually had before she would do something defiant. She was going to have to be ornery on her own time. There was no way I was going to allow her to make a scene and get me into trouble.

I grabbed Julia's hand and dragged her back over to the bike. I let go of her arm long enough to stand the bike straight, mount it, and push back the kickstand.

"Get on," I commanded.

She stood there, staring into the bakery window. I knew she wanted him to see her. I believed he already had, but was pretending he hadn't.

"C'mon, Julia," I said more firmly. "Ain't no need in making a scene. You're gonna get us both in trouble."

"Who is that tramp?" she grumbled.

"Julia!" I whispered loudly.

Just as she hopped on, Mr. Richardson looked over at us. He looked her right in the eyes and continued on with the young lady as if nothing had happened. He never missed a beat.

Neither of us said anything as we rode back to the house. We'd had no fun for most of the day, and worst of all, we didn't even get the butter cookies.

"Mouse, you think my Daddy has a girlfriend?" Julia asked, finally breaking the silence.

"I don't know, Julia. Looked like it."

I hated to be the one to agree that it looked like exactly what she thought it was.

"You think I should say something to Momma?"

Her voice quivered as she asked the question. I grabbed her hand before shrugging my shoulders. I figured it wasn't the worst that could happen to her momma, considering what my father had done to mine.

"There may be a good reason for what we saw. Might be best to let grown folks figure they own stuff out."

Julia nodded and then burst into tears. I didn't know much about relationships, but it seemed to me that a married man shouldn't go around buying things for another woman and allowing her to kiss him on the cheek. I put my arm around Julia's shoulder and allowed her to cry.

Dinner had been served, and Suga and I were straightening up the kitchen by the time Mr. Richardson made it home. I'd hoped that we would finish before that happened, but I had no such luck.

Mr. Richardson came in with a bouquet of the prettiest pink roses I'd ever seen in my life and two white boxes with purple ribbons—one for Mrs. Richardson and one for Julia, Suga, and me to share. When he handed one of the white boxes to Julia, he gave her a wink like they shared a secret. Julia took the box and turned away from her father's kiss on the forehead. Mrs. Richardson watched her daughter with a confused look on her face.

"Wonder what's gotten into her," Mrs. Richardson commented.

"No telling. You know how you women are," said Mr. Richardson.

"What's the special occasion?" she asked.

Mrs. Richardson was delighted, eyeing the flowers and the other box.

"No special occasion. I just wanted to bring sweets for my sweets," he said evenly.

He'd come bearing gifts because he wasn't entirely sure what he would be walking into. Now that he knew Julia hadn't told on him, he could play it cool.

"Aw, isn't that adorable?" Mrs. Richardson squealed.

She opened her box and teased, "Julia, Daddy brought home those butter cookies you love so much."

Julia smiled sweetly at her father, but her eyes said she wasn't happy. "Thank you, Daddy," she said curtly.

Suga looked over at me, and I gave her a look. She nodded. She'd understood that meant I would tell her all about it on our walk home.

Mrs. Richardson and Suga went into the kitchen, and Julia headed back to her room. I was left in the dining room with Mr. Richardson.

"What were you two doing so far from the house?"

"We just wanted to get some of those butter cookies."

"Did you ask anyone if you could go to that store?"

"No, sir. We didn't plan it, but when we got out that far, we just decided to go to the store," I explained.

I was starting to get nervous about where this conversation was going. I was trying not to lay the blame for being at that store at Julia's feet, but

I'd been warned against getting into trouble because of Julia's whims.

"You two shouldn't be that far away from the house without someone knowing where you are. Anything can happen to two young girls by themselves. You stay on this side of the tracks, you hear?"

"Yessir," I answered quietly.

"Alright, see you tomorrow," he concluded the conversation.

I went into the kitchen, and Suga was drying her hands on the dish towel, signifying her day was done.

"I'll be right back. I want to go tell Julia goodbye," I told Suga.

"Don't be all night. My back is worrying me sum'mn awful. I'm ready for this baby to be born. I'll be outside."

I ran back to Julia's room.

"I'm going. You okay?" I asked Julia.

"I'm fine," she responded.

"Your daddy just warned me that we shouldn't have been down there by ourselves and not to do that again."

Julia didn't say anything. She just looked at me with her eyes squinted. I thought that warning probably made her mad all over again.

"I'll see you tomorrow," I said.

I didn't want to make things any worse.

"What the heck was that all about?" Suga asked as soon as we were down the road a bit.

"Julia and I rode into town for some of those cookies Mr. Richardson brought home. He was at the shop with a pretty blonde lady who kissed him on the cheek. Julia saw the whole thing, and she was hot fire mad. Mr. Richardson saw us too," I told Suga.

Suga's head jerked in my direction.

"I told you to stay outta trouble, Mouse! If Mr. Richardson think you gone cause trouble, he might fire me, and then what's gone happen to us?" she almost yelled.

"Mr. Richardson wasn't mad. He just told me Julia and I shouldn't go down there by ourselves and don't do it again!" I almost yelled back. "Besides, I don't think he wants Mrs. Richardson to know what we saw. He knows if I told the truth about it, Julia would back it up. Julia is so mad with her daddy, I don't know what she might do."

Suga shook her head.

"Mouse, don't leave the house no more without telling me where you going. Anything coulda happened," Suga warned.

"Okay. We hadn't really planned where we were going. We just kind of ended up down there."

"Warning come before destruction. That's what the Bible say," she chided. "Ooooh, the baby kicking. You wanna feel?"

I nodded with excitement. I had never felt a baby in the stomach.

Suga took my hand and placed it on the side where the baby must have been resting. At first I didn't feel anything, then there was a sharp bump against my hand. I jumped and snatched my hand away in surprise. Suga grabbed her belly and laughed.

"This baby here is strong," she said, grinning.

I was amazed at a real, live human being in her stomach.

"How do women get pregnant?"

Suga walked quietly for a few paces.

"You remember what you saw me and yo' daddy doing the morning after we moved into the apartment?"

I nodded.

"That's how," she said matter-of-fact.

"But you were just bouncing on top of him," I said confused.

"You know how you have an opening 'tween your legs?"

Again, I nodded.

"Well, a man has sum'mn to put inside the opening 'tween your legs."

I walked quietly beside her for a moment, considering what this meant.

"And that makes you pregnant?" I asked with a scowl on my face.

"Only if all the conditions right," she said thoughtfully.

I shrugged my shoulders.

"So, is that what all the girls were doing with the customers at Ms. Sookie's?" I questioned.

If that's what had made Ray lose his mind and disobey Ms. Sookie's order, that must have been what all the men were getting when they came to visit.

Suga stopped walking. She spoke calmly without looking at me.

"Don't never ask me about what I did at Ms. Sookie's again."

"I didn't mean to say anything bad. I just want to understand," I said solemnly.

I really had not meant to hurt or offend Suga.

She continued walking. "Yeah, that's what we did with all them men," she responded softly.

"Well, you must have been good at it, because they kept coming back."

Suga bursted out laughing. I didn't understand what was so funny, but I was glad she wasn't angry with me.

The whole mess with Mr. Richardson had affected both me and Suga. Suga looked at Ray with distrust when he returned home from work. She still served him dinner with a smile, but she seemed to be a bit more reserved than she'd been when he promised her a better life once the baby arrived.

That night, I thought of Sunny and how young she was when she got to Ms. Sookie's. She was the youngest in the house, yet she was working the same way all of the other girls were. Suga must have been close to that age when she started working. I went under the couch and pulled out my suitcase. I opened it, reached in, and unwrapped the elephant from the cotton handkerchief in which it was wrapped. I rubbed the elephant and wondered if my friend was okay.

The next morning, Julia was bold enough to ask if we could go into town. Mrs. Richardson was so involved with trying to get invited to the Summer

Social that she wasn't paying much attention to what Julia was saying.

"Sure, dear. You and Hannah go on and play. I have to make some phone calls and go see Mrs. Sanderson. Your daddy's influence helped them get into that house. They will kindly be reminded of that if I don't receive an invite to the social. Everyone else has already received their invitations, and I've already bought my dress," she prattled on.

Julia didn't care about any of that. All she heard was, "Sure, dear." Anything after that was just noise.

I heard the whole conversation because Suga had propped the kitchen door open. I was sitting at the table cutting up tomatoes for our lunch sandwiches pretending like I was unaware when Julia walked in kitchen.

"Momma said we can go into town," Julia stated, looking at me for a response.

"But I told you yo' daddy said we couldn't," I said confused.

"He didn't tell me that," she responded.

"He told *me* that," I said with a raised voice. "If he catches us down there again, I'm going to be the one in trouble, and Suga too."

I was annoyed that Julia didn't seem to care how another trip into town would affect me and Suga.

"Fine. I'll go by myself. I have to see if…" She looked over at Suga. "If the same thing will happen again."

"She knows," I said quietly.

Julia's eyes got big and her nostrils flared. "You told her?"

"Suga won't say anything," I assured her.

"I sure as heck won't. I can't afford to lose this job, so I ain't gonna cause no trouble," Suga said, inserting herself into the conversation.

Just as quickly as she'd turned around to add her two cents, she turned back to the sink and continued washing the dishes from breakfast.

"You still shouldn't have told, Mouse."

I'd disappointed Julia.

"Sorry. Suga picked up that something was wrong, and she asked me about it."

I shrugged my shoulders, not knowing how I could fix what had already been done. Julia rolled her eyes and left the kitchen.

"You going to talk to her?" Suga asked.

"No. There's no talking sense into her when she gets like that. She's going looking for trouble."

"Best let her find that on her own," Suga concluded.

I heard Julia stomp out of the house and slam the front door. Mrs. Richardson sat in the den oblivious that her child was upset. Either that, or she just didn't care to find out why.

I spent the rest of the morning helping Suga clean up the kitchen from breakfast and the early afternoon preparing for lunch. The food had just been put out when Julia came into the kitchen through the back door.

"What's for lunch?" Julia asked.

"Turkey or ham sandwiches, cucumber and tomato salad, butter cookies, and some fresh lemonade," Suga responded.

Julia nodded her head and went to go wash up. She didn't say a word to me or acknowledge my presence. When she sat down at the table, I returned the favor.

"How was your trip into town?"

Suga was trying to break up the awkward silence.

"Fine."

"That's nice," Suga said eagerly. "Was it busy out today?"

"Not particularly."

Julia's response was sharp, signifying she was done answering questions.

I looked at Julia long and hard. I understood that she wasn't happy about her daddy's behavior. I was the princess of disappointing fathers, but that wasn't permission to be mean to us.

"Be mad at your daddy all you want, but don't take it out on me and Suga. That's not right."

Julia put her sandwich down and exhaled.

"You're right. Sorry, Suga. Sorry, Mouse. I just feel helpless. Whatever daddy was doing with that woman was wrong, but I don't want to hurt Momma by telling her. I'm not sure she'd believe me anyway," Julia said softly.

That was the first time Julia had called her Suga instead of Lizzy. Suga didn't correct her.

"Who wouldn't believe what, darling?" Mrs. Richardson asked as she walked into the kitchen.

It was good that Julia's back was to the living room entrance into the kitchen because her eyes were stretched to the size of two apples.

"Um, I wasn't sure you'd believe I wanted to attend the Summer Social with you. I know I said I didn't want to go, but I've changed my mind," Julia lied.

"Well, that's wonderful, dear. I think my little visit with Mrs. Sanderson did the trick. Our invitation should be coming soon. We'll have to find you a beautiful dress to wear."

I snickered inwardly. Julia hated the idea of having to be a show pony for all of her mother's friends. Now, she'd lied her way right into being miserable on a perfectly good Saturday afternoon.

"Lizzy, I'll take my lunch in the den," Mrs. Richardson instructed.

"Yes, ma'am."

As soon as Mrs. Richardson left the room, Julia whined about the trouble she had gotten herself into.

"Great! Now I've got to go to this stupid social."

"What is it anyway?" I asked.

"A stupid event where we get all dressed up, drink tea, and eat little stupid cucumber sandwiches with the crusts cut off. Last year was the first year I was old enough to go, and I hated every minute of it."

"It don't sound so bad," Suga teased.

Suga knew full well that Julia was more rough-and-tumble than sugar and spice.

"I guess it's not for folks that look like us," I said, furthering her embarrassment.

"Well, not really," Julia responded. "But it sure would be better if you could come."

"Ooooooh, I can't wait to see Miss Julia in a frilly dress," Suga laughed.

Julia turned bright red in the face, which made Suga and I laugh even harder. She eventually gave up being mad and laughed with us.

The next day was more of the same. Julia went into town without me, only this time when she returned, she'd found exactly what she'd been looking for. She raced back into the house, grabbed me by the hand, and pulled me outside to our spot in the backyard.

"I saw them again, Mouse. Daddy didn't see me this time. He kissed her on the lips, Mouse. Full-on, on the lips," she said bitterly.

"Are you sure, Julia?"

"Sure? I saw it with my own two eyes!"

"Okay. Keep it down, unless you want Suga and your Momma to come find us," I warned. "What are you gonna do?"

"I don't know, Mouse. I don't know. You think Suga will know what to do?"

"I think Suga will want to stay out of it, just like I do," I responded.

Julia threw up her hands and sighed.

"Talk to your Daddy," I suggested.

"I'm gonna talk to him alright."

Julia was fuming mad. Her temper was just as fiery and her red hair, and there wouldn't be much I could do or say to keep her from tearing into her daddy if that's what she set her mind to.

"Let's go back into the house and eat some lunch. Maybe you will feel better after you get something in your stomach."

I hoped food would ease her mood, but Julia moped all through lunch and the rest of the afternoon. She came to the kitchen every once in a while for a snack or something to drink, but spent the rest of the time in her room. I wasn't allowed to spend time in her room, so I stayed in the kitchen with Suga. I was beginning to regret asking to spend my remaining days of summer at their house. I would be having much more fun with the Alexanders and Jimmie.

Suga would glance at me from time to time with a look of pity on her face. She knew I didn't want to be here helping her with dishes and cleaning. Even though I wanted to ask about going back to Ms. Bernadette, I knew Julia was going through a rough time, and I didn't want to abandon her.

"Hello, everyone," Mr. Richardson announced as he swept into the house. He came in, once again, bearing gifts after having seen the other woman. Pink roses and two boxes of butter cookies were becoming a telltale sign of his indiscretions. "I've got treats for my sweets!" he announced.

Mrs. Richardson looked somewhat dismayed.

"Thank you, dear," was all she offered, along with an obligatory peck on the cheek.

Julia didn't even come out of her room.

"Well, that was certainly lukewarm. And where's my little girl?"

"Julia, your daddy's home," Mrs. Richardson called out. "I'm sure she's just fiddling around in her room."

"Good evening, Lizzy and Hannah. What's for supper?" he asked.

"We made pot roast, mashed potatoes and gravy, green beans, biscuits, and a sweet potato pie," Suga responded.

"Well, sounds mighty fine. I'm gonna go wash up, and I'll be ready for dinner. Julia, get washed up and come on to the table." Mr. Richardson yelled.

"Yessir," she responded.

I could hear the anger in her reply.

Suga and I set the table hurriedly and then returned to the kitchen.

"I got a bad feeling, Mouse. Let's gone get this kitchen cleaned up so's all we gotta do is put the food up and wash they dinner plates," Suga whispered.

"Yeah, Julia saw her daddy with that woman again. This time she saw him kiss the woman on the mouth," I told Suga.

Suga gasped and put her hand over her heart. She shook her head, then turned to the sink and started running warm water for the dishes. I began collecting the pots, pans, and cooking utensils we'd used to prepare the meal. Once the sink was half full of warm, sudsy water, I began scrubbing while Suga wiped down counters and took out tupperware to store the leftovers.

Once I finished, I pushed the swinging door just a bit so there was a small crack. If I got my angle right, I could see through the family room and into the dining room without being noticed.

Julia stared down at her plate, swirling around something she hadn't eaten on it. Mrs. Richardson stared off into space with her hands resting on the table. Mr. Richardson was eating his food with not one care in the world. Julia looked up and watched him with obvious disgust. If he'd taken a moment to look at her, he would have lost his appetite.

I eased the door shut.

"You want me to take out that pie?" I asked.

"I got it."

Suga carefully lifted the pie in its beautiful baking dish and backed out of the kitchen. She returned with raised eyebrows and head shaking.

"That Julia is looking at her daddy like she could kill him," she said.

When dinner was finished, we cleared the table. Julia's plate had barely been touched.

Suga and I worked quickly and quietly, but as I was going to put all of the food in the refrigerator, Suga stopped what she was doing.

"Mouse, you think you can sneak down the hall and get Julia here before we go?" she asked.

"I think so."

"Go," Suga commanded.

I pushed the door again to see if both adult Richardsons were in the living room. Mr. Richardson was holding the paper up between his hands, which hid his face. Mrs. Richardson was seated in the chair beside the couch, focused on her needlework.

I slipped out of the door and into the hallway as quiet as the rodent I'd been nicknamed after. I pushed myself against the wall and slid down to Julia's open door. She looked up when I moved to stand directly in the light of the doorframe. I put my finger up to my mouth and then motioned for her to follow me.

As we got to the end of the hall, I peeked at the Richardsons again to find them in the same exact positions. I eased back into the kitchen with Julia close behind.

Suga motioned for Julia to sit down at the table, and then she motioned for me to keep watch at the door.

"Julia, you ain't gone like what I gotta say, but you need to hear it," Suga began. "What yo' daddy doing ain't right, but it ain't none of your business."

I heard Julia making the beginning sound of a protest, but then it abruptly stopped. When I glanced back, Suga had her hand up and was shaking her head. I turned my eyes back to the crack in the door, but my ears were all hers.

"First of all, if you tell the truth, it's gone crush yo' momma. If it's gone come out, you let it come out all by itself. And if it ever does, you take it to your grave that you knew. You hear me?" she asked Julia.

I heard no response, but I assumed Suga received one, because she continued.

"If yo' Momma find out you knew and didn't tell her, it's gonna sting even worse. Some things better left unsaid. If you tell her, she gonna see you as the one putting her in a bad situation. She gonna have to choose whether to stay so she can keep you in comfort but be shame at the choice, or leave and struggle by herself to take care of you and her. If it come out, that needs to be between her and yo' daddy," she concluded.

Julia sat there for a minute in silence. I glanced back again because I just couldn't help myself, and I saw her wipe her face.

"Ok, Suga," she said.

Now that Suga had allowed it once, Julia had begun calling her that whenever Mr. and Mrs. Richardson weren't around.

Suga walked over and hugged Julia and kissed her on the head.

"Straighten up your face before you leave outta here," Suga said sweetly. "Mouse, go tell the Richardsons we'll see them tomorrow."

I did as Suga asked. Mr. and Mrs. Richardson barely acknowledged my existence.

Julia was gone, and Suga was ready to go when I returned to the kitchen.

"You think Julia will be able to keep quiet?" I asked her.

"I don't know, Mouse. That little girl is headstrong as a mule, and she so angry with her daddy, but I don't think she wanna hurt her momma like that. That's a bad choice for a child to have to make. I know how that feels."

I considered what Suga was really saying. I thought better of asking her how she knew judging by the look on her face.

"Why do men marry a woman and then go with another woman?" I wondered out loud.

"Who know why a man do anything," Suga said with a shrug. "Men do all kinds of things, and most times they don't even know why they doing it."

"Makes it seem like men are pretty stupid," I mused.

"Who said they ain't?" Suga asked with a laugh.

Ten

School started without much fanfare. Ms. Bernadette was my teacher, as promised. She stayed behind while Jimmie was stationed in Florida. They hadn't yet set a date for the wedding, but she didn't seem to be in any rush. She really didn't want to leave Hemings.

I made a few friends, which was easier when I wasn't the new girl showing up in the middle of the school year. Charlene had become my best friend almost immediately. She was the funniest person I'd ever met. Ms. Bernadette would often look over at our desks and give us the stink eye, which was all it took to make me quiet. Charlene, on the other hand, usually went home with a note pinned to her blouse. She took whatever punishment her parents gave her and went back to her usual antics the following week. They didn't punish her too harshly. Her grades were just about as good as mine, which I couldn't figure out because she was always clowning around. She'd finish her work quickly so that she could be a distraction to the rest of us.

Nita was my other friend. She was a tiny little thing, the shortest student in the class. However, she had the biggest mouth. Nobody ever bothered her because she'd raise the alarm, and everyone would stop what they were doing to see what was happening. Nita wasn't just loud for no reason; she had the voice of an angel. She could sing so pretty it would bring a tear to all the grown-ups' eyes. Our classmates would just sit in awe. Sometimes on the playground, we would all gather around, and Nita would sing us "At Last" by Etta James or "Will You Love Me Tomorrow" by The Shirelles.

As Suga got more and more pregnant, I spent less and less time with Julia. When I arrived at the Richardsons', I'd have to help Suga wrap things up for the evening. We'd walk home, and I would have enough time to help Suga make dinner, do my homework, bathe, and get my clothes ready for the next day. Suga and Ray had been saving as much money as they could since she would have to take a few weeks off when the baby was born.

Suga planned to get back to work as soon as she could. Mrs. Richardson told Suga she was entitled to six weeks, but she would appreciate it if Suga could return sooner. Ruby was willing to come back a couple days a week to fill in, but she had too many babies now to leave them with her momma everyday. I figured Suga didn't want Ruby to get too comfortable back in the Richardsons' house.

I worked odd jobs on the weekends to help where I could. I would weed the Richardsons' garden, as Mrs. Richardson was too prim and proper to do any work that required you to get dirty. Mr. Richardson was uninterested in that type of work, and Julia was busy with her friends. I also collected soda cans and turned them into the recycling plant. I gave any money I made to Suga.

I was sitting on my little stool, tending to Mrs. Richardson's flower bed when Julia and three of her new friends came to the house.

I waved.

Julia gave a slight nod, but kept walking.

"Who's that?" asked the blonde girl at the front of the pack.

"Our cook's girl," Julia responded.

I couldn't believe my ears. I turned back toward the house so none of them could see my face. My throat tightened and my eyes began stinging, but I refused to allow them to see me hurt. I understood that Julia and I hadn't spent much time together since the summer, but the "cook's girl?" That's all Suga and I were to her?

I pulled weeds as slowly as I could, careful to check each flower bed twice. The girls left about an hour later. I put my bucket of tools and my gloves in the garage and knocked on the kitchen door. Julia answered.

"Your cook's girl?" I asked.

"What was I supposed to say?" she defended.

"That I'm your friend."

"Are you? I've barely seen you since we started school, and when I do, you have to work," Julia said bitterly.

"I've been trying to help get ready for the baby. We have to save so we won't fall behind once the baby gets here. Sorry my family doesn't have money like yours does. You could have come to see me, too, you know."

"Julia, what's going on?" I heard Mrs. Richardson ask from the swinging door by the living room.

"Nothing, Ma. Hannah was just saying hi before she had to leave," she said, turning back to look me in the eyes.

"Oh here, give her this and thank her for coming to weed the garden. Lord knows that's not a job I want or can do with this delicate skin of mine."

Julia reached back, got the three dollars, and turned to hand them to me. I took them from her hand, and then she closed the door in my face.

I stood on the doorstep for a few moments, shocked. I had been warned that this would happen at some point, but I'd thought better of Julia.

It was only a few months before that Julia, Suga, and I had had a good time helping her pick her dress and hairstyle for the Summer Social. We weren't there when she actually got dolled up, but she made sure we had felt a part of things by doing a dress rehearsal the night before. Suga did her hair, I painted her nails, and we made sure the dress was hung without a single wrinkle. Now, we'd been reduced to just being the help. Or was that what we'd always been? Though I was devastated, it wasn't something I would share with Suga or Ms. Bernadette. They would be gracious enough not to say, "I told you so," but I was sure they would be thinking it.

By November, Suga was as big as a house. I was out of school the whole week of Thanksgiving, so the three days prior, Suga and I spent preparing the Richardsons' meal. Suga was trying to make the meal foolproof so that all Mrs. Richardson had to do was put things in the oven Thanksgiving morning. Suga had me write down her instructions, step by step, to try to avoid any errors. Julia stayed out of the way.

Suga was becoming suspicious after two days of no Julia.

"Something going on with you and Julia?"

"No," I responded.

"She was coming around me just fine, then soon as you get here, she disappears," she stated.

I knew Suga well enough to know she was fishing. I shrugged my shoulders in response. She left it alone.

Since Suga already had to prepare one Thanksgiving meal for the Richardsons, Mrs. Althea and Mr. Kenneth insisted we all come to their house for Thanksgiving. Jimmie would be home for the holidays and would come to pick us up since it was getting too cold, and Suga was too slow for us to walk. That morning, Ray and I dressed quickly. I helped Suga get ready while he sulked on the couch. While he enjoyed Mrs. Althea's cooking, he didn't like being around them much.

I didn't understand why Ray felt that way about the Alexanders. It had taken Suga awhile to warm up to them, but now she and I fell right in with the rest of the crew. Ms. Bernadette had even thrown Suga a small baby shower to help her get the rest of the things she needed. Suga had cried and cried, she was so overwhelmed at what we'd done. She was surprised that I had kept the secret for weeks. I wished he would come around like Suga had.

We arrived to the smell of warm cinnamon apple cider, turkey, dressing, collard greens, macaroni and cheese, candied yams, potato salad, shrimp perlo, hoppin' john, shrimp salad, and cornbread. And my goodness, the dessert! There was every kind of cake and pie you could imagine.

Mrs. Althea and Mr. Kenneth came to the door to greet us. Ms. Bernadette wasn't far behind. They each took turns hugging us all, and the ladies had to rub Suga's belly.

"I'm ready for this baby to get here," Suga confided in her women friends.

"Don't you rush that baby. He will be here soon enough," Mrs. Althea fussed.

"He? How you know the baby a he?" Suga asked, amused.

"He sitting low," Mrs. Althea responded.

Suga laughed, and Ray beamed.

"I don't know how, but Momma does have a knack for knowing what a child will be before it's born," Ms. Bernadette confirmed.

"Well, whatever this baby is, it's hungry," Suga said, rubbing her tummy with both hands.

We washed our hands and made our way to our seats.

"Let us all join hands," Mr. Kenneth said in a serious voice.

Once everyone was connected, he began his prayer of thanksgiving.

"Heavenly Father, we come to you as humbly as we know how. We thank you for your grace and mercy throughout this year. We thank you for your kindness and your forgiveness, for we all sinners, unworthy of your precious love. Now Father, we thank you for this wonderful meal that has been prepared. We pray that you will bless it to nourish our bodies, and we ask that you bless the hands that prepared it. These and many other blessings we ask in your son, Jesus, name. Amen."

Everyone else joined in with a solemn, "Amen."

"Now, let's eat!" Jimmie yelled.

He clapped his hands and rubbed them together. Everyone laughed, but we all felt the same way.

The only sound that could be heard during the first round was silverware on fine china. No one found their voices until folks started going back for seconds.

"Mrs. Althea, you showl put your foot in these collard greens," Ray said.

Suga cut her eyes at him. He never carried on much over her cooking. In fact, I could count on one hand the number of times he'd complimented anything.

"Mmm hmm, baby. And that potato salad might be the best you ever made," Mr. Kenneth agreed.

"Actually, I made the potato salad," Ms. Bernadette announced.

"Oooooh weeeeeee! You gonna be cooking like this when we get married?" Jimmie asked.

"I learned from the best," Ms. Bernadette answered.

Mr. Kenneth looked over at Jimmie and winked. They shared a laugh.

Everyone was stuffed after round two. The ladies went into the kitchen to clean the dishes while the fellas and I cleared the table.

"Suga, you go sit down," Mrs. Althea fussed. "Me, Bernadette, and Mouse can handle this. You gone get off your feet."

"I can help!" Suga said.

"Nonsense. Ray, tell your woman we got this," Mrs. Althea demanded.

"Suga, the ladies got it. And the menfolks even helping. Set on down and rest," he instructed.

"Yeah, better rest now. Won't be too much rest to be had after that little boy get here," Mrs. Althea finished.

Suga sat down on the couch. Ray took the small footstool that was next to the lounge chair and put it in front of her. She lifted her swollen legs up onto it.

Suga's legs weren't the only thing that looked swollen. Her face was swollen, and her nose had spread across her face. Her breasts were bigger. Her hips were wider, and her navel was poking out. She looked almost double her normal size. I had never been close to anyone who was having a baby, so I didn't realize how being pregnant changed a woman's body. Seeing how pregnancy affected a woman made me unsure I'd ever have a child.

Before long, Suga and the men were asleep in various spots in the den. Mr. Kenneth was even snoring. Mrs. Althea and Ms. Bernadette had a good chuckle over all the noise he was making. No one had even tried to tackle dessert yet.

The three of us washed, dried, and put away the dinner plates. The dessert plates would remain out until the cakes and pies had been devoured, or at least sampled.

Suga was the first to stir from her nap. She woke up rubbing her belly and yawning.

"Suga, I know you must be ready for some dessert. What you want me to bring you?" Mrs. Althea asked.

"I'll get it, Mrs. Althea," Suga answered wearily.

"You stay right where you at," Mrs. Althea chided. "Now, what you want?"

"I'll take a slice of that coconut cake, and I think the baby want a small slice of chocolate," Suga said with a grin.

I thought it was funny she was blaming her greediness on the baby. Having known Suga before she got pregnant, I knew she could eat. She would have had two slices of cake under normal circumstances. It was a miracle she'd stayed so thin.

I wondered if she would return to her normal size once she had the baby.

I ate a big piece of chocolate cake. I was so stuffed, I was miserable. One person should not be allowed to eat as much as any of us had eaten.

"Well, Mr. Kenneth and Mrs. Althea, we should be heading on back. Me and Suga both gotta go to work in the morning. Thank ya kindly for your hospitality. We showl appreciate it," Ray said.

"It weren't no problem at all, Ray. We was glad to have you. Y'all pack up some of this food to go! Jimmie gotta eat at his folks' house, too, and ain't no way me, Kenneth, and Bernadette gonna eat all this food," Mrs. Althea begged. "You know you gonna want some of those collard greens tomorrow. Greens taste better the next day."

"Yes, ma'am. Mouse, go on and pack us some stuff up to go."

Suga got up and came to help me. She knew better than I did what he wanted and how much. We worked quickly to get the food wrapped up in paper plates and covered with foil. We had to put the juicy stuff, like the greens and candied yams, in containers that Suga promised Mrs. Althea she would return by Sunday.

"Ms. Bernadette, would it be okay if I came here tomorrow instead of going with Suga to the Richardsons'?" I asked.

"Mouse, Ms. Bernadette probably got plans. You shoulda asked before now," Suga said.

Ms. Bernadette looked at Jimmie, who nodded his approval.

"Suga, it's fine. Mouse, Jimmie and I had plans to ride over to Huntsville tomorrow, but I don't see why you can't come."

"Naw, y'all two lovebirds go 'head. Mouse can go with Suga like was already planned," Ray spoke up.

I pouted the whole ride home. We each took baths and prepared for the next day. I went to bed livid that I would have to spend the day pretending as if everything was okay between me and Julia.

When Suga and I arrived at the Richardsons', you would have thought that World War III had broken out in their kitchen. There were dirty dishes, pots, and silverware all over the place. The floor was sticky. One of the pots looked like a bomb had exploded in it, and the oven looked even worse than that.

Suga took one look around the kitchen, and her lips tightened. I knew that look to mean she was chewing up her words so they wouldn't spill out of her mouth and get her into trouble.

"Lizzy, you and Hannah must get this kitchen cleaned up. I just didn't have the energy to do it yesterday after all that cooking," Mrs. Richardson said.

Mrs. Richardson feigned as if she was so tired.

"Yes, ma'am," Suga said.

I could detect the attitude, even if Mrs. Richardson could not. When Mrs. Richardson left the kitchen, Suga sat down in a chair from the table and surveyed the entirety of the damage.

“Mouse, I can’t do all this by myself. This kitchen shouldn’t even look like this!” Suga shouted in a whisper. “All she had to do was to heat up the food, put the leftovers away, and wash the dishes. She couldn’t even do that?”

She just shook her head. Tears began to well up in her eyes.

“Suga, I will help you. Julia and I aren’t speaking anyway, so I have plenty of time to help you work. It won’t take us that long. I promise.”

Suga just nodded her head, but I could see the weariness in her face. She either didn’t catch my comment about Julia, or she was too frustrated to care. I was glad that Ray had insisted I come with her today. If she had been alone, I don’t know what she would have done.

“Let’s start with dumping all this leftover food that wasn’t put away,” she directed. “Such a waste,” she said with a shake of her head.

Suga and I worked tirelessly the entire day. No one in the family bothered us. They didn’t even come in for food. They went to the local diner for lunch and picked up some take-out for dinner. By the time we were finished, the kitchen sparkled. The inside of the stove looked brand new, and all the dishes had been washed, dried, and put away. The floor was mopped and no longer sounded or felt like we were walking across flypaper. Neither Suga nor I could figure out what had been spilled on the floor. It was a good thing it was Friday, because Suga would need the whole weekend to recover from all that work.

We walked home even slower than usual.

"I'm glad we got those leftovers. If Ray expected me to cook tonight, I would pass out," Suga commented.

"I'm beat too. I can't believe they left that kitchen like that."

"Chile, don't be surprised by nothing white folk do," Suga warned. "And don't think I didn't hear you say you and Julia ain't speaking. What's wrong wit' y'all?"

"We just don't have nothing to say to each other."

That was all I had the energy to tell her. Suga nodded, knowingly.

We returned to the normal routine after Thanksgiving break. The next month of school was uneventful. Everyone was on their best behavior because Christmas was right around the corner, and no one wanted to be on Santa's naughty list. Even Charlene avoided the notes home to her parents. She and Nita would tease me, because whenever they asked me what I wanted for Christmas, I just told them I wanted a healthy little brother or sister. I really didn't care about a new doll or fancy clothes. I just wanted someone I could love who might love me back the same.

The day school let out for Christmas break, you would have thought captives had been set free. Children were wrapped up in winter coats, running through the halls of the school, cheering and screaming that it was Christmas. I was happy for the break too. I loved school, but the baby would be coming any day now. I wanted to be there when it happened.

When I got home, Suga was sitting at the table looking as if she was about to burst. The Richardsons were taking it easy on her and had already made plans to spend Christmas just a few hours' drive away in Lincolnville, Illinois with Mrs. Richardson's sister. They told her Ruby would start her schedule as soon as they returned.

Suga greeted me as I walked in the house.

"Hey, Mouse."

"Hey, Suga. How are you feeling?"

"Just tired. The baby has really been kicking up a fuss today."

She absentmindedly rubbed her belly. I walked over and placed my head on her tummy.

"Hey, there. You ready to come out and meet us?"

I spoke into Suga's belly.

There was a kick so hard, my head lifted slightly off of Suga's stomach. We both laughed.

"Well, I'on' know if that was a 'yes' or 'no', but it sure was a strong kick," Suga chuckled.

There was a knock on the door and Ms. Bernadette pushed it open.

"Hello, ladies."

"Hey, Ms. Bernadette. Whatchu doin' here?" Suga asked.

"I came to grab you ladies for a sleepover!" she responded.

"A sleepover?"

Suga and I questioned in unison.

"Yep. Grab some night clothes and some clothes to wear back tomorrow," she instructed.

"Ms. Bernadette, this baby has been moving something awful today, I'm tired, and Ray is going to get worried if he come home and I ain't here. Mouse can go with you, but I think I'm gonna stay here," Suga responded.

"We'll leave Ray a note. He'll be fine. How many times have you told me he always comes home late on Friday nights?" Ms. Bernadette looked over at me and said, "Go on and gather some clothes."

I was excited to be having a sleepover, even though I didn't know what one did at such an affair.

"C'mon, Suga. I'm definitely not leaving you here all alone. Anything could happen. If Ray wants to cause trouble about it, you let me handle it. You two shouldn't be here alone with that baby so close to coming. Plus, I just think my momma misses y'all when she hasn't seen you for awhile."

"Mouse, grab me some night clothes. Where Mr. Kenneth and Jimmie gone be?" Suga asked.

"Daddy is gone fishing with some of his church buddies, and Jimmie is outside, but he's dropping us off and going back to his parents' house. He's got an early morning tomorrow," Ms. Bernadette answered.

Once I had our clothes packed, Ms. Bernadette helped Suga up out of the chair and we rode to the Alexanders' house. Jimmie pecked Ms. Bernadette on the lips and waved goodbye at me and Suga.

Both Ms. Bernadette and I helped a waddling Suga manage the stairs. She had to sit down once we got to the top to rest a bit.

"My goodness. That baby gonna be juicy when he get here," Mrs. Althea said, coming to the porch door. "C'mon in here and let me make you some hot tea."

We moved Suga to the living room and got her settled with her feet propped up and a steaming cup of peppermint tea.

"So, you and Jimmie picked a date yet?" Suga asked between sips.

"Not yet. He'll be at his station for another year or so, and I'm not sure I want to move to Florida," she said, glancing over at me.

"You betta go be with yo' man," Suga chided. "A fine, military man like that… hmph. It's tail chasing him all around that base."

"Suga!" Ms. Bernadette squealed in surprise.

All three of the ladies howled with laughter. I continued to sip my hot chocolate.

"Well, she ain't lying. But I don't think Jimmie is that kind of man. He chased behind Bernadette for two years before he even got a date. He wouldn't take any other girl out. Told all his friends, his momma and daddy, and me and Kenneth she was gonna be his wife," Mrs. Althea explained.

"That's sweet," I interjected. I was feeling a bit left out of such grown up talk.

"Yeah, that's sweet, but he a grown man now, with needs. Don't stay away from that man too long, Ms. Bernadette," Suga warned again.

Suga inhaled sharply. Both Mrs. Althea and Ms. Bernadette's heads jerked toward her.

"What's wrong, Suga?" Mrs. Althea asked.

"Nothing. Just had a sharp pain, is all. I'm fine," she answered.

When neither of the women took their eyes off of her, she spoke again.

"I'm fine!"

Their shoulders relaxed, and they returned to the conversation.

"Well, I do want to get married soon, but I don't want to have to follow Jimmie around from base to base. I'd rather stay here and teach children I know. I really hope when it's time that he chooses not to re-enlist," Ms. Bernadette said in a worried tone.

"You tole him that?" Suga pried.

"Not in so many words," Ms. Bernadette said.

"Lawd, menfolk don't pick up on hints, chile," Mrs. Althea said. "You better tell Jimmie how you feel. You two just getting started. You can't go down this road of marriage hiding your real feelings from one another. He told you whether he plans to re-enlist yet?"

"He said he wasn't sure what he'd be able to do for work if he got out now. I know he's worried about being able to provide for us," Ms. Bernadette replied.

"Well, Bernadette, that's something y'all two need to get clear on before you get married. If you don't want the same things, that could cause big trouble," Mrs. Althea warned.

Suga inhaled sharply again.

"Suga, are you having contractions?" Mrs. Althea asked with squinted eyes.

"I don't know," she responded, her eyes growing wider at the thought.

"What's a contraction?" I asked.

"Contractions are like really, really bad cramps, and they mean the baby coming," Mrs. Althea answered. "The last time you made that sound was only a few minutes ago. Did your water break already?"

"I don't know!" Suga responded, alarm in her voice. "Last night, I got up because I thought I peed myself. There was some liquid running down my leg, but this baby done made me wet myself a little bit before."

Suga was beginning to breathe rapidly, but Mrs. Althea continued questioning.

"Have you been feeling these pains since then?"

"Yes, ma'am," Suga said with a nod. "They didn't really hurt like they do now. I just thought it was a little bit of cramping. When I seen movies and shows of women having babies, they hoop and holler like somebody killing them. I didn't feel nothing made me want to do that."

"Okay, Suga. I ain't trying to scare you, but I think you been in labor since last night. If that's so, you could be about to have this baby, and with none of the menfolk here, we don't have no time to get you to a hospital. By the time the ambulance get here, you gone be done had this baby," Mrs. Althea said. "I need to take a look down there and check you, okay?"

Suga nodded as she tried to breathe steadily.

Mrs. Althea took the end of Suga's dress and hiked it up to her waist. Suga was wearing panties, so Mrs. Althea pulled them to the side. I was scared but curious and stood right over Mrs. Althea's shoulder. When Suga's flower came into full view, I thought I was going to pass out. It was swollen ,and her skin looked impossibly stretched and angry. I could see the shape of the head pressing on her body from the inside, but only a little bit of dark, curly hair was visible within the parting of the folds.

"We gonna have to do this here and now. Bernadette, go call the ambulance. Mouse, go grab all the towels you can find in this house. I'm gonna go grab some gloves and the plastic cover for the dining table. Suga, you just sit here and breathe as slow and deep as you can. You don't push until I get back and tell you to. Not a minute before."

Mrs. Althea had taken command like she was running a ship.

Suga nodded. Tears welled up in her eyes, threatening to fall. Mrs. Althea took notice that she was afraid.

"Don't you worry, Suga. This ain't my first time bringing a child into this world. My grandmother was a midwife. I ain't done it in awhile, since hospitals done got more and more friendly for black folk, but I been seeing chil'ren into this world since I was twelve. I won't let nothing happen to you or that little boy. Don't you be scared."

Mrs. Althea nodded her head to reassure Suga. She mimicked a nod while inhaling and exhaling slowly. She was readying herself for what was ahead.

I was frightened. Ray wasn't here, and Suga looked like an alien was trying to exit her body from between her legs.

As Mrs. Althea and I both headed out of the room, she pulled me to the side.

"You think you can get in touch with your daddy?"

"I can call Mr. Hamilton and ask him to check to see if he's home yet," I answered.

"Good. If he ain't, tell Mr. Hamilton to leave him a note that this baby is coming tonight and to get over here as soon as he can."

I made it to the phone mounted to the wall right outside of the kitchen just as Ms. Bernadette was hanging up from calling the ambulance. I dialed Mr. Hamilton's number.

"Hello," Mr. Hamilton grumbled.

"Hello, Mr. Hamilton. This is Mouse."

"Do you know what time it is? Why are you calling here at this hour?" he said gruffly.

"Mr. Hamilton, Suga and I are at the Alexanders' house, and Suga is in labor. The baby is coming now. We don't even have time to get her to the hospital. Can you see if my father is over in the apartment?"

"Oh! Yes, just give me one minute."

I heard the phone drop and scurrying sounds in the house. I heard Mr. Hamilton ask himself where his shoes were. I heard his back door open and close. The following silence seemed like it lasted for an eternity. When he finally returned, I heard him shuffling over to the phone.

"He's not there, Mouse, but I have an idea where he might be. I'll get a message to him and tell him to get on over there as soon as possible."

"Thank you, sir."

I hung up the phone and ran to find the towels. By the time I had gathered all of them, Mrs. Althea and Ms. Bernadette had gotten Suga onto the plastic cover. She was on the floor, propped up by pillows and cushions piled up underneath the plastic. Her underwear had been removed, and her legs were spread wide apart. Ms. Bernadette was behind her holding her steady, and each of her feet were propped up in a dining chair.

"Now, Suga, the next time you feel that hard cramping, I want you to bear down and push like you trying to take a poop. You hear me?" Mrs. Althea commanded.

Suga nodded. Her face was beginning to bead with sweat.

"I feel one coming," she growled through gritted teeth.

"Then push!" Mrs. Althea yelled.

Suga made the most God-awful guttural sound I'd ever heard. She sounded like something you'd hear in a scary movie. I sat mesmerized, holding the towel Mrs. Althea had given me to catch the baby in.

Suga's flower looked even more stretched, and a small head was beginning to protrude from the opening. My stomach began churning. Mrs. Althea looked at me and shook her head.

"Mouse, I know you never seen nothing like this before, but you gotta stay strong. You can't pass out or throw up your guts. We don't have time for that. If you can't handle helping me on this end, switch sides with Bernadette."

Ms. Bernadette's eyes stretched to the size of saucers. She didn't want to be on the receiving end any more than I did.

I shook my head and took a deep breath.

Suga began to pant. Mrs. Althea raised the back of her hand to Suga's forehead. A look of concern briefly washed over her face.

"Okay, Suga. We need another big push. When you feel the next contraction coming, you tell me, and we gone push together," Mrs. Althea said, looking Suga deep into her eyes.

"I can't do this, Mrs. Althea," Suga began to cry.

"You sure can. That little lady holding you up back there is here because I could, and if I could, so can you," Mrs. Althea encouraged.

"I can't," Suga whimpered.

"You got to," she told Suga.

"You can do it, Suga," Ms. Bernadette said, using a cool wet rag to wipe Suga's forehead.

"You can do it, Suga," I echoed.

Suga looked at me, and I nodded my head. She nodded back and took a deep breath.

"Another one is coming," Suga squealed in a high-pitched voice.

Mrs. Althea raised up on her knees and leaned forward.

"Push!" she yelled.

As Suga pushed with all her might, Mrs. Althea laid her forearm across Suga's lower belly. She applied pressure at the same time Suga pushed. When she looked back down, the head was out.

Mrs. Althea rocked back onto her legs. She took her hands and gently eased them inside of Suga, pulling the jelly-like mass of a baby out of Suga's body. She put the baby on the towel I was holding. She stuck her gloved finger in the baby's mouth and wiped around, then she wiped the face and used q-tips to clean out the nostrils.

The baby was quiet and unmoving.

"Why my baby ain't crying?" Suga asked, panic in her voice.

Mrs. Althea kept working silently. She gently flipped the baby forward onto her left hand and she rubbed the baby's back fiercely with her right.

"C'mon, little boy. C'mon, little boy," she whispered over and over again.

Finally, the sound came. Ms. Bernadette and I breathed a sigh of relief. Suga began to cry. Mrs. Althea beamed with joy and pride.

She wrapped the baby like a sandwich, with the umbilical cord hanging out from the bottom, and passed him to Suga.

"Here's your precious baby boy. Say 'hi' to your momma, little one," Mrs. Althea cooed.

He was still hollering when she placed him on top of Suga's stomach. She rocked back on her legs and sat and watched mother and son for a moment.

The doorbell rang. I ran to the door and peeked out through the side window. It was Ray. I opened the door and he came rushing in.

"Where Suga?" he asked in a frenzy.

"She's in the living room."

He rushed past me. When he saw Suga and the baby, he fell down beside her and looked at the baby in her arms with amazement.

"My baby boy," he said.

We sat around and stared at the three of them until the emergency rescue team arrived. They finished up by allowing Ray to cut the umbilical cord and helped Suga to push this gross lump of stuff into a bucket before loading her up into the ambulance. Ray jumped into the ambulance with her.

"Ray, Mouse can stay here as long as need be. We'll take good care of her," Mrs. Althea told him.

"Thank you. And thank you for all you done to get my boy here safe," he told her with tears in his eyes.

"It was no problem at all. I'm glad something told me to get them over here tonight, or they..." Mrs. Althea's voice trailed off. "I'm just glad I was with her and was able to help. Been a long time since I had to do that, but it felt good."

Mrs. Althea, Ms. Bernadette, and I spent the next couple of hours marveling over the miracle of birth while we cleaned up the mess the miracle had made. While watching my little brother being born was beautiful and was something I would never forget, I didn't think I ever wanted to go through that again, not even to have my own child.

The next afternoon, Jimmie came over and took the three of us to the hospital to check on Suga and the baby. Ray was asleep in the lounge chair next to the bed, and Suga had the baby up to her breast.

"There they are!" Mrs. Althea said excitedly.

"Hey, y'all," Suga said.

She looked worn out. Her hair was all about her head, her eyes were puffy, and she looked a weird kind of swollen. Different than the swollen she'd looked while she was pregnant. I walked around to the other side of the bed and gave her a hug. I looked down at the baby. His eyes were closed, but he was sucking hard at her nipple.

"He's a hungry little something," she informed us. "He weighed in at eight pounds and three ounces and was twenty-one inches long! Mouse, I told you he was gonna be strong."

Suga beamed as Ms. Bernadette placed the flowers we'd brought on the small nightstand between Ray's chair and the bed. He didn't even stir when she passed by him.

"My goodness, he sure is beautiful. You decided what you gonna name him?" Ms. Bernadette asked.

"Ray, Jr. R.J. for short," Suga said with a smile.

Suga and R.J. were released from the hospital three days before Christmas. Since neither one of them would be able to leave the house for a few weeks at least, Mrs. Althea sent Christmas dinner to our house early. The whole family sent one gift for each of us. Ray pretended he didn't care about the socks he'd received, but Suga and I loved our bags filled with fruit and nuts and our beautifully embroidered handkerchiefs. R.J. received a cute little stuffed teddy bear.

Though Ray and I would never be what we were before we left Mapelwood, I longed for the love and adoration he showed R.J. Every time he beamed while looking at R.J., I remembered how he'd once looked at me. It reminded me of the man he used to be, and I hoped for R.J.'s sake he could truly be that man again.

Eleven

It was an adjustment getting used to the wake-ups every two hours. Suga and I hopped to action whenever R.J. cried, fumbling and stumbling around in the dark. Ray's early mornings didn't lend themselves to being up all night. He slept right through the crying, feeding, burping, changing, and rocking back to sleep. Suga had to breastfeed, so there was no sleeping through for her. Sometimes, once she'd feed R.J., I would tell her to go back to sleep, and I would burp and change him. Then, I'd lay there and run my fingers through his dark, curly hair until he fell back to sleep. I'd put him back in the crib and try to sleep until the next feeding. I was in love with him from the moment I held him, so I didn't mind the sleepless nights.

Ms. Bernadette minded my sleepless nights; they were beginning to catch up to me in school. She didn't punish me for my nodding off or embarrass me when I'd fall asleep. She'd just call my name and tell me to see her after class. She'd ask me how we were all doing once all of the other children were out of the classroom. She even offered to let me come stay over at her house a couple of nights just so I could get some rest, but I told her I would be okay. There was no way I could leave Suga to deal with R.J. all by herself.

Besides, R.J. was so cute, and he was such a sweet baby. I didn't want to be away from him. I was content to watch over him like a good big sister, though I had expected a new baby brother to be more exciting. I thought he would smile and laugh at my silly faces, but most times, he didn't really seem to actually see me. Half the time he looked cross-eyed. Ms. Bernadette had to explain to me that it takes a while for a baby's eyes to focus. After the newness wore off, I was too exhausted to worry about excitement. I almost felt like I'd had a baby too. Tired or not, I did my best to help Suga care for him. Even through sleepless nights, I kissed him, rubbed his tummy, and wrapped him up so he wouldn't catch cold in our drafty apartment.

The only thing I hated about caring for R.J. was those cloth diapers. They were a lot of work. The pee-pee diapers weren't so bad, but his poopy diapers were the worst. Suga washed most of the soiled ones during the day. If there were any dirty diapers when I got home, I would wash them so we'd never run out. I'd have to scrub them extra hard because we had to use a milder detergent on his clothing.

Suga was in her own world with R.J. She talked with Ray and me on the off chance she was awake outside of feeding the baby. The only time he wasn't superglued to her was when she just needed to rest and me or Ray took him off her hands. He would whine and whimper for a while but would eventually calm. I wanted him to feel connected to me in that way, but I knew it was a different kind of bond. He would love me, but never the way he loved Suga. I understood why the bond was different each time I watched her breastfeed. She was so loving and tender with him. It was the only part of the process that made me think that having a child of my own one day wouldn't be so bad.

When our days began to feel normal, we began to have visitors. All of the Alexanders came by to see Suga and the baby. Jimmie and Mr. Hamilton visited, and Mr. Hamilton brought over a cute blanket that had animals on it. All the men had spoken to R.J. in that baby talk voice, but none of them wanted to hold a baby that small.

Mrs. Richardson and Julia even came to see R.J. They brought a small play toy for R.J. and some groceries for Suga and me. Julia sat perched on the edge of the couch, like you would do when visiting someone's house that was nasty. Our home was clean, so her behavior annoyed me. I wondered when she'd changed from the girl who didn't mind playing in the dirt with me to this snooty white girl.

Any hopes I had of the two of us making up were dashed.

Mrs. Althea was over every time she got a chance. She couldn't get enough of R.J. I could tell she was working hard not to intrude on our bonding with him, but she wanted her own close connection with him as well. On the last Saturday of Suga's house arrest, Mrs. Althea and Ms. Bernadette came by and sat with us. R.J. was laying on the makeshift pallet we'd made out of blankets.

"Suga, what you gone do with R.J. when you go back to work on Monday?" Mrs. Althea asked.

I already knew where this was headed. She'd picked a perfect time for the conversation because Ray was out working overtime.

"I ain't decided, Mrs. Althea. He still on breastmilk, and when he ready to eat, he ready to eat. He can get mighty worked up when I'm taking too long. I don't know if Mrs. Richardson is gonna want a crying baby around the house," Suga responded. "We was trying to put him on formula, but he don't seem to like it."

"Oh, I got a trick for that. You got a pump, right?" Mrs. Althea asked.

"Yes, ma'am," Suga said with a nod.

"Pump your milk and start mixing the formula with the milk when you feeding him. Just put less and less breast milk in every time until you giving him all formula."

"Okay, I'll try that," Suga said happily.

"If you want, I can keep him. He's such a good baby, it won't be any trouble at all," Mrs. Althea volunteered.

"How much would you charge us?" Suga asked.

"Nothing!"

Mrs. Althea almost shouted as if she was offended.

"No, Ray ain't gonna allow that. We gone have to pay you something."

"Well, y'all figure out what you can pay, and that will be just fine with me," Mrs. Althea finally said after some thought. "Y'all come by tomorrow afternoon and have dinner, and we'll iron out the particulars."

"Yes, ma'am."

We waited until we thought the Alexanders were home from church before we headed over for dinner. Jimmie was back on post, so we had to walk. R.J. was bundled up with so much material, you almost couldn't see his round little face. The rest of us bundled up as best as we could. I felt like a popsicle by the time we made it to the house.

"Oh, y'all get on out of this cold and warm up! I've got some tea already on," Mrs. Althea fussed.

While she was fussing, she was reaching for R.J. He wasn't old enough to reach back, but his eyes traced every inch of Mrs. Althea's face. He didn't cry or recoil. He was satisfied to be taken from his mother by her. Suga kissed him on the cheek before handing him over.

"Hey, Ray. Hey, Mouse!"

Mrs. Althea wanted to make sure we did not feel overlooked for her affection.

"Hey, Mrs. Althea," we said in unison.

She looked back at the two of us and chuckled.

Ms. Bernadette was in the kitchen, and Mr. Kenneth was seated at the table. They greeted us, and Mrs. Althea took R.J. over for Mr. Kenneth to look at him.

"Hey, there little boy," Mr. Kenneth said in his deep baritone.

R.J.'s head turned to find the sound.

Ms. Bernadette came in and snuck a kiss on his cheek. Even though I loved R.J., I felt a little like he was stealing away the people who loved me. Ms. Bernadette must have picked up on my feelings because she came and hugged me and kissed me on the cheek as well. I smiled and hugged her back.

"Wash up, everyone, and let's eat," Mrs. Bernadette announced.

We all washed our hands and took our seats. R.J. was nestled into some pillows and blankets on the floor so that we could all eat without trying to hold him. He was content, peacefully cooing so that we'd look up from time to time to talk to him.

Ray began the conversation about R.J.'s care.

"Well, Mrs. Althea, we figured out a price for you to watch R.J. during the week while I'm at work."

"Now, Ray, just so you know, I told Suga it wasn't necessary, but she said you would insist," Mrs. Althea stated.

"Suga was right. Johnsons don't depend on nothing and nobody but themselves. I don't want nobody to ever be able to say I owe them nothin'."

Ray spoke boldly, proud of his resolve.

"Well, alright then."

Mrs. Althea lips were pursed and her eyes were slightly squinted. Everyone knew it wasn't Mrs. Althea's way to hold anything over anybody.

"We can pay you twenty-five dollars a month to watch R.J. We'll make sure he has milk and clean diapers each morning when he dropped off."

"That sounds just fine, Ray. It is my pleasure to watch that little one, but I won't say the extra money won't help us out around here."

I had watched Mrs. Althea long enough to know when she was helping things along. She always seemed to get just what she wanted, all the while her intended target thought they'd come up with the idea.

"Alright, that's settled. Suga, you deal with drop-off and pick-up. Mouse, you can come here straight from school and wait with R.J. for Suga to get off."

Ray was really confident that he was running the show.

"Alright, Ray," Suga said with a side glance in his direction.

"Yessir," I responded.

We enjoyed the rest of the meal talking about other things. We sat around with the Alexanders for a couple of hours, then we headed home to prepare for the week.

Ray went for a nap, taking R.J. with him. Suga and I prepared for the next day. She stopped and looked at me as I was ironing my clothes for school.

"Mouse, I don't know what I'd do without you. You been such a help to me in this past month, and I don't even know if I even once said thank you. Some days I'm so tired, I don't know if I'm coming or going. Your daddy help as much as he can, but you there even when I tell you I'm fine."

I didn't know what to do or how to respond. I kept ironing.

"I know you ain't my child, but don't you never think R.J. is taking your place. I love that little boy more than life itself, but I love you like that too."

My throat felt like it was closing. I held back the tears and managed a nod. We finished the rest of our preparation in peace and quiet, enjoying the little time we had before the nighttime feedings would begin.

Twelve

R.J. was four months old by the time spring was in full swing. Suga had started adding cereal to the milk because breastfeeding and formula wasn't holding him anymore. He was turning into a little cherub as a result. His face was rounding out and his little arms and legs were getting folds. I was amazed at how much he had grown and changed in such a short period of time. I was so mesmerized by everything about him, I almost didn't notice how much the town and its people were gearing up for the upcoming event.

Hemings was alive with the activity of preparing for the festival. Suga was baking apple pies at both the Richardsons' and at home, though she was only credited with the latter. Mr. Alexander was using his truck to help haul wood downtown for the repairing of old festival booths and building of new ones. Mrs. Althea was constantly mixing some kind of batter for one good thing to eat or another. I'd get to smell a different treat every day when I got to her house after school. It was torture not to be able to taste the end result. The sweet, lemony scent of her pound cake batter made my mouth water.

Our side of town was especially excited because this would be the first year that black folks were allowed to participate in the festival from beginning to end. We were usually left to enjoy Sunday after church according to Ms. Bernadette. That meant most of the good food and prizes were long gone, and we would be left with the scraps. Jimmie thought we were being included as a way to keep us quiet about integrating the schools.

Ms. Bernadette tasked me with helping her make the paper flowers for the church's float, which meant work for my little hands just like everyone else's.

"Here, Mouse. Let me show you how to make these. First, you need two-ply toilet paper. Tear off about three squares and fold it accordion-style, lengthwise. Like this. See?"

Ms. Bernadette looked at me for confirmation, and I nodded slowly.

"Once you have it completely folded, tie it in the center with a twist tie. Lastly, pull the layers of the toilet paper apart, and voila!" she exclaimed, proudly holding up her paper masterpiece.

"That's really neato! How'd you learn how to make these?" I asked.

"Years of working on floats," she said with a tilt of her head and a roll of her eyes. "Do you think you can handle making these until your hands cramp up?"

"Sure," I responded, nodding my head.

Ms. Bernadette sat with me and worked just as hard, checking my work along the way. She was pleased with the flowers I was turning out. We only took the occasional break for snacks and for Jimmie to come and tease us, like he was going to destroy all of our hard work.

By the end of the evening, I was miserable, and my hands hurt from all that delicate work. We gathered the flowers gently and put them in big containers. Ms. Bernadette would carry the flowers to her church in the morning, where they would begin the work of attaching the flowers to chicken wire that would be connected to the old truck they would be using. She'd explained the whole process, much to my disinterest. I didn't want to see another piece of toilet paper any time soon, not even to wipe my own tail.

Ms. Bernadette and Jimmie dropped me off at home. Suga and R.J. had already made it to the house, but Ray was not there yet.

As soon as I walked in, R.J. started cooing, kicking his legs, and waving his arms.

"Lawd, this boy loves his sissy," Suga said with a smile.

"I love him, too," I said as I walked over to him. "Hey, R.J.! How was your day today? Did you miss me?"

R.J. squealed with delight as I tickled his fat little tummy. He was such a happy baby. All I wished for was that his life would never know moments like mine had. I wished for him to have Suga for as long as he needed her. Even though our father treated him differently, I didn't hold it against him.

"You want me to take him and give him a bath?" I asked Suga.

"Yeah, this little boy want me to sit and talk to him all day like you do. I gotta finish cooking dinner 'fo yo' daddy get home," Suga replied.

I took R.J. and propped him on my budding left hip as I went to the bathroom to run some water in the sink. R.J. wasn't big enough to put in the tub yet.

I gathered his wash rag, soap, and towel. I checked the temperature of the water with my elbow to make sure it wasn't too hot, like Mrs. Althea had shown me. Mrs. Althea had shown me and Suga lots of things about tending to R.J. Suga only knew a little more than I did about babies.

When the water was the right temperature, I pushed the stopper in so that warm soapy water could fill the bowl. As the water rose, I took off R.J.'s clothes and Pamper. He watched my every move with old, wise eyes.

"My R.J. loves bath time. My R.J. loves bath time," I sang to him.

He smiled, and I smiled back. I loved when Suga had too much to do and asked me to give him a bath. It was our own special time. Sometimes, if Ray got home at a decent hour, he would take over. I preferred when our special time was uninterrupted.

I spread out R.J.'s towel on the counter and laid him on top of it. I dipped the wash rag into the warm water, squeezed it out, and wiped him down from head to toe, rewetting and wringing the rag as needed. I wiped eagerly but carefully under his chubby chin, in the folds of his arms and legs, and in between his cute little toes. I turned him over and wiped down his back and bottom as well.

Once I wiped him down again with regular warm water, I dried him off, rubbed him down with a light coat of Vaseline, and put a little powder on his chest. He was already beginning to fall asleep when I handed him back to Suga for his last feeding of the night.

I watched intently as she fed him. Suga had to keep rubbing his cheek to stimulate him to suckle at her breast. By the time she put him up on her shoulder to burp, Ray was walking in the house.

"There's my boy!" he exclaimed.

"Ray!" Suga whispered loudly. "I swear, if you wind this boy back up, you gone be up with him all night."

Suga issued her threat with squinted eyes. Ray knew she meant business. He walked around Suga so he could look R.J. in the face. He leaned over and gave him a kiss on the cheek.

"I'm going to go wash up before I eat dinner."

He kissed Suga on the cheek.

"Hey, Mouse," he said as he went into the bathroom.

I didn't even bother to return the greeting. He wasn't really listening for it anyway. Since the baby had come, he only acknowledged me from time to time.

Suga looked over at me with disappointment. I knew she felt bad for me. She'd grown to love me, and I had grown to love her. She didn't understand our dynamic, Ray and me. As long as she didn't know the whole truth of how we'd come to meet her in the first place, she never would.

It was Friday and finally time for the real fun to begin. I didn't know what to expect because I'd never been to anything like it before. It was like a holiday—no school, and most businesses closed early so families could enjoy the activities. Ray, Suga, and I walked the couple of blocks to be in the heart of all that was happening. R.J. was alternated between Suga's hip and Ray's arm as we headed up the few blocks to the entrance.

All the local churches, organizations, small businesses, and individual craftsmen had booths. The main road was closed to traffic, and the various booths lined either side of the street, settled pretty close to one another. The smell of fried food was the first temptation to hit our senses, even though the food vendors began somewhere in the middle of the whole set-up. The trinkets, art, jewelry, clothing, and accessories were the first booths we encountered. I'd already been warned not to touch anything because we could not afford to buy any of the stuff they were selling. We kept a steady pace moving as quickly as we could around people who'd stopped to touch a fabric or ask about the price of an object.

A sparkly wind chime with sea creatures caught my attention as we walked through. I thought of Nana Margie's porch and wished she could have met R.J. Of course, if she hadn't passed, there wouldn't have been an R.J.

As we entered the section with the food options, my eyes grew big at all of the choices. There was seafood, BBQ, soul food, burgers, pizza, corn dogs, smoked turkey legs, and sweets galore. Everybody had special prices, and every sign indicated what that booth had was the best, or the most famous, or the award-winning recipe. I wanted to eat my way down the entire street.

"Let's walk all the way through and see what they got before we spend any money," Ray told Suga.

Suga nodded, and we all kept walking. I spotted the First Baptist booth, and my eyes landed on a slice of Mrs. Althea's famous red velvet cake. I already knew she'd baked five of them for the festival and hadn't even kept one for the house, which meant there hadn't been any tasting done by me. Not even bowl drippings. My mouth began to water just thinking about that cake. I'd only tasted it once, and that was all I needed to know Mrs. Althea had the best red velvet cake ever. I nudged Suga and pointed over to the First Baptist booth. Again, Suga nodded. I'd found her to be my greatest ally in getting things I wanted. She had a way of dealing with Ray that had stopped working for me the moment we left Maplewood.

We made our way toward the rear of the festival. The dunk tank, due to the watery mess it made, was at the back. We managed to make it to the tank for Jimmie's shift. Apparently, he'd already been dunked a few times. His blue and white t-shirt, with some type of bird on it, was soaked and sticking to his body, and his swim trunks were plastered to his thighs. He sat perched on the bench, hovering just above the water, taunting anyone who dared throw baseballs at the red-and-white target on the side of the tank. Ray bought three tries to dunk him at fifty cents a turn, but failed each time. We stayed there until he was able to see someone dunk Jimmie. He had a good laugh when Jimmie finally hit the water.

When Jimmie's shift was over in the dunk tank, he caught up with us. By that time, we'd shared a couple of hot dogs and a slice of Mrs. Althea's cake. Jimmie bobbed for apples and won a stuffed bear for R.J. and a yo-yo for me. I had no idea how to use a yo-yo. Ms. Bernadette was missing all the fun, but she was preparing for the parade.

I caught a glimpse of red hair out of the corner of my eye. I turned in the direction of the flash, and there was Julia. She was with Mr. and Mrs. Richardson. They waved at Suga, and she headed their way with R.J. I stayed back with Jimmie. Julia looked in my direction but did not wave or smile at me.

Though everyone was allowed out at the same time, you could tell which sections were for which groups. The booths had been smartly laid out so that there would not be much mingling. The food booths seemed to be the neutral zone, where color didn't matter; only hunger.

"Hey, Mouse. You wanna go find a good spot to see Bernadette in the parade?" Jimmie asked.

"Yeah," I chirped.

Jimmie and I walked along the parade route until we found a section where the two of us could stand in the very front.

"You get all the good candy when you're up front," Jimmie confided in me.

The parade was kicked off by the mayor speaking over the loudspeaker at the main stage platform.

"Welcome one and all to the Hemings Spring Festival! I'm Mayor Birch, and we're gonna kick things off with our annual parade! The whole town has been working hard on these beautiful floats, and I know my wife and her friends have been baking their pretty little heads off for y'all to have wonderful goodies to eat. Come on over to the dunk tank and see if you can drown me for fifty cents, why don't ya'! Have fun at this year's festival, folks!" the mayor shouted with joy.

That was the band's cue. The drum major blew his whistle to signal the band to play, and the parade was off to its start. The floats were all so pretty. When the First Baptist Church float came into view, I felt pride well up in me. Not only were the flowers I'd made beautiful on Mr. Thomas' truck, but Ms. Bernadette looked like an angel. She was seated on something chair-like that was covered in soft and fuzzy white fabric. Her dress was white, and she wore a long sheer white shawl that lifted gently in the breeze of the truck's slow movement. Her hair was in loose curls, and she had on a tiara that sparkled in the sunlight. She wore a white sash with blue glittery letters that read "Miss First Baptist" diagonally across her body. Sandra, one of the small children Ms. Bernadette taught in Sunday school, sat on a smaller version of the same covered chair with a smaller version of the same outfit, and her sash said, "Little Miss First Baptist."

Mr. Alexander was on the back of the float tossing out handfuls of candy. When he spotted Jimmy and me, he tossed two handfuls our way. Jimmie and I grabbed up as much as we could before a swarm of nearby children came to collect their portion.

I checked my bag, and I'd grabbed some of the best candy. There were pieces of Bit O' Honey, Peanut Butter Bars, Pixie Sticks, SweeTarts, Now & Laters, and I even got an Astro Pop. I had a few small boxes of Swedish Fish, which I would give to anyone who wanted them. I couldn't for the life of me understand why anyone liked those nasty candies. If R.J. was old enough, I'd share with him, but he hadn't even cut his first tooth yet.

Once the parade was finished, Jimmie walked me back over to Ray and Suga.

"I'm gonna go catch up with Bernadette, Mouse. We'll come find y'all."

"Okay, Jimmie," I replied.

Ray, Suga, and I walked around for hours, enjoying the blinking lights, the bells and whistles, and the smell of all the wonderful eats that engulfed us. It was overwhelming but exhilarating at the same time. Whenever R.J. became fussy, Suga would take him off-a-ways from all that stimulation and either cover up and feed him or try to rock him into calm. He was easy enough to soothe.

By late afternoon, we'd spent all the money Ray intended to spend on food. But when Suga saw the funnel cake stand, her eyes grew big. I'd never had one, but it looked like a treat we just shouldn't walk away from.

"You want one?"

Ray looked at both of us. Suga and I both nodded.

Ray strode over to the stand and ordered one funnel cake. Suga and I waited patiently as they cooked the batter to order and sprinkled it with powdered sugar while it was still hot. Ray came back with the sweet treat, and we found a picnic table to enjoy the sticky mess it would make of our fingers. For a brief moment, we felt like a real family. Ray was even nice to me and made sure I'd eaten as much of the funnel cake as I'd wanted.

Mr. Kenneth, Mrs. Althea, Ms. Bernadette, and Jimmie found us as we were finishing up our dessert.

"Well, we'll leave the rest of this for you young folk. Suga and Ray, y'all want us to take little R.J. with us?" Mrs. Althea asked.

Suga looked at Ray. He gave a slight nod, and Suga happily handed R.J. over to Mrs. Althea.

Suga didn't have many breaks from being a new mommy. I helped out where I could, but between school and homework, I wasn't able to be as much help as I would have liked.

Since we wouldn't have to worry about getting R.J. to sleep, that left the five of us able to stay out for the fireworks show.

"Let's go back toward the center of downtown. That's where we'll get the best view of the fireworks," Jimmie suggested.

We all followed his lead, even Ray.

About a block away from where we were headed, Ms. Bernadette noticed an odd little tent. I had been by this spot at least three times that day and hadn't noticed it. The tent was red-and-white striped, with a poorly-carved wooden sign above the opening that read, "Pearl's Palm Readings, $1.00."

"Let's go in there, Jimmie," Ms. Bernadette said, grabbing Jimmie by the arm.

Jimmie looked skeptical.

Suga looked at Ray.

"Unh unh! I ain't wasting perfectly good money for some crazy woman to shake a chicken foot at me and tell me some stuff I already know!"

"I think I sense a couple of chickens, alright," Ms. Bernadette said.

Suga laughed and nudged Ray, who responded by squinting his eyes. He didn't like being called a chicken.

"Ain't nobody chicken. Them people are rip-offs. They can't a bit more tell the future than me. Hell, even a broke clock right twice a day. Half that crap they guess," Ray argued.

"Well, there's nothing to be afraid of then. I'll even pay the dollar for you and Suga," Ms. Bernadette said.

What did she go and say that for? Ray saw no other choice but to prove he wasn't afraid.

I was.

"We can pay our own dollar. C'mon, Suga. Let's get this mess over with."

Ray stormed into the tent.

We all followed close behind. Inside, seated at a small wooden table was a woman of average size. Her skin was an ashy reddish-brown and looked paper thin. Her hair was wrapped up in a beautifully-colored silk scarf, but there were long, silver tendrils hanging down from the sides and back of it. She wore a gold necklace with coin-sized medallions hanging from it. Her clothes were long and flowing. The tent was dim, but her eyes were bright. Candles were placed all around the tent, casting the most odd shadows around the makeshift room.

"C'meah," the woman waved us forward. "My name Ms. Pearl, seer and conduit of dem dat gone on. What message from dem you ah seek?" she asked.

Ray pointed at Ms. Bernadette to pay her dollar and go first. Ms. Bernadette began to dig in her purse for the dollar, but Jimmie pulled one out of his pocket and leaned forward to hand it to Ms. Pearl. She motioned him to drop it in the empty glass bowl sitting off to her right.

Ms. Pearl pointed for Ms. Bernadette to take a seat in the chair directly across from her. Ms.

Bernadette took the seat as instructed. Ms. Pearl reached across the table with her hands, palms up. Ms. Bernadette followed suit. Ms. Pearl took and inspected each, turning them so she could see clearly.

"De left hand show me what God plan is. De right show me where you be 'pon de path he set down before you. See heya?" Ms. Pearl asked Ms. Bernadette as she pointed to a line on her left palm. "Dis heya show me God planned fuh you to help chil'ren. Dis line heya show me you 'posed to have two of yo' own wid de love of yo' life," Ms. Pearl said softly.

Ms. Bernadette looked over at Jimmie, who was grinning from ear to ear.

Ray began fidgeting. Ms. Pearl had gotten one thing right, and I was sure that was making him nervous.

Ms. Pearl took Ms. Bernadette's right hand.

"Ah," she said with a chuckle. "So you do work wid chil'ren. You teach?"

Ms. Bernadette nodded with amazement.

"He gwan breed you soon," Ms. Pearl nodded towards Jimmie. "Firs' baby come in a year or two."

"How can you see that from lines in my palm?" Ms. Bernadette asked in shock.

"Same way you kin look 'pon de chile and know what it need widdout it evah tell you," Ms. Pearl responded.

Ms. Bernadette's eyes grew soft with understanding.

"Dey'll be a time of separation 'tween you and yo' loved one, but it won't be long. Things will be diff'ent, but diff'ent don't mean bad," Ms. Pearl continued.

"Separation? Why would we be separated?" Ms. Bernadette said with alarm rising in her voice.

"I can't tell all dat from yo' hand. I'm just preparing you for what I see. I might could tell from his, but anything else you wanna know gwan cost you another dollar," Ms. Pearl said sternly.

Ms. Bernadette withdrew her hands from Ms. Pearl and stood up from the table. It seemed she was now unsure of the decision she'd made to come into this tent. She looked over at Ray and stretched her eyes.

Ray motioned for Suga to sit in the seat, but she shook her head violently. He motioned for me to sit. I knew from his glare there was no way he was sitting in the chair, and leaving without any of our family getting our palms read was out of the question.

I sat in the chair, and he passed one dollar to Jimmie to drop in the jar.

"Well, ain'chu precious," Ms. Pearl said with a smile.

Her mouth was full of empty spaces.

"Gimme yo' hands," she said as she reached across the table.

When she touched my hands, her body jerked as if a bolt of electricity had gone through it. I jumped back, trying to take my hands with me, but her grip was too strong. Her eyes rolled into the back of her head and then her head dropped backwards.

After one horrifying moment of the rest of us looking around at one another, her head lifted slowly. She turned her gaze slowly until her eyes rested on Ray.

"You haven't done right by Mouse, Ray."

It couldn't be. Surely the sound I thought I heard coming from Ms. Pearl's mouth was a hallucination. My mind had to have been playing tricks on me. All these years I'd tried hard to remember the sound of my mother's voice and had failed. As soon as Ms. Pearl spoke, I remembered. It was almost as if her voice had never left. Tears started stinging my eyes, but I refused to cry. I had to focus on the rest of what she would say.

Everyone's attention turned to Ray. His eyes grew to the size of baseballs, and he started sweating and breathing heavily.

"You took me from my baby. A girl child has a tough time learning to be a woman without her mother. That won't go unanswered, Ray."

It was like Ms. Pearl was a ventriloquist's dummy, and Momma was somewhere in the great beyond, pulling her strings.

Ms. Pearl turned her head toward me, and when I looked in her eyes, I gasped. It was my mother's gaze looking back at me. I felt as if my head was swimming. I thought I was about to faint, but Ms. Pearl held me steady.

"You're such a strong girl, Mouse. I'm so proud of you, my love. I've watched you since you left Maplewood. Ms. Janie, Mr. Earl, and Ms.

Sookie took good care of you. I made sure of it. I'm always with you. I'm always with you," the voice said sweetly.

With that, Ms. Pearl released my hands, and her whole body slumped down into her chair. Everyone was frozen.

Ms. Pearl slowly seemed to regain her own consciousness. Once she was able to gather herself, she turned and looked at Ray.

"Leave dis heya tent and donchu nevah come back."

Then she turned to me and said, "You couldna save her. You was too lil', and it weren't fa you to do. You 'pose to be who you 'pose to be 'cause of wha' happen to ya."

Her voice was raspy and dry, like that of a chain smoker. She got up from the table and walked into a room in the back. She did not return.

"I told y'all this was a buncha bullshit!" Ray yelled.

I sat quietly. I wanted to savor the sound of my mother's voice as long as I could.

Suga seemed to be shrinking away from Ray. Jimmie grabbed Ms. Bernadette by the hand and began to pull her out of the tent. I was stuck to the chair.

"What she talmbout, Ray?" Suga asked.

"Suga, I know you don't believe that shit," he said accusingly.

"What she talmbout, Ray?" Suga asked again louder, her voice quivering.

Suga stood, her body visibly shaking. I could not tell if it was fear, anger, or some other unrecognizable emotion that had taken hold of her.

"I ain't defending myself from no half-crazy old woman!" Ray screamed.

"It's the truth," I said without knowing I would.

The sound of my own voice had startled me. I looked over at Suga.

"He killed her. He shot her because he was drunk and mad and jealous of a man who didn't mean no more to my momma than a friend would. Right in the head. I saw it myself, with my own two eyes."

It felt as if a fifty-pound weight had been lifted from my shoulders. They straightened in reaction to the lightness.

Suga grabbed both sides of her face and screamed. She turned and ran out of the tent.

"You a liar! You always been a liar!" Ray yelled at me.

"No, you've always been the liar. Making up a new name and a story about our lives as if it was nothing at all. Like she never existed. I tried to forget what happened. I tried to forget her. I figured one awful parent was better than no parent at all, but I can't keep hiding the truth of what you did to my momma. You should pay for killing her," I said quietly.

"You shot my mother, while I watched from the doorway of y'all's bedroom. I watched the life drain out of her, and you wiped me off and put fresh clothes on me like it was nothing," I said with my voice cracking halfway through. "What kind of person does that?"

I waited for an answer. When none came, I resigned myself to never really understanding what could have driven him that far. I stood up, feeling like my behind had been released from the chair. A calm I hadn't felt since before the awful day of my mother's murder laid itself gently on my back. I felt able to breathe easier. I inhaled deeply, turned, and walked out of the tent.

Suga was nowhere in sight, but Ms. Bernadette and Jimmie were right there waiting on me. It was clear they'd heard what I'd said to Suga by the looks on their faces. They grabbed me and headed straight toward Jimmie's car. No one asked any questions, and no one pressed me to talk during the walk to the car. Ms. Bernadette and I sat inside the car in silence while Jimmie went to talk to his police officer buddy.

"Is that why that car backfiring at the lake frightened you the way it did?" Ms. Bernadette asked while we waited for Jimmie.

I nodded.

"I'm so sorry, Mouse. How long ago did this happen?"

"I was seven-and-a-half."

"So, you two have been moving from town to town ever since?"

Ms. Bernadette looked like she was in shock. I'd only glanced at her because I was afraid of what I'd see in her face. I didn't want her love for me to be replaced with pity.

"Yes."

I really didn't feel like having a conversation, but I knew they would all have questions. I was worried about Suga hating me for not telling her the truth.

"How long has Suga been with y'all?"

"We met Suga in the last town," I answered. "I need to find her."

"I'm sure she went to the house to get R.J. Let me see how much longer Jimmie will be," she said, getting out of the car.

She returned to the car within a couple minutes.

"Jimmie's friend, Officer Ronald, is going to come to the house to get some more information. They are going to have to confirm there was a murder in Maplewood fitting your description before making an arrest. Are you willing to talk to him?" she asked.

"Yes, ma'am."

We rode to the house. Just as Ms. Bernadette thought, Suga was there with R.J. Mrs. Althea was rubbing her back, and Mr. Kenneth was standing in the doorway, looking confused. Suga was holding R.J. so tightly it looked like it was hard for him to breathe.

When I got out of the car and walked up the porch, I stopped in front of Suga. Her eyes were bloodshot. Mrs. Althea got up and guided the others into the house.

"The police are coming for me to tell them what happened. Once they match us up to Maplewood, they are gonna arrest him," I said after taking the silence as long as I could.

"How I'm 'posed to take care of my son, Mouse?" she whimpered.

"Keep working at the Richardsons'," I said with a shrug of my shoulders. "I didn't have time to think any of this through. I didn't know this was going to happen," I whispered.

"Why you ain't tell me this before now?" she hollered. "You was like my child too, Mouse!"

"How was I supposed to tell you? We've been on the run since I was almost eight. He threatened me over and over again not to tell. For all I knew, he would have killed me, too, if I ever told. If I ever thought you were in danger, I would have told you. But he loves you and R.J."

"And he ain't love your momma?" Suga asked sarcastically.

The police car pulled up as I was trying to come up with an answer.

Suga was about to get up to go inside.

"Please stay with me," I said quietly.

I reached out and touched her hand. Suga eased back down onto the seat. The rest of the family came back to the porch and listened quietly as I laid out what had happened all those years ago. I answered Officer Ronald's questions about our whereabouts after the murder. He wrote notes the entire time I talked. Mrs. Althea kept wiping her eyes, Mr. Kenneth sat on the steps with his hands folded in his lap, Jimmie held Ms. Bernadette, and Suga rocked R.J. like she was soothing him from a bad dream. When I finished, I felt spent. Ms. Bernadette left Jimmie and came over and hugged me. Her touch put a small crack in the dam I'd built around my emotions, and a portion of my pain came flooding out. What started as a sob soon turned into an all-out wail. R.J. woke and started wailing.

"Gimme that child," Mrs. Althea told Suga.

Suga handed him over, and Mrs. Althea took him in the house to settle him down.

Suga rose from the chair, I thought to go inside, but instead, she came over and wrapped her arms around me as well. The three of us sobbed while fireworks burst in the sky of downtown Hemings.

When the three of us finished crying, Mrs. Althea came to the screen door.

"Y'all come inside. It's getting late. I done put that baby down for the night, so y'all might as well stay here until morning. You don't need to go back to that house alone either; neither of you," she said sadly.

"Yes, ma'am," Suga and I said in unison.

"Jimmie, can you and Daddy take them to the house tomorrow?" Ms. Bernadette asked.

"Yeah. I'll call Ronald in the morning to see if they picked up Ray before I come by here. You good to go with me, Pop?" Jimmie asked Mr. Kenneth.

"Yep," he answered.

"Well then, that's settled. Bernadette, come help me change the linen in the guest bedroom. Suga and Mouse can sleep in there. I'll grab some towels and washcloths so's y'all can bathe," Mrs. Althea said.

"I'll go grab y'all some shirts and shorts to sleep in," Ms. Bernadette added.

Suga and I laid in bed, wide-eyed and smelling fresh. R.J. laid between us, sleeping like a little angel, unbothered by the day's revelations.

"I'm sorry I didn't tell you," I said into the ceiling.

"I don't blame you. You was scared. Tell the truth, there was something in yo' daddy I was a little afraid of myself. I just couldn't put my finger on it. He never treated me badly, other than getting too drunk every now and again. I never much liked the way he treated you, even when we wasn't close. I thought maybe it was just because you was a girl, or maybe you reminded him of your momma. Either way, I prayed for this baby to be a boy," she said.

I hadn't known she wanted R.J. to be a boy because she was afraid of how my father would treat the baby.

"We had the best relationship before he killed Momma, sorta like how he is with R.J.," I told Suga.

"I was worried you was gonna hate R.J. when I saw how much he love him," she confided. "But you been a good big sister. R.J. love him some you."

I could see her teeth in the dim light of the room. It was the first time I'd seen her smile since she'd heard the truth.

"He's a sweet baby. I never wanted any bad to come to him. I prayed for him to have you for as long as he needed. Even though I can't forgive Ray for what he did, I hate that R.J. won't grow up with him around," I told Suga.

She reached across R.J. and touched my arm.

"I'm sorry you seen that side of your daddy, and I'm sorry you lost your momma like that. I lost my momma, too, but least I know I can go find her if I just wanted to see her face," she said quietly.

Nothing more needed to be said, and we drifted off to sleep.

The next morning, we awoke to the smell of breakfast cooking. Both Suga and I looked around the bed because R.J. was not there.

"R.J.?" Suga said.

She hopped up and yelled, "R.J.!"

I jumped up and began yelling too.

Ms. Bernadette came running into the room with a laughing R.J. in her arms.

"He was crying, and you two were so exhausted you didn't even hear him. I changed him and gave him some milk, and we've been up playing since early this morning," she explained.

Both Suga and I relaxed. I could look at her and tell she'd had the same fear that Ray had broken in and taken R.J. I, for one, was immediately afraid that he may have hurt the Alexanders. Neither of us shared what we'd thought may have happened during the night. In that moment, I learned that some things were better left unsaid.

"Y'all come and get some breakfast. Momma has been up cooking, and she's gonna send y'all out of here with full bellies."

Ms. Bernadette chuckled, none the wiser that I thought R.J. had been taken and she had been harmed.

Suga and I washed up for breakfast after our early morning scare. Our clothes from the day before had already been washed and pressed and were laid out on the bed when we were finished in the bathroom.

Now that R.J. had seen his momma and me, he was not too keen to let us out of his sight. He'd put up a fuss with Ms. Bernadette until we were done getting ourselves together. As soon as we sat down to eat, he wailed until he was placed into Suga's lap. He was satisfied there as long as he could keep his eyes on me.

Now that he was settled, I began to eat my food. I was mid-bite of a slice of bacon when Jimmie tapped on the door.

"Morning, everyone," he greeted.

"Morning, Jimmie," everyone replied.

He walked over and kissed Ms. Bernadette on the cheek.

"I spoke to Ronald, and they were able to get in touch with an Officer Wallace in Maplewood who confirmed Mouse's story. Ronald and two other officers are going to be headed over to the house to pick him up in a few minutes," Jimmie informed all of us.

Suga put her fork back down on her plate before she'd eaten the food that was on it. It seemed she immediately lost her appetite. I finished my slice of bacon.

"Suga, if you want to leave R.J. here with me, that's fine," Mrs. Althea said.

"Lord knows Ray don't deserve it, but I feel like I should let him say goodbye to his son. Mouse, you going?" Suga asked.

I hadn't really thought about it. Part of me never wanted to see my father again, but another part of me felt I owed it to my mother to see him taken away in handcuffs.

"I'm going."

Mr. Kenneth got up from the table and went out of the room. All of the adults exchanged looks that I couldn't read. When he returned, the black handle of a pistol stuck out of his waistband.

"C'mon, y'all," Mr. Kenneth told Suga and I.

Mrs. Althea and Ms. Bernadette stayed behind while the rest of us piled into Jimmie's car. We took the short ride to Mr. Hamilton's house and waited on a side street until the squad cars arrived.

Officer Ronald, followed by two other officers, walked up to the door of the apartment. He knocked on the door. There was no answer.

He knocked again, this time with, "Ray Maynard, this is Officer Spencer. I need to speak with you for a moment. Open the door!" he yelled.

The door opened slowly, and there stood Ray, looking disheveled and defeated. It wasn't until I saw him that I exhaled.

Jimmie and Mr. Kenneth both opened their car doors. Mr. Kenneth let Suga and me out on his side. As we walked toward the small apartment, Mr.

Hamilton came out of his house to see what all the commotion was about.

"What in the hell is going on here?" he asked.

"Hey there, Mr. Hamilton. Let me talk to you for a minute."

Mr. Kenneth quickly pulled him to the side.

"Ray Maynard, I have a warrant for your arrest for the murder of Hope Maynard. You have the right to remain silent," Officer Ronald began.

I didn't hear anything but the clicking of the handcuffs on his wrists after that.

"Officer, can he have a minute to see his son?" Suga asked.

"Just one. We've got a long drive ahead of us to get him back to Maplewood," Officer Ronald responded.

Back to Maplewood? For a moment, I thought about whether I could go, but what would I be going back to? I had no family left, and it had been years since I'd spoken to any of my friends. I didn't even know if the people I knew and loved were still in Maplewood.

I hadn't even thought of what would happen to me here. The fear of being alone and homeless began overtaking me. What had I done? If I had pretended Ms. Pearl was crazy, everything would have been okay.

Suga leaned over so that R.J. could touch Ray. Of course, Ray could not reach for him, but he leaned his stubble-filled face out for R.J. to slobber on. R.J. hadn't yet gotten the concept of a kiss. The bristly hair on his cheek made R.J. scrunch up his face and pull back.

"I love you, boy," was all Ray could muster.

Ray looked at Suga. She said nothing. Her face gave no sign of emotion. He looked over at me. I mirrored Suga. He turned and allowed himself to be taken to the police car.

By the time they got him loaded in the car, Mr. Hamilton had gone back into his house, and Mr. Kenneth had returned to Jimmie's side.

"I spoke with Mr. Hamilton, and you and the children can stay here for less than what y'all was paying with Ray here. He'll work out the details with you before the first," Mr. Kenneth informed Suga.

"Thank you, Mr. Kenneth. Thank you both for bringing us back here," Suga said as if she were embarrassed.

"That's what family is for," Jimmie told her.

Mr. Kenneth nodded. They both hugged us, walked us to the door, and waited until we were safe inside before leaving to head back to the Alexander household.

Thirteen

There was a wad of money and a note on the table inside the house. Suga handed it to me to read.

"I ain't know how to tell you. Here's all the money I had left, and there's one more paycheck coming from the mill. Send Jimmie or Mr. Kenneth up there to get it," I read aloud to Suga.

"'I ain't know how to tell you,'" Suga parroted. "I ain't know how to tell you I killed my wife and let my girl child see me do it," she said dryly.

I started chewing the one fingernail I had left after yesterday's craziness.

"Guess I'll go get groceries after I get off work Monday," Suga said to no one in particular.

R.J. was sprawled out on a blanket on the floor, preoccupied with chewing on his newly-discovered toes. Suga just stared at him absent-mindedly.

"I'm not going back to school," I told Suga.

"What? Where you get some foolishness like that?"

She had a scowl on her face.

"I need to work to bring some money into the house."

I wanted to sound like a grown-up, but I was upset at the thought of quitting school. I knew I had a responsibility to help take care of R.J. since Ray could not.

"Mouse, you a child. Now, you my child. I appreciate any help you give me with your baby brother, but you ain't quitting school. You going right back to that school come Monday."

I knew from her tone not to press that any further.

"And stop biting your fingernails. I thought you quit that nasty habit," she added.

"I thought I did too," I mumbled under my breath.

Suga and I moped around the house the rest of the day. We drifted from room to room like ghosts, the only sound coming from our feet sliding across the floor. R.J. was swiftly attended to with the slightest cry, but there were no silly games played to make him or each other laugh. Suga just stood at the sink, looking blankly at the wall at one point. I left her be. What was there for me to say?

Suga had left some lima beans soaking before we left for the festival on Friday, so she decided to cook them with a leftover ham bone. Lima beans weren't my favorite, and whenever Suga made a pot of them, they lasted for three whole days. Without Ray here, they would last even longer. I was not looking forward to a whole week of lima beans.

I'd learned how to make Suga's cornbread. Three scoops of self-rising flour, two scoops of self-rising corn meal, one egg, some milk, some sugar, and a whole stick of melted butter. "Some" was the only measurement she could give me for the milk and sugar, so I'd figured out how much "some" was through trial and error. I started making the cornbread once the beans only had about forty more minutes of cooking.

I was mixing the ingredients together while worrying about how we were going to make it. Times were about to be lean with Suga trying to keep a roof over our heads and feed us on her one salary. I knew the Alexanders wouldn't let us starve or be homeless, but I couldn't help but be angry that we were in this situation thanks to Ray. I still had Maynard blood running through my veins and didn't want for us to have to rely on other people to make sure we were okay.

When the beans and cornbread were both done, Suga and I sat down to eat them in silence. Suga cradled R.J. in her left arm while she ate with her right. The beans were salty, and my cornbread was slightly overdone, but it was a meal that we were both thankful for nonetheless.

Sunday morning, Suga and I ate cornbread and jelly while R.J. nursed. We continued to mope with the only laughter coming from my sweet little brother. We entertained him as best we could, considering neither of our spirits were very high.

A knock on the door came around noon. I hopped up to answer it. When I opened the door, I found Ms. Bernadette standing there in her Sunday best.

"Hey, Mouse," she said with a smile

I was glad to see her, but I wasn't sure why she'd stopped by.

"May I come in?"

I'd forgotten my manners in the shock of her visit.

"Yes, ma'am."

I stepped aside so she could come into the apartment.

"Hey, Suga."

Ms. Bernadette walked all the way into the room.

"Hey, Ms. Bernadette. What brings you here?" Suga asked.

"Jimmie's outside in the car. We came to pick y'all up. Momma cooked so much food, and she wants to see y'all faces. You know she's fallen in love with that baby boy of yours."

Suga looked over at me. I shrugged my shoulders. As much as I loved the Alexanders, I wasn't sure I was up to being around them. Sometimes the strength of their love for one another made me feel like I was all alone on a deserted island. There was no one alive who loved me like that, and I hadn't felt that type of love in a long time. I knew they all cared for me, but they weren't mine. No one was mine to keep for very long, but maybe R.J. would be different. I wanted to give R.J. that type of love. I knew Suga would give it to him, but it wouldn't hurt to have two people who loved him beyond what words could express.

"Y'all know if I go back home without you two, Momma will have my hide."

Ms. Bernadette stretched her eyes wide and tilted her head.

Suga looked down at her clothes, and I looked at mine. We certainly weren't dressed for Sunday dinner at someone else's house.

"Not one of us cares how you two are dressed. We are family."

Ms. Bernadette had come with all her tools to fight any complaint or objection we may have had.

"Okay, but at least give us a minute to change clothes," Suga said.

She was resigned to the fact that Ms. Bernadette was not leaving without us.

"I'll be in the car," Ms. Bernadette sang.

Suga changed while I put some decent clothes on R.J. We'd allowed him to lay around in his onesie up until now. I threw on some half-decent clothes once I was done with R.J. and pulled my hair into an Afro puff at the back of my head. The three of us loaded into the back seat, and we were off to get some good food and relief from our blues.

Mrs. Althea must have been trying to heal all our wounds with her cooking. If our wounds hadn't been so deep, she just might have done it. That was the best food I'd ever had in my life. Her fried chicken was the prettiest golden brown, with the crispiest, most flavorful skin. Her biscuits were so light and fluffy, I thought they might float right off the table. The mashed potatoes and gravy were creamy and smooth. Even the green beans were tasty, with a bit of a tangy flavor I'd never tasted before.

The family chatted about the morning's message. Suga and I didn't say much other than to ask for more food. We knew we had a week's worth of lima beans and ham ahead of us, so we were trying to enjoy the moment as best we could. Mrs. Althea was sneaking R.J. mashed potatoes every chance she got while Suga pretended not to see. R.J. was quickly becoming a fan of the starchy food, soft enough for him to gum and swallow.

I looked around the table at them all and was suddenly filled with an emotion I couldn't describe. It was as if someone was trying to pour something into a hollow container, but it couldn't be filled because there was a hole in the bottom. I hopped up from the table and ran outside.

"Mouse!" Suga yelled after me.

Suga stood up to follow me, but Mrs. Althea raised her hand.

"I'll go talk to her," she said.

She handed R.J. to Suga and followed me outside.

"What's wrong, lil' one?" Mrs. Althea asked.

By this time I was sobbing.

"Why couldn't I have a family like this?" I wailed.

"You get what God give you," she responded. "And you got to be thankful for that. God don't just give you blood family, you know. You've got Suga, me, Kenneth, Bernadette, Jimmie, and you know you got R.J. Why you think God surrounded you with all of us? You just as much my family as if you was my grandchild. I love you, Suga, and R.J. like y'all was my own blood. And long as any Alexander draw breath, you got family in Hemings," she finished.

That only made me cry harder.

"Everyone I love leaves, or I have to leave them," I murmured through tears, snot, and saliva so thick I thought I would choke.

"Well, that stops now. I can't promise we won't pass on. No one can promise you that. But I can promise I'll always be your family, no matter where you are. You understand me?" she asked, wrapping her arms around me.

I nodded.

She pulled me into a hug and kissed me on my forehead.

"You a mighty strong young lady. You been through more in your few short years than some been through in a whole lifetime. If what you seen didn't break you, nothing can. You, Suga, and R.J. can come here for anything you need, from a shoulder to cry on to a roof over your head, 'cause that's what family do for one another," she concluded.

We sat in silence for a little longer.

"Now, I made some peach cobbler that's got your name written all over it, and Kenneth picked up some vanilla ice cream. What you say we go give everybody some, including that little curly-haired boy," she said with a devilish grin.

I smiled and nodded back at her.

Everyone smiled when they saw me come back in, including Suga. When I sat down at the table again, she reached over and touched my hand. R.J. giggled at me and I took him into my lap. I tickled his little poked-out belly until he squealed with delight, which made everyone else laugh.

Mrs. Althea and Ms. Bernadette served everyone some warm peach cobbler with vanilla ice cream once our food settled. Afterward, we all sat out on the porch until the sun began to set.

"Well, I need to go get ready for work tomorrow, and Mouse needs to get ready for school," Suga stated. "Mrs. Althea, I'm not gone have the money to keep paying you to keep R.J., so I'm just gonna take him to work with me. He's a little older and shouldn't be as fussy now."

"You certainly will not!" Mrs. Althea yelled. "I only took that money because Ray wasn't gonna let it be any other way. You keep your money and keep bringing that baby by here every morning. You hear me?"

"Yes, ma'am," Suga said quietly.

"Bernadette and I will take you home," Jimmie interrupted.

"Thank ya'," Suga said with a nod.

"Y'all pack up some plates! There's still plenty of food in the house," Mrs. Althea urged.

"No, thank you. You've fed us plenty today. Besides, I made enough lima beans yesterday to last us until winter," Suga said with a chuckle.

I made a face, and everyone laughed. Even R.J. seemed to be amused. Suga swatted at me and pretended to be mad but ended up laughing.

We went home and busied ourselves preparing for the week. Suga ironed clothes while I bathed R.J. She fed R.J. and put him down while I made my lunch for Monday. There was just enough of that sliced ham left to make a sandwich.

Monday began as it normally did. Suga had squirreled away a couple of Mrs. Althea's biscuits, which she warmed and slathered in apple butter. Warm biscuits and apple butter was one of my favorites.

R.J. was wrapped close to Suga's belly like she wished he was still inside her. That made it easier for her to keep her hands free to carry her bags to work. His little arms and legs hung out of the openings she'd expertly crafted in her makeshift baby pouch made from a long silky scarf she'd had for ages. He looked around bright-eyed at everything he could see as we walked down the trail that led to both the Alexanders' house and the school. When we reached the fork, which would take us our separate ways for the day, I kissed R.J. on the cheek and told them both I'd see them later.

I prayed that no one had heard the news of Ray's arrest as I walked into Ms. Bernadette's class. She looked up as I passed her desk.

"Good morning, Hannah," she said with a smile.

"Good morning, Ms. Alexander."

I took my seat and class went as usual. Everything was fine until lunch time.

"Do I have anything on the back of my pants?" Charlene asked.

"No. Why?" I responded.

"Because everyone is staring," she answered.

"I thought it was me," said Nita.

I'd noticed that everyone had been watching our every move as we found seats at the nearest empty table. I knew exactly what it was about. I hadn't had time to tell either of them what had happened.

"It's not y'all, it's me," I assured them.

"You have something on the back of your pants?" Charlene asked, confused.

"No. My father killed my mother when I was seven, and we've been on the run. It caught up to him this weekend, and he was arrested and taken back to our hometown of Maplewood."

I wanted the telling of this over and done with. I spit it out as quickly as I could. I needed them to get over their shock quickly and get back to being my friends. I would have plenty of people looking at me with pity or disgust as it were.

Charlene busted out with laughter. Nita just sat there, staring blankly at me.

"Mouse, that is the craziest thing you have ever said! Where did you get a story like that?" Charlene teased.

When my face did not change, her eyes grew big and her voice dropped to a whisper.

"You're serious?" she asked.

"Can't you tell she serious, Dummy?" Nita asked, turning and looking at Charlene like she was crazy.

"Don't call me a dummy!" Charlene yelled.

I didn't know how the two of them had been best friends before I came along. I waited for them to stop arguing.

"Mouse. Oh, my Lord. What? How? I have so many questions," Charlene said.

"Well, save them for later. Right now, I just need you two to be normal," I told them.

"We're cool," Charlene responded.

"Yeah, we won't tell anyone," Nita added.

"I don't think you have to," I said dryly.

We ate lunch and talked as usual. The other students eventually went back to eating their food. No one was interested in asking me questions or making fun of me for now.

At recess, the three of us went to the nearby tree for shade. The boys were playing flag football, and the girls were not allowed to participate in that.

"So, you ready to talk?" Charlene asked.

"What I already told you is basically it," I responded.

I really had no desire to hash it out all over again.

"How did it all come out?" Nita asked.

"That lady, Ms. Pearl, at the festival. The palm reader," I answered.

"What palm reader?" Charlene asked.

"The one that had the tent over near the church," I said. "Y'all had to see her tent. It was red and white," I explained.

"My family didn't get there until late," Nita said. "Daddy had to work, and Momma ain't no fan of the heat. We got there just in time to see the fireworks and get a few snacks. I didn't see no red-and-white tent."

"Mouse, I didn't see one, either, and I was there all day. I walked that entire fair twenty times over. Momma had me so busy running for the church, I couldn't have any fun. I didn't even see you that day," Charlene piled on.

Now I felt crazy. I knew me, Suga, Ray, Ms. Bernadette, and Jimmie couldn't have all imagined Ms. Pearl.

"It was the only red-and-white tent there," I said, annoyed. "Anyway, the old lady knew what Ray had done, and she said as much. Ms. Bernadette and Jimmie were there, and Jimmie went to the police."

They were both still skeptical about the tent, so I kept the detail about Ms. Pearl channeling my momma to myself. They would think I needed medical attention for sure if I shared that part.

"How come you never told?" Charlene quizzed.

"Ugh, you so stupid," Nita fussed.

Before the argument could begin again, I answered, "He threatened me. I was seven. I'd already seen what he was capable of."

I was hard-pressed to understand why people thought a seven-year-old with one living parent who'd witnessed that one living parent kill the other had the ability or opportunity to tell someone what had happened.

They both sensed that I was in no mood to keep defending myself.

"I'm sorry. I can't imagine I would have been able to tell either," Charlene apologized.

"That's fine. I don't want to talk about it. He's gone to jail. It's over."

They both nodded their heads and left the conversation alone.

There was a piece of paper on my desk when we returned to class. Every nerve in my body was singing. The white sheet of paper was turned face-down. I knew there couldn't be anything good on the other side. Nita reached out and turned it over. The note had a poorly-drawn scene of a man shooting a woman. I snatched the paper from her, balled it up, and threw it down. I ran past Ms. Bernadette's desk and out of the room.

I was too angry to cry, so I sat on the toilet seat, fully clothed, with steam rising from the top of my head.

Both Charlene and Nita came and found me in the bathroom two minutes later. They knew exactly which stall would be my sanctuary. They talked to me from the other side of the door.

"Mouse, you okay?" Charlene asked.

Nita sighed loudly. She was losing patience with Charlene's obtuse behavior.

"I'm fine," I said through clenched teeth.

"Ms. Bernadette sent us to check on you. She's trying to get to the bottom of who left that on your desk," Nita explained.

"She told us to tell you to go to her house and wait there with R.J. until she gets home," Charlene interrupted Nita.

"Fine," I mumbled.

"I have your school bag," said Nita.

I opened the door to the two of them looking scared of what I might do. I took my bag from Nita and walked past them out of the bathroom. I didn't stop walking until I made it to the Alexanders' house.

"Mouse, what you doing here this early? Where is Bernadette?" Mrs. Althea questioned when I walked in the door.

I walked past her, went into the bathroom, and closed and locked the door.

"Mouse!" she yelled.

I didn't have the strength to answer another question or look at another face filled with pity for the poor little parentless girl. I hated Ray for what he'd done and how he'd totally messed up my life. Mrs. Althea must have sensed I needed some time alone. She didn't even bring R.J. to try to coax me out of the bathroom.

There was a tap on the bathroom door a couple of hours later.

"Mouse, open the door, please," Ms. Bernadette said softly.

I walked across the bathroom and unlocked the door, but that was the most she was getting. She opened the door and came in.

"Mouse, I understand you are upset, but that was disrespectful for you to come into our house and not speak to my mother. You owe her an apology," she said calmly.

"Yes, ma'am," I responded.

"I know who left that drawing on your desk. They will be making an apology tomorrow in front of the class," she continued.

I interrupted her. "Please, Ms. Bernadette. Don't make them do that. It will only make things worse," I begged.

"No. That was cruel, and I won't stand for that kind of behavior in my classroom," she admonished. "When Suga gets here, we are going to tell her what happened. She should be aware that people know, and there may be trouble."

"Trouble?" I asked.

"Not really trouble. Folks just like to gossip, and people may treat you differently," she tried to explain.

I sat on the commode with my head resting on my fists and my elbows bearing down into my thighs.

"Now, c'mon out of this bathroom. There's a little face that is just going to light up when it sees yours," she said with a smile.

I followed her out of the bathroom and into the kitchen. Mrs. Althea was at the stovetop stirring a pot of something that smelled scrumptious. She had R.J. on her hip, and he started squealing as soon as he saw me. She did not turn around as she normally would have. I looked over at Ms. Bernadette, and she gave me a nod. I walked over to stand beside Mrs. Althea.

"Mrs. Althea," I said cautiously.

"Yes," she answered cooly.

"I'm sorry for coming in the house and not speaking to you. I got picked on at school, and I was really angry," I explained.

"I accept your apology, Mouse. Don't let it happen again. You got every right to be mad at how you were treated, but that doesn't give you the right to take it out on the people that love you. You understand?"

"Yes, ma'am. It won't happen again."

She pulled me against her free hip into a half hug. She turned so R.J. could babble at me. I took him out of her arms and plastered his face with kisses. He giggled. I took him over to the table and sat down across from Ms. Bernadette.

"Okay, Mouse. Let me hold R.J. so you can go work on your homework," Ms. Bernadette instructed. "There's a few things you missed after you left class. I put the papers you need on the desk in the study."

When Suga came to pick us up, Ms. Bernadette informed her about what had happened in school. Thankfully, she left out the part about me storming past Mrs. Althea without speaking.

Suga didn't bring it up until we were home.

"Mouse, don't you let them kids upset you. What happened ain't none of their business, ole nosey…" she trailed off.

Heat traveled up from the soles of my feet to the top of my head. My whole body felt like it was on fire. I exploded. I pounded my fists on the table and screamed at the top of my lungs.

"I lost my momma. I lost my home! Everybody is looking at me like I'm an orphan. He's ruined everything!"

I had said the words before I could catch myself.

R.J.'s eyes were wide. He seemed to not know what to make of the noise for a moment. Then, he began to cry out of fear. I'd frightened him.

Nobody here had done anything bad to me. The person who deserved this outburst was sitting thousands of miles away in a jail cell. I'd never once shown him this type of emotion. His presence helped me keep a leash on my anger, but now I could be free of it. That freedom felt good for a moment, but now I felt horrible for blowing up.

Suga just sat there blinking back tears. I hadn't seen her cry about any of this since she'd found out.

"Not everything."

She looked over at a crying R.J.

"No, not everything," I agreed after awhile.

Maplewood

Fourteen

Twenty-Five Years Later

Ray and I stared at each other through the glass. It was 1986 and the first time I'd seen his face since he'd been hauled off in handcuffs. He spared me the cruelty of a trial. I'd even heard that his lawyer wanted to ask for a reduced sentence of life-in-prison since he was confessing to the crime, but Ray prevented him from doing so. He said that he would take whatever punishment the state of Georgia saw fit to give him. That turned out to be the death penalty.

Ray's big almond-shaped eyes, the color of rich molasses with lashes enviable by most women, were hard and cold—same as they were when I had last seen them. His skin, smooth and brown as

Crown Royal, had been replaced by skin creased and ashen with time and emptiness. His fingers, once strong and self-assured, now shook with nervousness as he held the receiver to his ear. Then it struck me—if it were not for the way that that kind of life aged a person, R.J. would be Ray's spitting image.

I had yet to reach for the phone on my side of the glass. I thought I had dealt with what had happened all those years ago, but that was proving to be untrue. Memories of Momma flooded my mind, and my stomach felt like it was in my feet. I felt the tips of my fingers to see which I could chew.

You're not a little girl anymore, I thought to myself. I stretched out my fingers and laid them against my thighs. I'd broken that habit before I was sixteen. I wouldn't allow myself to revert to it for comfort now.

I picked up the phone.

"Hey, Mouse," he said with ease, like he'd just spoken my name yesterday.

I simply stared at him.

"I hoped you would come," he spoke again after an awkward silence.

"Why?" I asked.

It was the only word I could manage.

"I wanted to ask for your forgiveness. I didn't mean to hurt you or your mother. I was out of control. I didn't know nothing about being a man, and the little I did know I wasn't measuring up to. It felt like I was losing everything, including your momma, and I didn't know how to handle it," he explained.

"So you thought your best choice was to murder her, and to do that in front of me?"

"That's just it. Wasn't no thought. I wasn't thinking about her, you, or even myself, for that matter. I just knew how I felt, which was lost and like the whole world was crumbling around me. I know now that I was what they call 'depressed,'" he offered. "And when I pulled the trigger, I didn't even realize you were in the room. I didn't see you until after. I'm so sorry I did that to both of you."

"I can't have a normal relationship," I blurted out.

He didn't respond.

"One day, everything was beautiful ,and the next, you snapped, because everything wasn't going your way. How can I trust anyone?" I demanded.

"Please forgive me," he said with a quivering voice. "Don't measure nobody else by me. Everybody is different."

"And knowing what you had done… what you were capable of… why did you involve Suga? The truth almost killed her. R.J. is the only reason she made it through that. I watched her watch him for years, silently praying that he didn't have the capacity to be like you," I said.

He ignored what I said.

"How is R.J.?"

"How do you think? A father he can't even remember is about to die for a crime committed before he was even born. He's confused, hurt, concerned for me. He's all mixed up. I'm just glad he's had so much love surrounding him that there's no room for anger. Jimmie and Mr. Kenneth picked up your slack," I said bitterly.

He flinched.

I'd known that would sting. I'd wanted to hurt him. I looked at him. A little piece of me felt sorry for him, knowing what he was about to face.

"You thank them for me next time you see 'em," he said through a clenched jaw.

"Mr. Kenneth passed two years ago, but I'll be sure to tell Jimmie," I responded.

"Mouse, you got to let go of that anger," he admonished.

"Why? You let go of the guilt?"

"Naw, I'll never get rid of that."

"Then don't tell me what to do with my feelings. That's between me and God."

"You still believe in God?"

I laughed.

"Maybe not the way most people do, but God is the only way I came out of that fucked-up mess you made of my life," I answered. "I know you expected me to come in here all weepy and mousy, ready to forgive you for what you did, but you only remember me as a child. You don't know me now. In fact, you never really knew me then."

"I know you a high-powered lawyer. You done prosecuted many a murder case," he said proudly.

It caught me off-guard.

"How do you know that?"

"R.J. used to write me and send me newspaper clippings. I put that picture of you leaning on the table in a courtroom on the wall in my cell. I look at that picture many hours of the day. I'm proud of you, Mouse," he said quietly. "I guess Ms. Pearl was right. What you been through helped shape you into who you was supposed to be."

"So, I suppose I should be grateful for what happened?" I asked incredulously.

"No, no, no. That's not what I mean. I'm just saying, even though it was horrible, God turned it around and made it into something good. You get murderers off the street."

"Too bad I couldn't do it with my own father."

"In a way, you did. You could have lied about it that night," he said with a shrug. "If that night had never happened, I never woulda turned myself in."

I shook my head.

"Not even after Ms. Pearl?" I asked.

"Naw," he answered. "I wouldn't have wanted to leave you and R.J.."

"Me? You barely even looked at me after we went on the run," I half-yelled.

"And why you think that was? I loved your momma more than the breath in my lungs, and every time I looked at you, I was reminded of what I done. I couldn't stand facing her every day," he choked out. "I love you, Mouse. I know that's hard for you to believe, and I don't blame you. If you never hear nothing else I've said to you your whole life, know that I love you."

He put his hand up to the glass. His face was wet with tears. I didn't realize that mine was as well until I felt a teardrop hit my chest. He hung up the receiver and called for the guard. He never took his eyes off me until he had to turn and walk through the door.

That was the last time I saw Ray Maynard alive.

Afterward, I sat alone in a cold waiting room, preparing myself for what would happen in the next few hours. I would watch my father die; a witness to his execution. Everyone but Suga and R.J. had offered to take this journey with me, even Mrs. Althea, who could barely walk these days. I would have said no even if R.J. had offered. I knew it was my journey to take and mine alone.

Watching electricity course through Ray's body was more traumatic than I'd thought it would have been. In my lifetime, I'd watched one parent execute the other and the other parent be executed by the state. Afterward, I sat in the car for what felt like hours, paralyzed by a strange feeling. On one hand, I could rest knowing the debt he owed for taking my mother's life had been paid. On the other hand, I was now officially parentless. I'd felt that way for a long time, but the reality was Ray was still alive. Now, there was no one.

I finally put the keys in the ignition and began to drive. I drove for twenty minutes before I realized I was headed toward Maplewood. The prison was only about forty-five minutes outside the small town, though I'd initially had no plans to head that way.

I hadn't eaten in two days, and I was beginning to feel lightheaded. There was a cluster of bright lights up ahead, so I decided to stop. As I got closer, I saw what I thought to be a ferris wheel.

"I look ridiculous pulling up to this fair in this car and in these clothes, but I'm hungry, and a little emotional eating will do me just fine," I said aloud to myself.

I parked the white Volvo as close to good lighting as I could. It was just like my car, but it was a rental, and I wasn't interested in paying for it being stolen or damaged.

I was sure I'd be throwing away my beautiful stilettos after walking around the fair for any length of time. Mrs. Bernadette had taught me a lady didn't wear scuffed-up heels. I locked the car and headed into the fair to find the greasiest, most unhealthy food I could to help me chase away the "both my parents are dead" blues.

I decided to start with a corn dog. I sat down at the nearest table. I carefully opened the mustard and ketchup packets, because neither condiment would wash out of this fabric easily, and my dry cleaner would charge me extra for a tough stain like that. I swirled the two sauces together until they were a funky shade of brown and cheerily dipped my corn dog in the mixture before each bite. That first hot bite was the epitome of satisfaction.

A young black couple with a small boy were seated at the table next to mine. I thought of Ray, Suga, and R.J. that day at the fair. The mother, who had on a dress in the most striking shade of yellow, looked up and saw me staring. She smiled. I returned the gesture.

I started to feel weird at a fair all by myself, dressed like I was headed to court. I finished my corn dog, wiped my mouth and hands on the napkins that were on the table, and threw my cardboard dish and trash away.

Just as I turned to head back to the car, I had to stop in my tracks. Something unexpected grabbed my attention. It was small, compared to the others, but it still stood out. A tiny tent with red and white stripes. There was a poorly-carved wooden sign above the opening that read, "Pearl's Palm Readings $1.00."

I walked closer in disbelief. It sure looked like the same tent. This couldn't be the same Ms. Pearl. She was old back then; she would be ancient by now.

I walked gingerly into the tent. There she was, sitting in a chair that faced the entrance. The room was dimly lit with candles. Her hair was wrapped the same, and her face didn't seem to have changed much at all. Her eyes were different. They had turned a cloudy blue and almost seemed to glow. I was about to turn and run out of the tent.

"C'meah, chile, and saddown. Ms. Pearl don't hafta see to know dat's you, Mouse. I knew you come back to me. Ray went on t'day?"

I pinched myself to see if I was awake. I thought that perhaps somehow the day's events had sent me into some type of hysteria.

Ms. Pearl chuckled.

"You ain't dreamin', chile," she said softly. "And you ain't crazy."

Surely I was losing my mind. I sank down into the wooden chair.

"How did you know that?" I asked, confused.

"Same way I know anything. Spirit tole me," she answered. "Spirit tole me you come to me soon."

Ms. Pearl wore a grin as big as a Cheshire cat. The years had not been kind to her teeth; she had even fewer than she'd had the first time we met.

"Yes, ma'am. He finally paid today for what he did to my momma," I answered.

"Oh chile, you know betta den dat," she mused.

"What do you mean, Ms. Pearl?"

"He been pay fuh dat e'r day since he pull de trigga. Yo' momma soul left quick; yo' daddy soul die one day at a time."

I sat quietly.

"Don't make it right, but he suffered fuh what he done. Dat make you feel betta?" she asked.

"No, ma'am."

"Didn't think so," she said simply. "You tell him you fuhgive him 'fore he go?"

"Why would I do that?" I asked angrily.

"You gotta leave dat in de past now, chile. You wanna soar, you gotta drop de dead weight," she replied. "Hand 'em heya," she said as she reached across the table with both her hands.

I was hesitant. My life had changed drastically the last time I'd allowed this woman to touch me. But it had also been the last time I'd heard my mother's voice. I placed my hands gently in hers.

Ms. Pearl's head jerked back and then dropped sharply forward. I inhaled deeply, afraid of what was about to happen.

"Jes kiddin'," Ms. Pearl said.

She looked up at me sideways with one eye peeked open.

I snatched my hands back as Ms. Pearl howled with laughter. I couldn't help but laugh myself.

"Gimme back ya hands, close yo' eyes, and say what I tell you ta say," she commanded.

I reached back across the table.

"Fatha, you done de best you could fuh me. It hurt me what you done to my mutha, but I fuhgive you," she said.

I stayed quiet. I felt a harsh squeeze of my right hand.

"Father, you did the best you could for me. What you did to my mother hurt me, but I forgive you."

"I pray you fine peace on de otha side," she continued. "I release you. Be free, fine what you could not fine heya."

"I pray you find peace on the other side. I release you. Be free, find what you could not find here," I finished.

Like my first experience with Ms. Pearl, I felt lighter when she was done. Ms. Pearl startled me out of my exploration of this feeling.

"Dere's somethin' waitin' for you in Maplewood. Res' you'self dis ebenin'. Love be waitin' fuh you 'round de corna," she said.

"Love? Ms. Pearl, I am not looking for a man," I said dryly.

"You don't neva know what you looking for 'til you fine it," she said with a wink.

I pushed the chair back and stood up. I walked around the table, placed my hand on Ms. Pearl's shoulder, and leaned down to give her a kiss on the forehead. She patted my hand.

I turned to walk out of the tent, but before I stepped out, Ms. Pearl cleared her throat. I turned back around to find her pointing at the empty bowl where she collected payment. I dropped the fifty dollar bill I had in my pocket in the bowl and left the fair.

I stopped at the nearest hotel that didn't look like the kind where I'd be sharing the bed with unwanted critters. I could afford better, but this would have to do. My exhaustion would not allow me to drive any further. I wrapped my long hair, bathed, and passed out.

I felt like I was floating while watching a movie on a screen. I looked all around the room, trying to figure out where I might be. Then I saw her. There was Momma dressed in all white, sitting in a chair. She was surrounded by the softest mist, making it difficult at times for me to see her clearly. She was laughing and smiling. She seemed so happy, happier than I'd ever seen her in life. Daddy walked up beside her. He was dressed in off-white. She reached for his hand. He looked as if he was afraid to touch her. She gave him a nod to let him know it was okay. He reached out for her. They joined hands and smiled at one another. They both turned and looked at me. I felt a warm, tingly sensation at seeing the two of them together. When I awoke, my pillow was soaked with tears. I laid on my wet pillow and took in that they were finally both at peace.

Though I'd slept almost a full eight hours, I was still a bit tired. I got up, dressed, rode the elevator downstairs, and grabbed a boiled egg and a slice of toast from the continental breakfast offered by the hotel.

As I drove closer to my destination, my hands started sweating. I was surprised that I still remembered the way. I pulled up beside my old house, wondering if whoever owned it now had been given the history of the house. I hoped they would be nice enough to allow me inside.

There was an old man sitting in one of the porch chairs. They looked like the same chairs from my childhood.

"Hello, sir. Do you know the owners of this house? I'd like to speak with them," I said.

"I'm the owner," he replied.

The voice sounded so familiar. I squinted my eyes as if that would help me remember.

"Mister Johnny B?" I questioned.

"The one and only," he responded.

"It's Mouse!" I screamed.

I couldn't bear to remind him of what he'd used to call me.

"Lawd! Girl, come on over here and give me a hug!" he said with the same amount of enthusiasm. "When my nephew told me your story was all over the news, I knew you would come back."

I grabbed his neck and hugged him tight.

"I didn't know what had happened to you, Mouse. I was the one found your momma, and I was afraid the worst had happened. I looked for you until I 'bout made myself sick. Then when I couldn't search no more, I came back and worked until I could buy this house and save it just in case you came back."

"Uncle Johnny, what's all the fuss?" a tall, handsome stranger said, rounding the corner of the house.

I couldn't take my eyes off of him. His walk was confident, bordering on slick. His broad shoulders alternated forward with the opposing leg. His eyes were bright and full of mischief. I almost felt transported back in time—he looked so much like a young Johnny B.

"This here is Mouse!" Johnny B yelled, as if this man should know me.

"For real?" he exclaimed. "Wow, you came back. Uncle Johnny hoped you would. I've heard so many stories about you," he said nervously.

"That's my nephew, Daniel," Johnny B informed me. "He helps me keep this place up in his spare time, which he don't have a lot of. Couldn't ask for a better nephew."

"Nice to meet you, Daniel. Please, call me Hannah. Very few people call me Mouse these days," I said with an outstretched hand.

He took my hand in both of his.

"Are you thirsty?" he asked.

"No, I just had breakfast at the hotel. But, thanks, " I replied.

"What happened to you for all those years? Where were you?" Johnny B asked.

I told him everything that had happened after we left Maplewood, from Ms. Janie to the execution. They both sat quietly and took it all in.

"That's some story," Daniel said, shaking his head.

"Yeah, I'd think the same if I hadn't lived it," I agreed.

"I should never have left that day. I knew your daddy wasn't himself," Johnny B mumbled.

"Don't. There's nothing any of us can do about that day now. They are both at peace. We might as well be too," I said to comfort him as well as myself.

"You turned that tragedy into something good by getting the worst criminals off the street though. That's really pretty amazing," Daniel said bashfully.

I smiled awkwardly. I couldn't find any words to say. Johnny B looked back and forth between the two of us and then got a devilish grin on his face.

"Mouse, Daniel and I were gonna fry up some fish I caught last week for dinner. Would you like to stay?" he asked.

"We were?" Daniel asked, confused.

Johnny B shot him a look.

"That's right! We were. Grits, hushpuppies, the whole shabang," Daniel said, nodding.

"Um… I really hadn't planned on staying," I said.

"My sister, Theresa, made a chocolate cake. It's almost as good as your momma's," Johnny B enticed, turning his head and raising his eyebrows.

I laughed. "You always did drive a hard bargain."

"I've got to get some things from the store, Mouse—I mean, Hannah. Would you like to come with?" Daniel asked.

"Actually, if it's not too much trouble, I'd like to go into the house," I answered.

They both understood what I was asking.

"I can wait to go to the store," Daniel offered.

"No, please go. I'll be fine, and if not, your uncle is here," I said.

As he passed me, he placed his hand on my shoulder. Without a word, I knew he was offering his support for what I was about to face. He walked over to the blue-and-white truck parked in front of my car. He stood hesitantly by the door and looked at me. I nodded. He got in his truck and drove down the road.

Johnny B rose slowly from the chair. It took a minute for him to stand fully erect. When he did, we were eye-to-eye, and I could see he still had the same spirit. He opened the door for me to enter the house.

"Ain't much changed on the inside. I just did my best to keep the house in good condition and keep the taxes paid," he said. "Either Daniel or myself comes over at least once a week to open it up and check everything out. Every now and again, we'll have dinner over here."

"You don't even live here?" I asked.

"No, I stay a few miles across town with Theresa," he responded.

"I'm grateful you kept it up, but it seems such a waste that you are paying for it and not living here," I said.

"I couldn't live here feeling like I coulda stopped your daddy. I figured if you were ever able to return, it would be up to you to decide what to do with this house. You can burn it to the ground if that will help ease you from the pain of what happened here," he answered.

Johnny B's eyes began to water. He seemed to be overwhelmed with emotion. He stepped back and allowed me to walk in. I stood quietly in the foyer. I looked around, and Johnny B had told the truth. It was very much like it was before my whole life changed. Same curtains, same carpet, everything. I walked into the kitchen, and it was still the shoebox-sized room it had always been.

I walked over to the stairs. I felt a little weak, so I reached out and grabbed the railing. It was still strong. Johnny B stood right behind me.

"Want me to go up there with you?" he asked.

"No, I think I've got it," I answered.

He stayed at the bottom of the stairs as I walked up, turned right, and stood in front of the closed door to what had been their room. I turned the knob and pushed the door open.

Was I really ready to face the moment that Hope Maynard lost her life and the moment that I lost my sense of safety?

I turned the knob and pushed the door open. Everything that happened that day flashed before my eyes, like I was traveling back in time. I felt like seven-and-a-half-year-old Mouse as that fateful moment played out in my mind. Where Ms. Bernadette had put a crack in the wall years ago, being in this room again broke the dam. The anger I felt toward Ray engulfed my whole body. I felt like I was on fire. I beat the wall that Momma last leaned against. When I tired of hitting the wall, I fell to my knees and I let out a wail that didn't even sound human to my ears. I wailed until I couldn't. When no more sound would come out, I sobbed. The pain of watching my momma die went through every fiber of my body. I felt it in my fingertips, my toes, and even my hair seemed to hurt. I sank down to the cold floor, where I laid and cried. I cried for the little version of myself. I cried for my Momma. I cried for R.J. and Suga. I even cried for the daddy I remembered before the murder. I must have cried myself to sleep.

When I awoke, I was on the couch downstairs, and I could smell fish frying. I sat up and looked around. Dusk was beginning to fall.

I got up and went into the small bathroom at the foot of the stairs to freshen up. I looked in the mirror and almost gave myself a fright. My hair was disheveled, my eyeliner and mascara were smudged, my eyes were red, and my lip gloss was totally gone. My mouth felt like it had been stuffed with cotton while I was sleeping. My contacts were so dry from all the crying, it felt like I had sandpaper attached to the inside of my eyelids. I rinsed out my mouth, then I rubbed my eyes with my wet fingertips, which would help with the dryness for a moment. I used a paper towel to wipe away the smudged make-up.

Daniel's face lit up when I wandered into the kitchen.

"There she is," he sang.

I smiled. "How did I end up on the couch?"

"I carried you down and put you on it," he answered matter-of-factly.

I was embarrassed.

"I'm sorry," I said quietly.

"For what?" he questioned.

I didn't really have an answer.

"I mean, you're not all that light, but I work out. It wasn't too bad," he said with a chuckle.

I laughed while eyeing the ingredients for a successful fish fry on the counter.

"Where is Mister Johnny B?" I asked.

"Oh, probably watering the plants or something. He lets me handle the kitchen," he answered casually.

"It smells good in here. You seem to know your way around in one," I said suspiciously.

"I should. I own four restaurants."

"Really? What's your specialty?"

"Don't sound so surprised! Southern food with a twist. Aht, aht, aht. I see you getting your hopes up. This is just a quick and simple fish fry today. You'll have to come to one of my restaurants to fully experience my skills," he teased.

"Honestly, I'm so hungry right now, I'm sure I'll be impressed with whatever you put together," I joked. "Where are your restaurants?"

"I have one here in Maplewood, one in Miami, Florida, one in Hazelhurst, Michigan, and one in Lancaster, Pennsylvania" he answered.

"Hazelhurst? That's not far from Hemings, which is not far from Castleton, where I practice," I told him. "What's the name of your restaurant chain?"

"Southern Tastings," he answered.

I was shocked. I'd been to the Hazelhurst restaurant several times with colleagues. It was midway between Hemings and Castleton. The food was amazing. I tried to hide how impressed I was.

"You've been, I see. How was it?" he asked.

"It was good," I answered coyly.

"Good? Now I know you're lying," he said confidently.

We both burst out laughing.

"Okay, okay. It was amazing."

I raised my hands in defeat.

"Now was that so hard?"

"Actually, it was terribly painful," I teased.

"You two are having too much fun in here," Johnny B said as he walked through the back door.

"We just discovered I've eaten at Daniel's Hazelhurst restaurant."

"Oh yeah, my nephew can burn. Taught him everything he knows," Johnny B bragged.

"Don't let my momma hear you saying that," Daniel teased Johnny B.

"Anything I can do to help?" I asked.

"Have a seat," Daniel responded.

"He don't like nobody in his space while he's cooking."

Johnny B raised his eyebrows and rolled his eyes.

"I saw that, Unc," Daniel said, tossing the dish towel that was in his hand at his uncle.

The three of us ate and talked and laughed until ten o'clock at night. It reminded me of the energy that had been in this house before everything changed.

Daniel popped my hand when I tried to help him clean up the kitchen. I couldn't do anything but laugh.

"Well, fellas, thank you so much for the wonderful meal. I need to head back to the hotel and get ready for my flight tomorrow."

"Mouse, I'm glad you came to the house," Johnny B said.

"Me too," Daniel added.

"Me too," I said.

"I'm not rushing you to make any decisions, but this house belongs to you whenever you're ready."

Johnny B looked at me with a seriousness I'd never seen from him.

"Thank you, Mister Johnny B. I can't even think about this house right now, but I truly appreciate all you have done to keep it in such good condition. Once I've had time to get back and put some things in order, I'll call you to work out the details of repaying you for all of this."

"Repay?" he exclaimed. "No, Mouse. You never have to repay me for taking care of this house. I loved both your parents, and I love you," he said sadly.

"I love you, too, Mister Johnny B," I responded.

I decided I wouldn't argue with Johnny B about the house right then, but I wouldn't allow him to work all his life to take care of a house in which he never lived.

I hugged him tight and gave him a kiss on the cheek.

"Daniel, walk Mouse to her car."

Johnny B issued that instruction with tears in his eyes.

"Yessir," he responded.

We walked slowly to the car.

"You know I have to repay your uncle for all he has done," I said.

"He's a stubborn old man. Don't think we didn't try to talk him out of hanging onto a house he never intended to use or rent. He stuck to his guns about keeping it, so I think you have a very slim chance of getting him to take any money. I think it was his way of easing his guilt while holding onto the hope you would return. We didn't move back here until I was in my teens, but I could tell that what happened took a toll on him," Daniel shared.

"Honestly, I don't even know what I'd do with the house," I responded.

"Don't worry about it right now. You've got enough to work through."

We'd made it to the car. Daniel stood awkwardly by the door with his hands in his pockets. He seemed like he had something else he wanted to say, but was undecided if he should say it. I laughed nervously at the silence that hung between us.

"So… since you aren't far from Hazelhurst, I'd love to cook for you the next time I'm there."

I wasn't sure if he was actually asking me out or just being nice. I didn't know what to say.

"I'm sorry if that was inappropriate, considering the circumstances," he said nervously.

He'd mistaken my silence for disinterest. I heard Ms. Pearl's voice ring in my ears: *love be waitin' fuh you 'round de corna.*

"I'd like that," I answered shyly.

Castleton

Fifteen

A week after my trip, I drove to Hemings to visit the family. R.J. and his wife drove thirty minutes from their home to meet me there.

"Hey, sis," R.J. said as I got out of the car.

"Hey, baby bro."

I issued the standard pop upside his head that always accompanied my greetings.

"Uh, don't you think I'm a little old for you to do that to me now?"

"You'll never be too old," I said as I nudged him with my elbow.

I walked up and hugged his wife, Melissa.

"Hey, Mel."

"Hey, Mouse," she said. "You okay?" she whispered in my ear as we embraced.

I nodded my head quickly so she wouldn't linger. My tears came easily those days, and I didn't want to have an episode in front of R.J. or Suga. Neither one of them liked to talk about Ray. They both acted as if he had just been a figment of our imaginations.

When I walked into the Alexanders' house, Mrs. Althea was propped up in the living room. Mrs. Bernadette and Jimmie were seated on the love seat across from her.

"Hey, Mouse," they all greeted.

"Hey, y'all. Where's Suga?" I asked.

"She's up in her room," Mrs. Bernadette answered, looking at me with concern.

Suga had moved in with Mrs. Althea and was her live-in sitter. She hadn't taken the news of the execution date well and had taken to staying in her room when she wasn't doing something for Mrs. Althea. I'd hoped that would be temporary.

"I'll be back," I told the group.

I walked to Suga's door and tapped on it lightly. There was no response. I eased the door open, and she was lying in the bed, feigning sleep.

"I know you're not sleeping, Suga," I told her.

She rolled over and looked at me, but said nothing.

"He gone?" she asked a few moments later.

I was surprised that she asked anything about Ray. I nodded, and she rolled back onto her side, facing away from me.

"You can't just lay here in this bed pouting, Suga."

I sat down beside her on the bed.

"Don't think just 'cause you grown, you can start telling me what I can and cannot do."

"I don't, Suga," I chuckled. "I saw Ms. Pearl at a fair right outside Maplewood."

Suga sat up in the bed.

"Whatchu mean?"

"Just what I said. It was after… you know. I hadn't eaten in days, and I was starving, and this little fair was the first place I thought to stop. She was there in that same little tent."

Suga stared at me in disbelief.

"What she say?"

"She told me to forgive him and to let go of what had happened. Then, she helped me do it."

I grabbed Suga's hands.

"It might help you if you try to forgive him too."

"I don't know if I can, Mouse. If you and Ray hadn't come along, I woulda stayed right there at Ms. Sookie's, and I wouldn't have R.J., but a piece of me wish he woulda never came into my life. I really thought Ray loved me, but I ain't never even know him at all."

"He did love you, Suga. As far as knowing him, you knew some of the best parts of him. Parts I thought were lost forever until you gave him R.J.. I'm thankful I was able to see a little of that before he was arrested. That wouldn't have happened without you."

Suga began to cry. I hugged her and kissed her on the cheek. She laid back down on the bed and wept. I left the room and closed the door behind me. She needed to be alone to process things in her own way. She did not come and join the family fun. She didn't even come to say goodbye before I left, but I knew she would be alright.

I kissed everyone goodbye and drove the hour back to my house, passing Hazelhurst along the way. The thought of Daniel made me smile, which surprised me. I didn't trust men and didn't see much point in dating them, only to get disappointed or worse. That made me awkward and pretty much undateable throughout high school and college. Now, the thought of Daniel asking me out gave me a funny feeling in my stomach. I turned on the radio to get my mind off of Daniel and Maplewood.

I pulled into my garage, pushed the button to close the door, and sat in the car in the dark. It was hurtful to me that Suga was so unhappy. She'd cared for me after my father went to prison, and if it hadn't been for her and the Alexanders, I don't know where I would be. They'd all worked their fingers to the bone to provide and care for both me and R.J.. They saved for both of us to go to college. I wished that once Ray had confessed to what he'd done that Suga would have gone on with her life. For some reason, she got stuck. Grief has a way of cementing our feet to the ground wherever we're standing when it hits us. It takes hard work to get unstuck from that place, but we have to be willing to dig in. Suga was showing no signs of fight, but I had faith that she would.

I settled on that, grabbed my things, and went into the house. I decided a drink might help me feel better. When I dropped my keys in the little basket on the small table underneath the phone, I saw that the red light on the answering machine was blinking. I pressed play.

"Hi, Hannah. This is Daniel. Give me a call when you receive this message please. It's important."

I recognized his voice before he said his name, even though we hadn't spoken since the day we met. What could be important?

We'd exchanged numbers at the car before I left. I picked up the piece of paper he'd written his number on from the table and lifted the cordless phone from its cradle. I dialed the number, and by the second ring, he answered.

"Hello."

I paused, so soothed by his voice that I forgot to respond.

"Hello," he said again.

"Hi, Daniel. It's me, Hannah," I finally managed.

"Oh, I was about to hang up. I thought it was some weirdo who was gonna start breathing heavy on the other line," he joked.

I let out a nervous laugh.

"So, you said it was urgent that I return your call..."

Way to sound like you don't want to talk to him, I thought.

"Uh, yeah. Uncle Johnny is in the hospital. He's been having me get his affairs in order, and he wanted me to call you about the house," he paused. "He would like to go ahead and get it transferred over to you. I think he believes his time is almost up, and with no living heirs, even if he wills the house to you, it could get tied up in probate court."

"I see. Is he really sick? He seemed fine when I was there," I responded.

"Uncle Johnny isn't going anywhere. He's a tough old coot," he said with a nervous laugh of his own.

It sounded like he was trying to convince himself. I was getting the feeling that Johnny B was sicker than Daniel wanted to admit.

"I can come down Friday afternoon and get it taken care of. Is that okay with you?"

"Yeah, that sounds good. Uh, while you're here, I'd love for you to come by the restaurant."

"That sounds nice," I responded.

"Okay, it's a date," he said cheerily. "Talk to you soon."

"Good night."

"Good night," he responded.

I pressed the end button and placed the phone back in the cradle.

It seemed like it took Friday forever to arrive. I was worried about what state I'd find Johnny B in and anxious about seeing Daniel again. I got up at three so I could be at the airport by four for a six a.m. flight. As I was walking out the door, I noticed the light on the answering machine blinking again. It was a message from Daniel telling me to come straight to the hospital.

I was pulling my rental car into the parking garage of Maplewood Medical Center by mid-afternoon. I parked and found my way to room three-thirteen.

When I walked in, Daniel was sitting by Johnny B's bedside. His brows were furrowed, and the corners of his mouth were turned down. His body language said he was tense. There was a woman sitting next to Daniel with her hand on Johnny B's shoulder. Johnny B's eyes were closed. His breathing was labored, even with the tubes in his nose helping him inhale oxygen. Daniel looked up to see who was coming into the room.

"Hey, Hannah. Good to see you," he said softly. "This is my mom, Theresa."

"Hello, Mrs. Theresa. Nice to meet you. I'm sorry it's under these circumstances," I said.

"Nice to meet you too, Hannah. My brother is so fond of you. He talks about you all the time," she said sweetly.

"How is he?" I asked.

"We just learned he has stage four cancer. It seems he's known for a while but was hiding it from us. I know he didn't want us to worry, but he shouldn't have kept this a secret. Now, it's spread through his whole body, and the doctors have said there is nothing else they can do for him but keep him comfortable," Daniel answered.

"I'm so sorry," was all I could say.

"I'm so angry with you, old man," Mrs. Theresa turned and said to Johnny B. "If we had known, we could have helped you."

"Momma, you know how Uncle Johnny is. He's stubborn, and he felt like he had a debt to pay. He didn't want our help. We've gotten a second opinion, and that doctor said the same thing. Don't beat yourself up. Right now, we have to focus on making sure he has everything he needs to be comfortable."

Mrs. Theresa began to cry. I felt awkward, like I was intruding on family business.

"If you all have things you need to discuss, I can just go to the cafeteria or come back later," I offered.

"No, stay," Daniel answered.

"Excuse me, you two. I'm just going to go out for a little air," Mrs. Theresa said, standing up to leave the room.

"Okay, Momma," Daniel responded, standing as well. "I'll stay with Uncle Johnny until you get back."

Mrs. Theresa hugged her son, then turned and touched my hand before leaving the room.

"He really kept that from you both all this time?" I asked, astonished.

"Yeah. I'm not surprised. I knew something was wrong. He wasn't eating like he used to, and he was dropping weight, but every time I asked, he brushed me off. I sort of assumed he was just getting old. I know older people lose their appetites because they start having trouble tasting the food."

I shook my head in disbelief.

"I only just got him back," I said angrily.

"You're probably the only reason he's been around this long," Daniel confided in me. "I don't think you know how much he loved you and your momma."

"Who you calling old?" a voice croaked.

Both Daniel and I shifted our attention to Johnny B. His eyes were still closed, but he'd obviously been listening to our conversation.

"You, old man," Daniel teased.

"I ain't old," he responded slowly.

He tried to clear his throat. Daniel reached over and grabbed a cup of ice chips from the tray table in the corner. He spooned some into Johnny B's mouth. Johnny B sucked on the ice and smacked with satisfaction as if he'd just taken a sip of an ice cold soda. He opened his eyes, squinting as he tried to bring the room into focus. After a moment, he shifted his eyes to find me.

"What you doing here so soon?" he asked me.

His voice sounded a little bit stronger.

"I came to see about you."

"Daniel, I hope you ain't use me as no excuse to get her back down here."

"Well, didn't you tell me to get some things in order for you?" Daniel asked, confused.

"Oh. Yeah."

Johnny B responded oddly, as if he'd forgotten.

"Danny boy, give me and Mouse a minute," he managed to croak out.

Daniel gave him another spoonful of ice chips, put the cup down, and stood up to leave the room. Once Daniel was gone, Johnny B nodded at the chair across from him.

"Mouse, there's something I need you to do for me."

"What's that, Mister Johnny B?"

"Well, your momma got pregnant with you before she and your daddy got married," he started.

This was news to me. I'd never even thought of the timeline of their wedding versus my birth.

"When I came home from basic training, your momma was with me one more time; more out of guilt than anything else, I suppose. I guess you can tell what I'm getting at," he stopped.

I remembered Nana Margie telling me it took Momma and Daddy a while to tell Johnny B they were in love.

"You think I could be yours?" I said, completing his thought.

"It's a possibility," he said anxiously. "I wanna know the truth before I leave here. That's what's been eating me up all these years. I was fine not knowing if it meant I could watch you grow up happy and healthy, but it liked to kill me when he shot your momma and took you away."

I sat, stunned and speechless. Seemed like nothing in my life could be simple. Now, after watching the only father I'd ever known get executed, it was possible he wasn't my father at all. On one hand, it would probably be a relief. If I hadn't come from a killer's loins, I could lay to rest a lot of doubts and fears I had about myself. Could I have crazy hidden deep in my bones? Was I capable of killing someone? As the daughter of a killer, did I deserve to be happy and whole? On the other hand, it would enrage me that my life could have been so different. I was grateful for all the wonderful family I gained through tragedy, but what would blood family and a stable home right here in Maplewood have meant for me?

"Since you a lawyer and all, you think you could get one of them test done and see if you my daughter?"

"Sure, Mister Johnny B," I answered. "I'll come back and get what I'll need to get a test done."

We both sat in silence until Mrs. Theresa returned to the room. She looked from Johnny B to me with a puzzled look on her face, but she said nothing. She took her previous seat and watched her brother as he drifted back to sleep.

"I'll be back soon," I told her before leaving.

I was hoping I could avoid seeing Daniel on my way out, but he was coming toward the room down the same hallway I needed to take to leave.

"You leaving already?" he asked.

"I need to go take care of something."

He looked disappointed. I hadn't forgotten about dinner, but I couldn't go through with it considering that we could be first cousins.

"I'll be back a little later, but I'm going to have to cancel dinner tonight," I said as apologetically as I could. "Raincheck?"

"Sure," he said with a tight smile.

I was only going to share this piece of information if it turned out that Johnny B was my father.

I left the hospital and placed a phone call to my friend in the Crime Scene Investigation Unit back at home.

"Hello," she answered.

"Hey, Becca."

"Hey, Hannah. What's up?" she asked cautiously.

"I need to cash in that favor you owe me," I said calmly.

"Aw, hell. This can't be good. You sound way too cool," she said with a chuckle.

"I'm going to send you two buccal swabs, and I need DNA results back ASAP."

She was quiet for a moment.

"Okay. I think I can slide that in with the million other DNA samples I need to test for everybody's urgent case," she answered sarcastically.

"It's personal," I added.

"Ooooooh, the plot thickens. Okay, girl. I'll get it done. If you can get it here by Monday, I'll get you the results by Wednesday," she promised.

"Thanks, Becca."

What I was asking her to do was a gross misuse of my position, but I couldn't let Johnny B go to his grave without knowing the answer to a question he'd carried for my whole life.

I went to the nearest medical supply store to buy the oversized q-tips I would need to swab our cheeks, sterile bags, and some gloves. I needed to move fast in order to get the samples out before the end of the day. I rushed back to the hospital.

I needed to get my mouth swab out of the way before going inside. I put on a pair of the gloves, opened the box of q-tips, swabbed the inside of my cheek for thirty seconds, then carefully placed it inside one of the sterile bags. I sealed the bag and labeled it "Sample A."

I headed inside with everything I needed to collect Johnny B's sample stashed inside my huge purse. That purse had annoyed me on the flight because it was cumbersome, but I was suddenly thankful I'd brought it along on the trip. Mrs. Theresa was in the same chair, slumped over and sleeping. Johnny B was laying quietly in bed, staring into space. I was worried that he had transitioned, but I could see his chest was still rising and falling, though it was faint. He saw me come into the room, and a small smile lifted the corners of his mouth. He cleared his throat, which caused Mrs. Theresa to stir. She straightened up in the chair when she realized I'd returned.

"Theresa, can you go get me some more ice chips please?"

"Okay, Johnny," she said groggily.

As soon as she was past the door, I whipped into action. I put on my gloves and grabbed another swab. I instructed Johnny B to open his mouth. I swabbed the inside of his cheek, then put the swab in a sterile bag, sealed it, and labeled it "Sample B." I was done long before Mrs. Theresa ever made it back.

"Theresa, you and Mouse go get some rest. No need for y'all to be here staring at me. I ain't going nowhere for right now. I'll be here when you get back," Johnny B announced.

He and I were both anxious for these samples to be tested.

"You sure, Johnny?" Mrs. Theresa asked.

"Where I'm going?" he asked her.

"Okay, I think I'll go home and rest awhile. I'll call up here and check on you a little later," she answered.

She sounded as if she felt guilty but was ready for a break.

"I'll be back in the morning, Mister Johnny B," I added for good measure.

I kissed him on the forehead and rushed out of the room, giving Mrs. Theresa the briefest of goodbyes.

I took the samples to the nearest FedEx location I could find and paid a pretty penny to have it shipped. I called Daniel to see if we could take care of the business about the house before I headed back to my room.

"Well, it's almost lunch time. Why don't you meet me at the restaurant to grab some food while we go over the papers for the house?" he suggested.

He was not going to let me out of coming to the restaurant.

"Sure. That sounds good. See you in a bit," I answered.

I parked the car and walked into Southern Tastings. The interior of this location was even more beautiful than the one back home. The front of the restaurant was decorated like it was a front porch. It was dimly lit, and small lights were strung all around, giving me the feeling of being surrounded by fireflies, or what we called "lightning bugs" as children. From the vintage distressed wood to the bluesy music softly being piped through the sound system, it felt as if I'd just entered a grandmother's house.

"Ms. Maynard, Mr. Foster is waiting at the chef's table for you. Follow me," said the hostess.

She was young and very pretty. I followed her toward a part of the restaurant that was separated from the rest of the diners by a wall. There was a large rectangular table that was dressed for dinner service. Daniel was seated at a smaller square table that was casually dressed and close to a side wall.

Daniel stood up when he saw us headed his way.

"Glad you could make it for lunch," he said while helping me get seated.

"Thanks for inviting me. I'm just realizing I'm hungry," I said lightly.

"Yeah, I figured this would give us a little privacy. I had my servers set up this small table because we have a Chef's Tasting Table tonight for the local rotary club," he explained.

"Oh, that's nice."

I didn't know what to say. In a courtroom, I was a lioness. At that table, I felt like a lamb. I looked at the smile on his face and silently prayed the DNA test would come back negative. Until I received the results, I'd have to put my budding feelings for him on ice.

"So…" he started, tapping his finger on the table. "I have the paperwork for you to take ownership of the house."

He pulled out a black folder and placed it between us on the table.

"Yeah. Guess we need to take care of that," I said, reaching for the folder. "But can I order first? I'm really starving."

"I've already taken care of it," he answered.

"Uh, you don't know what I want," I replied.

I couldn't decide if I liked the fact that he was so sure of himself, or if I was annoyed he was taking control.

"I know my food. I ordered you the best items on the menu," he said with a devilish grin.

"Well, we'll see about that."

I gave him just enough attitude to let him know I was slightly displeased.

"I apologize if that seemed arrogant."

He leaned back, adjusting his shoulders. He seemed nervous.

Relax, I told myself.

I nodded my acceptance of his apology and began pulling the paperwork out of the folder to review it. Everything looked in order, so I began signing the necessary pages. Just as I was signing the final page, the food arrived.

He had not lied about ordering all of the best items. It seemed the two waitresses were bringing out nearly the whole menu. I looked up at him only to see him grinning in triumph. I couldn't help but laugh.

"You are going to send me back home about twenty pounds heavier," I chided.

"What's wrong with that?" he asked, amused.

"I'd have to buy a new wardrobe, that's what's wrong with that!"

All I could think about was bursting out of my size-ten clothes and having to move up to a size fourteen, but I shook my head and reached for a piece of fried chicken anyway.

The chicken was golden in color and drizzled with a little honey to give it just a hint of sweetness. The buttermilk biscuits were light as air. How he knew about my affection for apple butter I'd never understand, but there was a small dish of the delicious spread placed right next to the biscuits. The collard greens, which had been braised in apple cider vinegar, were tender and had just the right amount of smoked turkey. The candied yams were perfectly sweetened and even had pineapple in them, which was a treat I'd never experienced before. The baked macaroni and cheese was still bubbling hot and gooey. The only thing I would be able to do after this meal was go back to my hotel room and slip into a food coma.

I took the first bite and was transported to Sunday dinners with the Alexanders. This man could cook.

"You're not eating much," I said.

I'd been so wrapped up in my plate that I hadn't noticed until five minutes in that he had very small portions of just vegetables.

"Yeah, I don't eat this food everyday. I love to keep up tradition, but this isn't healthy for every meal," he said quietly.

He seemed a little sad.

"Are you worried about Johnny B?" I asked.

"Yeah… not as much as I'm worried about my mother. Uncle Johnny made a choice not to fight the cancer. While I don't agree, I respect his choice. I know Momma doesn't see it that way. She feels helpless, like she should have been able to do something to stop him. I just don't want her carrying that around once he's gone. I saw what hanging onto guilt that doesn't belong to you did to my uncle," he said quietly.

I understood. Guilt had been a constant companion of mine until I met Ms. Pearl.

"I know what you mean," I replied.

That's as much as I was willing to dig into about my own battle with guilt.

"Unfortunately, all you can do is support her in figuring that out for herself. You're not going to be able to convince her, but it will happen when it's supposed to," I offered.

We both sat quietly for a moment.

When I finished my food, Daniel nodded at the server, who quickly vanished. When she returned, he waved his hand over at the dessert tray.

"Here are our wonderful dessert options. First, we have bread pudding with a hot butter rum sauce, banana pudding, and our fan favorite, peach cobbler," he announced proudly.

"I'll take the peach cobbler," I said eagerly.

The server left and returned with warm peach cobbler with a scoop of vanilla ice cream on top. I had no idea how I would eat another bite until I tasted it. Then, I couldn't stop eating.

"Okay, I have to stop myself," I said, putting the spoon down with a third of the dessert left.

"Daniel, everything was truly delicious, and I appreciate you going through all of this trouble."

"It was no trouble. I'm sorry you couldn't come this evening," he responded.

I felt bad for not telling him why I'd cancelled our date, but that would just make things weird and complicated. I hoped Becca would have good news for me on Wednesday.

"Yeah, me too. Listen, I'm going to go by and see Johnny B in the morning, and then I'm going to head back home. I'd really like for us to keep in touch," I said.

"Sure," he replied.

His response felt a little like he really wanted to say, "Whatever."

We both stood up. I waited, not knowing whether I should hug him or just leave. He stepped closer and gave me a clumsy hug.

"Thanks for the amazing food and great company."

"Anytime," he said stiffly.

I left the restaurant and drove to the hotel. I had just enough energy to shower and get in bed. I turned on the television and drifted off to sleep.

The alarm startled me out of a deep sleep the next morning. I sat straight up in the bed and was lost as to where I was. It took a few moments for me to remember where I'd spent the night.

I washed up, got dressed, and headed to the hospital so I could chat with Johnny B before hopping on my ten a.m. flight. Thankfully, no one else was there when I arrived.

"Mister Johnny B," I cooed.

His eyes were closed and I couldn't hear him breathing, but I could see his chest rising and falling with each breath.

"Mister Johnny B," I called again.

"Mmmmmmm," he moaned.

His eyebrows furrowed, like I was interrupting him. His eyes fluttered open, but they took a moment to focus. Then, he seemed to stare straight through me for what seemed like forever.

"Hope, that you? Is this heaven?" he asked.

With me looking so much like my mother and the bright light shining down behind me, I imagine it might have given him the impression that he had gone on to glory.

"No, Mister Johnny B. It's Mouse, and you are still in the land of the living," I answered with a chuckle.

Johnny B blinked a few times, then seemed to return to himself.

"Hey there, Mouse. What you know good?" he asked.

"Nothing yet, Mister Johnny B. I won't know the results until Tuesday or Wednesday. I'll have to call you and tell you what the answer is."

"Okay. I was hoping to know sooner than that, but I guess you can't get it no faster."

I was sorry to disappoint him.

"I just wanted to see your face before I left. I have to go catch a flight."

"Well, I'm glad you was able to come," he said, managing a small smile.

"Mister Johnny B, I'm glad I was able to come too."

I kissed him on the forehead and turned to leave. Daniel was standing in the doorway.

"Hey, Hannah," he said cooly.

"Hey, Daniel," I said, returning the chilliness. "I was just on my way out."

"I see. I'll walk you to your car," he offered.

"You just got here. It's okay," I responded.

"My nephew is a gentleman," Johnny B croaked out with a dry, crackly voice.

Our walk was quiet. When we finally arrived at the rental car, Daniel drummed up the nerve to speak.

"Did I do something wrong?" he asked.

"No! Look. It's… complicated," I responded cryptically.

"Are you married or something?"

I laughed, which only annoyed Daniel. I put my hands on his shoulders.

"No. I'm not married. I don't even have a boyfriend. There's something I do have to clear up before I can think of anything with you. It has nothing to do with anything you did or didn't do. I hope you can give me a little time to handle it," I said sweetly.

"Once you get it cleared up, will you tell me what it is?" he inquired.

"I promise," I said, holding up three fingers stuck together with my pinky tucked under my thumb. "Scout's honor."

I thought about Johnny B, Daniel, and what the results of the paternity test could mean all the way home. I tried to distract myself from it by reading, listening to music, and reviewing some briefs, but none of it held my attention very long. I continued to struggle to stay focused throughout the week.

Wednesday rolled around, and I was on pins and needles waiting for Becca's call. By the time the phone finally rang, my nerves were frazzled, and the loud ring of my desk phone startled me.

"Hello," I said anxiously.

"Hey, girl," Becca said slyly. "So, whose DNA was that you sent me?"

"Becca, I called in that favor so I wouldn't have to answer any of your questions," I said sternly.

"Just thought I'd ask," she responded with a light chuckle. "The DNA is not a match."

I sat quietly.

"Hello," Becca said, concern in her voice.

"I'm here. Uh, thanks, Becca. You are the best forensic scientist I know," I said, massaging her ego.

"I'm the only one you know. When are we going out for drinks again?"

"Soon. I gotta go. I'll call you later this week," I said, rushing her off the phone.

As soon as she hung up, I dialed the number for the hospital and asked for Johnny B's room.

"Hello."

It was Daniel.

"Hi," I stuttered.

"Hey. I'm surprised to hear from you. What's up?" he asked.

"Is Johnny B awake?"

"Yeah, but they just gave him some medicine that makes him sleepy. I'm going to put the phone up to his ear and you better say whatever you have to say quickly," he advised.

"Okay," I said.

"He can hear you," I heard Daniel say faintly in the background.

In the foreground I could hear Johnny B's breathing. It was shallow with an eerie rattling sound.

"Hey, Mr. Johnny B. I got the test back. Turns out I'm not your daughter. I belonged to Ray Maynard, through and through," I said. "I'm glad to know you would have been happy if the results were different, and I'll always love you."

I heard a moan and a cough, then Daniel was back on the phone.

"What did you say to him?" Daniel demanded.

"Why are you angry?" I asked.

"I'm not angry," he said, dropping his intensity. "But, whatever you said, he didn't like it. He has tears streaming down his face."

"He thought there was a possibility I was his, and he asked me to run a DNA test. I just gave him the results," I answered softly.

"And?" Daniel asked, his voice an octave higher than usual.

"I'm not. I'm a Maynard," I said resolutely.

"So that's what the weirdness was about?" he asked.

His tone softened dramatically.

"Yes. I was a little freaked out," I said with a chuckle.

"Yeah, I'm glad you didn't tell me until now. That would have been gross."

We both shared a laugh.

"How's he doing?" I asked.

"I'm going to call you back from the nurses' station," he said.

I gave him the office number and waited for the phone to ring.

"Hello," I answered quickly.

"He's not doing well," Daniel said sadly. "They've moved to administering him morphine, which is the beginning of the end. They are only giving him another day or two."

"How are you?" I asked, knowing the answer.

"I'm okay. Hate to see my uncle going through this, and I wish I could make it easier for him. It's killing my mom, though."

"I understand," I reassured him. "Watching a loved one transition is never easy, no matter the circumstance," I said, thinking of seeing my own father die just weeks before. "I'm just a phone call away, you know. And if you want me to come back, I will."

"No, I think I've got it from here. I would be honored if you would return for his homegoing service," he responded.

"Absolutely," I answered.

"Well, I'm going to go back into his room. Is it okay if I call you this evening?" he asked cautiously.

"I'd love for you to call me this evening, Daniel."

We said our goodbyes and hung up.

I sat at my desk and allowed myself to feel the disappointment of Johnny B not being my father. Though I wanted to be free to see Daniel, it would have been nice to know that my gene pool had been made up differently than Ray Maynard's. However, even though I had his genes, I knew for sure I was the only person to decide who I would turn out to be.

"I choose to be loving, honest, and kind. And I choose to fight for justice for victims of heinous crimes," I declared out loud.

I grabbed my briefcase and headed off to court.

For anyone affected by abuse or domestic violence needing support, call the National Domestic Violence Hotline at 1-800-799-7233 or if you're unable to speak safely, you can log onto thehotline.org or text LOVEIS to 1-866-331-9474.

Acknowledgements

To my writing mentor, my literary sister, my co-conspirator, my best friends, and my publisher, this book would not have come to fruition without each of you. You inspired me, pushed me, talked me off the ledge, and encouraged me just when I needed you most.

To my family and friends, you mean the world to me. Thank you for having my back, even when you did not know what was in front of me.

~Mbinguni

www.ingramcontent.com/pod-product-compliance
Lightning Source LLC
Chambersburg PA
CBHW020556310726
48979CB00008B/1232/J

* 9 7 8 1 7 3 5 7 2 1 9 0 3 *